Fay Sampson was born in the fishing and farming village of Lympstone. She had her first children's novel published in 1975 and since then has had a further seventeen published, as well as two educational books and the first three books in this sequence of novels, *Wise Woman's Telling*, *White Nun's Telling* and *Black Smith's Telling*. She has taught adult education classes in writing and visits schools as 'writer in the community'. She lives in Birmingham, is married and has two children.

Taliesin's Telling

Book Four
in the sequence
Daughter of Tintagel

Fay Sampson

HEADLINE

First published in 1991
by HEADLINE BOOK PUBLISHING PLC

10 9 8 7 6 5 4 3 2 1

ISBN 0 7472 3568 6

Typeset by Medcalf Type Ltd, Bicester
Printed and bound in Great Britain by
Collins, Glasgow

HEADLINE BOOK PUBLISHING PLC
Headline House
79 Great Titchfield Street
London W1P 7FN

To Mark

Author's Note

In physics, Dark Matter forms an unseen world that is the inverse of the matter we observe. The two were created to exist in equal proportions. Together they hold the universe in balance. But when they come into contact, the result is mutual destruction. Morgan's story is the Dark Matter of Britain.

Legend makes Morgan the half-sister of Arthur and the wife of Urien. The historical Urien Rheged ruled in the late sixth century, some three generations after the suggested dates for Arthur. Taliesin was his bard; we still have some of his poems. But Taliesin himself became a figure of legend, and later poems of a more marvellous nature were attributed to him. I have honoured the bardic custom and telescoped the history of the sixth century to bring all the characters within the lifetime of Morgan.

Picts

ALBANY

Loch Lomond

Wall of Antoninus Pius

Alclud
(Dumbarton)

Din Eidyn (Edinburgh)

CLYDE

LOTHIAN

RHEGED

GODODDIN

Wall of Hadrian

Carlisle

Pennines

York

Elmet

Lindsey

Mon

Conway

Gwynedd

Chester

Lincoln

The Wash

POWYS

Pengwern

GARLOT

Angles

Brycheiniog

DYFED

Carmarthen

Gwent

GLEVISSIG

Caerleon

R. Severn

R. Thames

Saxons

London

Badon

Bath

Tintagel

Padstow

Glastonbury

Camelot

Winchester

Saxons

DUMNONIA

Exeter

Celliwig

0   50 miles

Peter McClure 1990

Chapter One

Well, what would you expect me to say? Lovely, she was. It is written on my soul, that first sight of Morgan the Wise. I, a young lad still, out of the mountains of Powys, fresh from the court of Cynan Garwyn. The prettiest bard in Britain. Farms to my name, a hundred horses trapped with silver, and a hundred purple robes, a hundred armbands of pure gold, and fifty brooches, and a sword to myself in a sheath set with precious gems, just for the look of the thing, you understand.

I exaggerate. But not much. I was worth that. I rode to Rheged with my harp on my back and the world at my feet.

And she? It was like coming home, full circle, as if I'd wandered in a mist, though I'd never set eyes on her and hers before. Or perhaps I had. We have been at the lighting of the stars, she and I.

I came to her from the mountains west of Severn. Slate and granite. Beautiful in the late afternoon. The lakes deep and dark, pregnant with old mysteries. Never mind that she was twice my years and more. Do you grumble about the age of a mountain, when the sunset fires the snow upon its crags? What is age to a woman like Morgan? She would be bewitching for a thousand years.

1

They tell me she also came from a slate and granite country. Cornwall. I believe them. The stones are in people. The soft, red, crumbling sandstone in the fumbling of the deep-bosomed Devon women. The pure, demure, clean maidens of the Dorset chalk. But Morgan the Wise. Slate and granite. We understand the darker side of life, she and I. The mountains under the rain. The cliffs endlessly baring their breasts to the storm. The Dark Hunt of the Lord of Annwn that hounds you through the nights and days. I was not always Taliesin of the Radiant Brow. I have come a wild dangerous way to fame since I was Little Gwion, though I wear the experience lightly.

Morgan was cold, some would tell you on Arthur's side. Hard. Unforgiving. Others say she burned inside with an unholy passion. But I was Taliesin. Late chief bard of Powys, though I'd been barely acquainted with a razor then. Before that, darling child of the great and terrible Mother Ceridwen, who loved me against her will. The breast of granite was like home to me. I thought I understood her, you see. I was young and clever, and not nearly as wise as I fancied I was.

Pretty pleased I was with myself that day. A lad, fresh out of the hills of Wales, and for all my history, nearly as green as a daffodil leaf about some things, though I'd have knocked you down for saying so, then. For wasn't I Taliesin, the sweet singer? The youngest poet in Britain ever to win the crown of king's chief bard? And the finest. And with the secret knowledge of Ceridwen's cauldron besides, for all they say one of my fathers was a saint. But that's another story.

So I halted at the gate of Urien's castle in Carlisle

in my new red tunic and my smart buckskin boots, and my precious harp, Healer, on my back, wrapped soft against the weather. I took more care of that harp than I did of myself. The gift of Cynan of Powys; the prince of cattle-harassers to the prince of poetry. Made my fortune already it had, this harp. And I had the scent of more to come. For wasn't Urien of Rheged higher spoken of than any king in the Island, since Arthur?

Since Arthur. There's a short line to carry such a stress of grief. The High King's not dead, but it was the nightmare every week of my life that the great climax of the tale of Britain had passed and no harper worth the echo of immortality was there to sing that name and send it ringing round the hall of time. Who but me should set the drinking-horns clashing a thousand years from now? Who raise the shout of Arthur that his fame shall not die? Who will tell of his grave and of his passing? Rein in your horses! Wait for me. Taliesin of the Radiant Brow is coming.

Powys first. Now Rheged. And finally?

A fine red castle, Carlisle. Great buildings of stone, and trimly kept. There's wealth here. A smart body of men and horses, by the look of it. And a king over them they respect. Nothing slack and shiftless. If he keeps his bards as handsome as his warriors, I'll do pretty well for myself here. I've seen stone castles in plenty west of the Severn, Caerwent, Carmarthen, Conway. But they were old, tired places, dreaming of lost Rome, and getting weed-grown in the cracks while they slept. I've sung Cynan's praises when he raided them, and got my share of the spoil for my song. But this palace is sharp, new-set. They mean business here in Rheged. And my poet's blood beats

out the rhythm of a praise-chant, for such activity
spells war. Angles in the east? Cattle raids on
neighbours? Who cares? How is a poet to grow rich
but out of fighting, when his lord and all his sons ride
out to battle and come home laden with loot and
yelling of victory? Or not, as the case may be. It's
all meat to the bard. I can rhyme you a very pretty
elegy.

So I let them lead me to the turret on the wall
where the king was taking the air, and I have a spring
in my step and my head held high and my chequered
yellow cloak thrown back to show them all my
finery. For aren't I Taliesin of the Radiant Brow, a
very presentable young man, a walking treasure-
house of jewels without and songs within that will
earn me more gifts yet?

We come out on the rampart, and I am hardly out
of breath, and I've readied my brightest smile before
I even see them. There's a flash of sky all round me.
Light spearing out of dark clouds to blind the eye
from spreading mere and sparkling firth.

Urien and Morgan. And it is not warriors and
raiding I think of once I see them both, though he's
a fine kingly figure, Urien of Rheged, in the prime
of life. A little serious, you might say, but who
wouldn't be, matched with a queen like that? It is
no joking matter. He's a braver man than I am, I can
tell you. Morgan has respected him. He is less scarred
than most who have lived that close to her.

All that in seconds, and I've turned from him,
drawn by a power I haven't felt since I fled
Ceridwen. It's a pity really, a generous, open-handed
king like that. Triumphant rustler, battle-provoker,
tiller-man of the ship of stewardship. But you do not

4

look at any man twice when Morgan the Wise is
standing by his side. Like a lone cromlech on a
mountain. Like a lone mountain in a plain. And green
eyes, like dragon's jewels, burning from the soul of
her.

Urien is talking to me, greeting me royally. Chief
of battle to chief of song. And it is no more to me
than surf on the beach when the moon is full.

Morgan is smiling at me. We face each other,
woman and boy – well, not much older I felt that
moment – and she smiles at me. Very sure of that
smile, she is. Green eyes, softening now, like moss
behind a waterfall. Lips curving like the rose. And
even as I go weak behind the knees I say to myself:
That's a very powerful smile. You've been practising
it. Only a moment it's taken you to make me yours.
For I have the knowledge, ever since I licked the
three drops of inspiration from the cauldron of
Ceridwen. I know who she is, and what is happening
to me. If she had spread her fingers and spoken the
words of power she couldn't have bound me more
surely than this.

Not that I'm complaining, mind you. When I feel
that smile lick out towards me like flame, consuming
my strength, I crumble willingly. She should be a
glorious queen. Yet more hungry than happy. I read
that in her eyes as the smile fades. Poor lady, so
that is the way of it. Too keen a fire for the damp
turves that surround you. Begging your pardon, my
lord Urien, but I think you take my meaning. You're
a plain soldier. A noble chieftain, to be sure, an
upright Christian – praised be the name of the
Trinity – brave and generous. Only, no magic in
those muscled hands. All honest daytime in that

face. She calls for moonlight to enhance her flames. And what is a young poet for but to make his lady happy if he can? Let her try me. I will be to her like new-cut ash to burn clean and true on her fire, and she may hold me to her bosom and kindle what sparks she will.

Her lips part now. Urien has finished speaking.

'Welcome to the City of Lugh of the Sunlit Brow, Taliesin.' Her voice wraps me in fur. Astonishingly difficult, it seems, to stand upright. 'You have come to us at a good time. My head is aching. Though your rank is higher now, you will not have forgotten yet the courtesies of a household bard. Your reputation goes before you. Follow me to my chamber and let me test how soft the charms you have to soothe it.'

That takes me back a bit. I have the poetic crown. I'd reckoned myself on the king's side when I was invited here. Chief Bard of Rheged, not the family harper, to sing in the women's room. But Carlisle, it seems, plays by different rules. I'd surrender the crown of all Britain, if Morgan said the word. I bow and smile. Well, I say to myself, you may have the body of a comely consort, but you show the will of a sovereign. You aim for what you want. You don't waste time beating about the covert.

Two chieftains here, then. Both light and darkness. I should tread softly on the sharp-edged bridge between their territories.

I look at King Urien. He appointed me. But he nods assent. He even smiles a little sadly. And, well, I think, you're a generous man. Rest easy, my lord. You'll have your dues of me too, and more besides. I'm not called the finest bard in Britain for nothing.

6

Until my life ages,
And death claims his wages,
I shall not cease yearning
Unless I praise Urien.

And so I go after Morgan to her chamber.

Chapter Two

Black lashes on white cheek, like a magpie's wing.
A great queen, and lovely still. I say still, because
now I am close to her I can see how the skin of her
neck is softly furrowed, like fine leather that begins
to lose its oil. She sleeps in the afternoon, her dark
hair loose upon the pillow. Let the music fade into
a breeze and the voice to a hum, and both fall silent.
She does not hear you. She does not need you now.

Is this all? I could have sworn she wanted more of
me. I read the hunger in her eyes. But here I sit
beside the bed in my new red tunic and my deerskin
boots. And if I'd been a virgin before, I'd be one still.
She asks more from life, and I am life, am I not? She
sleeps. I could reach out my finger now and trace the
bones of her face. Stone under moss. But I am afraid
to touch her. Not for herself. I think I understand
her. She would know I mean no disrespect. The
snowflake on the cromlech. The butterfly upon the
mountain. No disrespect.

But it is that thing squatting at the foot of the bed,
the shape of an old hag. 'Woman' is all the name I've
heard it given. Woman! Spent and shrivelled as the
skeleton of last year's leaf, watching me with jealous
eyes under a wimple that hoods the face more than
most, in a castle that seems full of handsome, high-

necked women. That's a sour whim of Morgan's to keep a thing so ugly in her bedchamber. Does it crouch and watch like that when the king comes to bed her?

Wait, Morgan stirs. Touch the harp lightly. Take up the song again. The most skilful bard in Britain shall sing your cares away.

No. Not even Taliesin can do that. There is great anguish here. See how she moans under the fine sheets and the heaping wolfskins. Passion and anguish. Taliesin is here; a little comfort. There is only one thing I am good for, besides the song, of course. But I will give it freely, not grudgingly, an acolyte to his goddess.

One word from Morgan. Low, but I recall that she is a queen. The hag shuffles out muttering and the voices of the ladies pause in the room beyond. Nothing that is done here is truly private; be sure of that. They will be discreet, though, these women. I have noted already how swiftly they move to serve her. They are her tribe, not her hirelings. Loyal to her as Urien's warband to him. Best not betray her, Taliesin. She goes a different way to Urien, but the bridge of honour must stand. The curtain falls again, and I see it draped where the old hag sits on the threshold, listening. Well, we both have our duties, she and I.

It is no trouble at all now to be off with the tunic and the boots and the breeches. And never mind the Woman outside. Does Urien know what he's keeping me for? Rest easy, my lord. I pay my dues.

There, it is done, and the tide ebbs for both of us. Here I am. Fine linen sheets, soft chequered wool, wolfskins above me. Naked and warm. And the

greatest queen of all lying beside me. For I have lived
with enchantresses. Ceridwen's potboy, in a previous
life. I've served this brood. I know power when I see
it. And Morgan's power is greater than any of them.
But she's still a woman, for all that.

Mind you, I could have done without her
watchdog, hunched in that fold of the curtain over
there. It's stirring, and a face scowls in at me through
a slit. The sun shafts on it for an instant and I see
what it is now. Oh, ye gods! That's worse than I
thought. Especially as he's looking at me as though
he'd like to drive a knife through my most sensitive
parts. Woman? That was the cruellest joke. Lucky
for me Morgan has him under her foot like a crushed
beetle. What had he done, to bring him to this? And
watch yourself, Taliesin, that you don't end up the
same way.

The nightmare has gone, I stroke her shoulder. Her
face is buried under the heaping of her still-black
hair. You did not think I meant that by the snow
on the crags, did you? Autumn is coming, but the
frost has barely touched her flesh. I sang of the
landscape of the soul. Her muscles are tight, even
now. I let my fingers stray among her hair. I am
satiated. I could sleep now, or go for a long walk
beyond the walls. But I owe her more. I will stay
a little. I am not so proud of my own craft that I don't
know what it means to be hired. I give value for the
gifts I get.

But for all that, I have left her still moaning. It is
not that I cannot satisfy, for it was well done. But
she is more spirit than body. And that says more than
you can ever know, who have not felt the passionate
surges sweeping through her. Yet the spirit was

somewhere else, more urgent still in its desires. And who is there in the world could satisfy that?

I settle my arm closer about her, and feel her tears warm and wet on my wrist. I leave her grief unspoken. I know my limitations. I am a young man, and good for one thing only. And the harp, of course. And both of those I do superbly well. But that is all.

I dress as before and go back to Urien's tower, and as I pass I try to nod and grin at Woman and those that have a better right to the name, only not too broadly. That would be unwise. Step softly, Taliesin, their eyes follow you.

I am glad to be out in the wind. I find Urien not on the wall but down by the smithy, talking to the armourer over a mailed kilt of leather and silver. He looks at me straightly. He knows, of course. I can tell this pains him. I would not willingly have hurt him; I like the man already. But what choice did I have?

A sharp intake of breath. I've been a fool. This is a king. The penalty for what we've done flashes before me.

But he rests his hand on my shoulder as we move from the furnace.

'Have a care, boy,' he says. 'She can break you as she has broken the others,'

I look up at his face. It strikes me again that, plain soldier though he is, he is a whole man, and kingly. There are few not of her side who could come close to matching her strength.

'But not you?' I ask.

'Morgan,' he says, baring his teeth, 'is not the woman to have married a fool.'

I like him for that grim smile. He's no weak

cuckold. I could respect this man. I shall do well here,
if I tread lightly.

> Until my life ages,
> And death claims his wages,
> I shall not cease yearning
> Unless I praise Urien.

Chapter Three

Modred. Morgan's blood. Anyone can see that with half an eye. He pulls up his horse on the racetrack ahead of the rest and swings neatly down. He soothes the sweating beast with a whisper, hands the reins to the ready groom and comes towards me, unhurried but purposeful. He looks pleased with life, but his breathing is steady. You wouldn't think he had just won a race. A young man under control, with deep reserves of power kept hidden, like a salmon that hangs flickering in the current. An arresting face. Darkly handsome. Morgan might have looked like that if Gorlois had ever sired a son. Black Morgan. Black Modred. But there's a difference, as I know before the end of the day.

He greets me courteously, and I see by that smile why everyone finds it so hard to refuse that family. So winning to the world, so bitter to each other. Brown eyes, flecked with green, like tarns in peat. They look deep into me, and seem to like what they find.

'Taliesin of Pure Song!' he smiles. 'Your harp declares you. Welcome to Rheged. The very blackbirds on the trees fell silent for despair the day we heard you were coming to Caer Lugh as Chief of Song. They tell me your bardic crown shines as bright as the Thirteen Treasures of Britain.'

I mumble some nonsense. For a poet, I'm curiously short of words today. My tongue trips and stumbles. I'm blushing like the smith's furnace. His hand on my shoulder now.

'How do things move in Pengwern? What does Cynan Garwyn of Powys plan this summer? Will he raid Brycheiniog or Cornwall?'

A lover of poetry and a soldier too. He is steering me across the courtyard as we talk. Hard to resist, Morgan's brood. I tell him what he wants. He offers me wine, but it is not that that loosens my tongue. I find it important that Modred of Good Counsel should think well of me.

I play a few englynion for him, and he gives me the goblet I have drunk from, rare green glass. He also knows more than a thing or two about harmonies. We stroll beyond the city walls.

'Is it true,' he asks, 'that your mother was an enchantress?'

Ceridwen, the Fair Beloved. And a shudder goes through me as I shape my lips to speak her name. Be careful, boy. Three times that one blessed you. She gave you body, life, and poetry, and all of them against her will. Do not presume that even this far from Lake Tegid she may not come to demand a reckoning, after all.

Still, I tell him. A bard is born to sing, and the inspiration of my awen is upon me. We sit on a boulder by the mere while I tune the harp.

I have had many births.
I have been a fierce bull bitterly fighting.
I have been a squirrel that vainly hides.
I have been a spearhead beaten on the anvil.
I have been a roe in an entangled thicket.

16

And before that? The light shines clear for a moment and I am the child Gwion Bach, set to stir the cauldron of mighty Ceridwen for a year and a day. The herbs seethe and the incantations of the goddess hiss like steam. She is brewing the liquor of inspiration for her son Morvran, the most ill-favoured man in the world, Morvran, brother to Creirwy, one of the three most beautiful women in the Island of Britain. From Ceridwen come ice and sunshine, cursing and blessing. You must understand she loves Creirwy and Morvran equally. The spell is her mother's gift to him. Granted he needs something. He's nothing else to commend him, with hair on him like the bristles of a boar. On the battlefield, there's no enemy dare look at him long enough to strike him.

There are two of us tend the magic, I to stir it, and blind Morda to chop the wood and stoke the fire. It is not for us, this inspiration; an ignorant boy and a sightless slave. But the year's toil has almost spun its hot hard circle and I grow clumsy with weariness. The paddle sticks and jerks. From the throat of the cauldron, three golden, boiling drops arch towards me. A dragon bites the finger of Gwion Bach.

Pain. Well, what would a boy do but suck his finger? I have never been the same since.

She knew, by the bursting of the cauldron. All else inside was poison once the poetry had fled. She knew, by the dying of the horses of Gwyddno Garanhir when the spilt brew had fouled the river. She knew that I had got her blessing and her son had lost it. She could have learned it in the shine of my face.

Terrible, the theft of knowledge. I won a vision, but Morda lost the eye that could not see before she

17

turned her wrath on me and found me missing. She came running, like a storm across the lake. And I must use that precious knowledge now to flee the giver.

Pain. Unmaking. Then the dark hard journey back into being. And always I must do it again. I am driven, hunted, pursued, As a hare I am chased by a greyhound, as a fish by an otter, as a songbird by a hawk. At last I become a grain of wheat trapped under the claw of a black, high-crested hen. I am swallowed, I am consumed. In the inescapable womb of Ceridwen I am made man.

She gives me flesh. I am Ceridwen's son now. I, the little robber, lie between her legs. It's all up with me. I'm a helpless baby, blind with her blood. Now I am washed with herb-scented water. They place me in her arms. The cheated mother looks on the brow of the thief whom she has borne, and loves me. The world is delivered of a miracle.

Not so easy, though, to forgive me. I am a pretty boy, but I am still the usurper of poetry. I robbed her son.

A last death. Sunk in a leather bag in the salt water of the estuary, the day before Beltaine. The cold takes my little breath away, a gasp of song. The river maiden Dubr Dulu hears it. She swims me on her bosom down the lapping tideway and leaves me hanging on the pole of Gwyddno's weir.

May Eve. And Gwyddno Garanhir's prodigal son Elffin finds the crows of ill-luck gathering about his reputation. His father gives him one last chance of fortune: the catch of the blessed weir on this sacred night, a rare inheritance. But it seems the young man is doomed to remain unlucky. The keepers shake their heads in disbelief. The famous trap is empty of salmon for him and there is only a satchel full of . . . me. The Child of the Radiant Brow, the pearl of poetry. Elffin takes me home and fosters me. I have rewarded him richly for that rescue.

I steal a glance sideways to test what effect I'm having. Modred is no fool. But I am startled by what I see. I am aware by the prickling of my hair-roots that I have plucked a chord deep in this man's soul. He is listening to me as though he were Adam and I were singing of his expulsion from Paradise. My song was no mere entertainment. This speaks for him. I summon my awen to do better for him yet. I see new visions.

I have been a prisoner in Caer Pedryvan, four-square, revolving.

I was with Mary Magdalene in the firmament.

I have been enchanted for a year in the foam of water.

I was with my Lord in the highest sphere when Lucifer fell.

That is not what he wants to hear.

'Who was your father?'

That stops me short. I laugh a bit. Fathers?

'They tell me one of them was a saint. You should ask my mothers.'

I get a laugh more bitter than my own for an answer.

Black Morgan. Black Modred. He and I walk back together. He is as generous as his sire . . . if Urien is indeed his father . . . and more than courteous to me now. His hand on my arm is warm. It tells me that we are brothers in some way. Very powerful stuff is poetry. I nearly said it changes things. But that

19

wouldn't be true, would it? It's not like magic. Poetry changes nothing; it uncovers the truth. It points up the pattern of the universe. Beneath the gorgeous trappings of hyperbole, we show you the bonework of reality. We embroider, but we do not reinvent the world. Poetry affirms.

So I suck my thumb of knowledge and nearly choke on a hiccup. His finger-clasp on my arm has grown chill. I see a little of what I have done. I am mischievous Gwion again. My little song has stirred the mud of the deepest lake in the narrowest valley where the sun has never shone. Beneath the attentive smile, under the nobility, Modred is damaged in spirit. I glance sideways and see the way his dark brows meet now over his eyes. I remember this is a warrior of reputation. You'd think twice, aye and thrice, before you crossed Modred in the council-chamber or on the battlefield.

Chapter Four

We part at the gate. Whatever passion it was I startled, Modred's got it reined in again. He's affable, considerate.

'Our kitchens will need to cook a rare feast this evening to match the banquet of song that you are inviting us to. I am eager for nightfall.'

He grasps my hand and crosses the court, and I see clearly enough where he is going. To the queen's quarters but not, I am sure, for the same purpose she called me. Closeness of another sort, Modred and Morgan. Is she his mother?

Black Modred, Black Morgan. Yes, there's a difference. Now I am under her window again, I can feel her darkness burning, like a lantern behind a shutter, like a smothered fire, like the stars in the darkest night of storm, if you could only tear away the clouds. As Ceridwen, so Morgan holds them both, with difficulty, by great power in her strong person. It is not easily done: the darkness with the light. You may not understand how this should be, those of you who have been brought up by the Church. Arthur and the bishops both use the vocabulary of the battleground. Our side or theirs, Heaven conquers Hell, as though God made the world to run by rules of war. I am a bard. Fighting's my metaphor as much as any spearman. But Christ and the Mothers speak another language, of buried corn, of circling seasons, birth and sacrifice.

Light and darkness. They are two halves of a whole, not good and bad, as you have been taught to understand it. They are two rhythms, created for each other, the voice singing one melody, the harp playing another. Together they weave one song, the penill. Most people, being small, serve principally one. I have been lucky. Made talented in childhood through this last birth, and footloose by my harp, I am free to wander Britain between the two. I am Taliesin, the charmed boy. I am not important in myself, though I wouldn't recommend you to say so to my face – we poets can chant a blasting satire! I am a dragonfly skimming the surface of deep water under the sunshine. I do not swim the deep, cold current of one, or soar in the high heat of the other. I live between the two, caressed by both, a thing without weight. Only my songs matter.

I have been reborn and know more lives than one. Some tell me my father was a white-frocked saint. Others call my mother Ceridwen the Crooked Witch. And I'm still waiting to meet the man who dares to tell me both stories in the same breath . . . Now there's a thought to take to bed with you!

But there have been those that married the hand and voice in full penillion. That could both swim and fly. Merlyn was one, who used magic to charm Uther Pendragon into Ygerne's bed and then set Arthur at the head of Christian Britain. He was a well-shaft deep into the old ways, a gateway to the new. It is not lightly borne. It takes great strength to hold the balance and not be toppled over. But where is Merlyn now?

Walk on, boy. People are staring at you. Do you want them to think their new bard's moonstruck?

Perhaps I am, though.

Morgan? Is there no one in the world who can part that curtain and let out the light in her? Be careful, Taliesin boy. It's early days yet. What is this light that leaps behind her door: the life-giving sunshine or a consuming fire?

But Modred. That's different. The light of courtesy and grace without. Darkness beneath. I have stirred something nasty under his bonfire pile.

Wait! They're coming out again, Morgan and Modred. Their heads are together. She steps with the swift grace of a wild mare on the moors, leading her colt. She walks right past me as if she hasn't noticed me. They pass through the gate, down to the forest, with that false Woman a few steps behind carrying a stick with a heavy head, like a cudgel. What do those two talk of together under the trees, with only the old hag to overhear? I feel astonishingly desolate, for one who's only just met her. There is no place for her harper Taliesin now. She will not teach me what she teaches Modred.

Well, there are plenty of pretty girls in this castle. I shrug my shoulders and look around. You can be sure there are bright eyes looking my way and hoping. If I had seen them first . . . But this day of my coming I only have eyes for my queen. Morgan's is not a face you quickly replace by another. Or a body. Later perhaps. But now . . . Besides, I'm prettier than any of them. I toss my head and smile a bit, and walk by as though I haven't seen them staring.

So I wash and dress in bright court clothes and

23

make ready to sing for my new king at suppertime.
The horses are penned for the night and the hall
seems full of prancing princes that smell like them
of sweat and leather. Urien's here. Only the face I
look for before all others is missing. Modred and
Morgan are not back, it seems.

A hospitable family this. Hands clasp my shoulder,
faces grin. Owain, Pasgen, Rhun, Agravain, Gaheris.
Siblings, cousins, foster-brothers. I can no more sort
them out tonight than a pack of circling hounds,
though I must have their genealogies off pat by
tomorrow. Rhiwallawn thrusts a great drinking-horn
into my hand, half of an auroch's head piece, bound
with silver and mother-of-pearl. The mead's good,
too. Gareth's doing a juggling trick with a pair of
sharpened daggers. It makes us gasp, and him too
when he gets it wrong. True sons of Morgan and
Urien, some of these must be, and others not. I watch
the fair and square ones, bow-legged, as if they still
straddled their horses, sure of sword and sturdy
drinkers of mead, outdoor men in a world of spears
and dogs. Rhun should be a scholar, by the look of
his finely-manicured hands. I suck my thumb and
spot the thread of dark Morgan's blood in some, like
a fallen hair on a pillow. Owain, now. We know that
name, of course, even in Powys. As like to Urien
outwardly as one buzzard to the next. But my awen
warns me he holds more dangerous power.

There are the women of course. Only I find it hard
to look them in the eye since this afternoon. One
young lady I shall search for in vain. Morfudd isn't
here, Morgan's famed daughter. She is married by
this, I'm told, and serving Gwenhyvar at Arthur's
court. A pity, though. One of the three most lovable

young women of the Isle of Britain, they say. Down, boy.

The young men shout and gesticulate as they wait for the meat to be served. His? Hers? I watch them, and cannot sort out the truth of it. They are already sitting at the board when Morgan enters at last, with Modred following. Urien rises and Modred hands her to her couch and goes to his own place. The high table for him, but a lower seat than most of the young men. Still, he rests his hand on each one as he passes and greets them with a smile and a well-tuned query.

To Gaheris, 'Your horse went lame, I think, or you would have beaten me today. Would you like me to look at his leg? . . . They tell me you've had a book sent from Ireland, Rhun. May I see it tomorrow? . . .'

They answer him soberly. He must be younger than any of them, yet I can see they respect him, and so do I.

It's been a long day, and I'm giddy with travel and strangeness; a long supper, and I am heavy with mead. But my time has come, and all those faces turn to me like daisies opening to the sun. My fingers quiver with anticipation. It has never yet failed. The music rises in me, more urgent than the push of manhood. Believe me, I do not lie. It must out.

I sing first, as I am bound, of the king's fame and feasting, and Urien is as open-handed as I've heard. A horned bull and a cow are no bad beginning. But my praise is colourless yet. I don't know the man and his deeds. He shall have better of me than this in the months to come. So I turn to the tales of Britain and her old glory. I sing of battles past, of days I was too young to see. All the fighting I've known was in my service to Cynan Garwyn. I can hardly praise the wars of the ruler of Pengwern in this hall. The cattle-herds of Rheged graze too close to Powys.

There is a greater name, though. Like the first drum-beat of Beltaine that wakes the dancing horse, like the first rain-drops at the end of drought, like the step of a sweetheart outside the door. Arthur. And the fists beat on the table and the throats roar out his name. And I know it's reality. This is Arthur's family.

We are all his family. Arthur. An incantation like the name of a god. A charm, a legend, and he is not even dead. Arthur. I have never seen him yet. He never came to hold his court in Pengwern. I could not follow the men of Powys to his muster. It is the stale verses of older bards that I must recite. And fear grows in me, like one who sees a wound that will not close, that I may have drunk those drops from the cauldron of inspiration in vain. I can weave the praise of Cynan and Urien, but it is not enough. The harp grieves with the weight of mightier songs unsung. For I am Taliesin, the marvellous bard of Britain. When will Arthur lead us again? Where is the matter of the great song I was born to sing?

My hands move on unbidden, my voice chants. My mind's somewhere else.

After Badon. Truce. The roads are free. In the north and west the people prosper. Forget the lost lowlands of the south and east, numb your heart to the thought that they were half of Britain. Blind your eyes to the women of the Cymry that have borne Saxon children.

After Badon. The Saxons settled in the east, an understanding. Our warriors do not fight across the wall of hills. Our Christians do not march to save

Saxon souls. The foreigners keep what they hold. And so do we.

A crippled peace. And where is Arthur now, that turned the tide and made us feel that we, the Cymry, were children of the dragon? The High King of all the Britons is almost forgotten. He has no territory of his own, who unites many. Who needs a general when there is no war? His kinsmen hunt the forests of the north. West, his boyhood friends have turned their spears on neighbours' cattle. Where are the battles of legend, the high glory, the warriors triumphant over the white-faced enemy? Where is the matter for the bards of Britain? Could it be that Taliesin was born too late?

Terrible thought. Drown it with the auroch's horn.

The mead goes round. It's someone else's turn to sing. Morgan looks up and smiles at me.

My sweet lady, there is a gentler side to my art. I can coax airs in the night to charm queens to bed. But they are too delicate to be sung in this hall. It might give rise to misunderstanding. Well, no, that's not my problem. If the world heard those songs, it might understand some things rather too well.

Urien knows already. And still he both loves and fears her. But that's not to say he'd want his grandson's grandchildren to hear these lays. And my poems will still be singing when the world is old. Rest the harp, Taliesin. He lifts his drinking-horn to you.

Tread circumspectly.

The domestic bard has had his turn. It is time to be on your feet again, boy. Pick up the harp once more and sing of the stag that Owain killed on the mountain, of the gold that Urien scatters with a ready hand, of the dun cattle in the pens of

Erechwydd. The songs that live are those we earn
our bread by. Those of the heart die when the singer
dies.

> Until my life ages,
> And death claims his wages,
> I shall not cease yearning
> Unless I praise Urien.

Chapter Five

I've hardly learned my way round the castle when the summons comes. Arthur will lead a spear-host beyond the Clyde. The troublesome Picts, worrying the heels of good Britons? The wave-bandit Irish, raiding for slaves and gold? The hunt for a famous boar? What do I care? What do any of us care? He rides again, the king of my dreams, and the young men are called to follow him.

They're wild with joy as they rush for their saddles. Owain and Pasgen, sons of Urien's blood, Agravain and Gaheris, sister's sons to Morgan. I have all their pedigrees versified now, except Modred, who calls Morgan 'Mother', and yet. . . I can see nothing of Urien in him, and I'm afraid to ask. I think I see the possibilities. Rhun won't ride with them. He wears a plain gown like a scholar monk. He'd sooner spend his time at the Abbey of the White House beyond the Firth.

Not Urien either. I seek him out. The wind is blowing my hair across my eyes. It cuts sharper in Rheged than I'm used to.

'Will you not ride with Arthur, my lord?'

His hand twists in the mane of the bay horse he's fondling. He's not so old; Arthur's his senior. You can see that he aches to be saddled with his sons. But he shakes his head.

'No. I am King of Rheged. I must fight for the land I hold, or for the Island's safety.'

'But Arthur's campaign!'

'Some fishing village in Strathclyde that pirates have looted? A hill in Lothian where the Painted People have placed their sign? Some high-handed chieftain who's kept his tribute back? I rode with Arthur once. We were both young then. We waded in blood on the beaches of Lindsey when the worm-ships came. We patrolled the high backbone of Britain in the mist and the rain. We stopped the Saxon right hand troubling our Cymric left. I fought at Badon. Those wars are over. The Island of the Mighty? A stew of quarrelling tribes. Dumnonia and Dorset, Gwynedd and Gwent, Elmet and Rheged. I steal their bulls, they take mine if they can. What should I care for the losses of Custennin, or Mark, or Rhydderch? I guard what I have. Lyvennet, Solway, Catterick. What's Britain now?'

I stare at him as if the gale had snatched my breath away.

What is Britain? No kingdom, then, but a dream, and beyond the Pennines a great amputation that aches still when the wind blows from the east? Only a dream, this Britain that we love. Only a dream, a vision that mocks our fractious history. I am a poet! I live by dreams. Britain is a country dreamed by Arthur when the night was blackest and the sun of Rome had set. Yes, Arthur is a man, they say, though strangely got. Arthur the warrior will die. But Arthur the dreamer will live on. As long as he sleeps under some British hill, so long that enchantment will endure. Britain, beyond all common sense, a kingdom of the heart.

'You will let me ride with your sons? I have brought my own horses. I'll stay out of serious trouble. I will sing of how Owain and Pasgen fought gloriously for Arthur . . .'

'You will sing of Urien Rheged guarding Carlisle.'

He shakes my arm then to make me laugh. 'Cheer up, lad! How about a cattle-raid against the borders of Powys? Would you back old Urien against Cynan's cowherds?'

I know he jests. There'll be no cattle-rustling till the young men come home. The tide of history is ebbing round me. I'm a young poet in an ageing king's court.

We wave the warband farewell, the women, children, cripples, veterans, Taliesin.

The yards are still. Spare horses start and throw their heads up when the buzzard screams. They're left at home, imagining, like me. Keen blood knocks on the doors of the heart in vain. My footsteps echo in empty passageways.

And Morgan? I learn that there are rhythms, seasons. I have my place in them. I am not always needed.

I get to know the women well. Too well, at times. Only one resists all my advances. Tegau Goldbreast, fresh and sweet as a jug of cream. But I'm a stalking cat that's smacked for trying to mount her table to come at her. Such soft blue eyes, such unintentioned promise in the curving of her side. And yet, nothing more. I think she teases, but she does not. Her candid face smiles serious reproof. A Christian maiden, in Morgan's bedchamber? Nearer to her than any, except that Woman. She's neither dark, nor damaged, a walking miracle of grace. I may dance

31

with her at night, but that is all. Poor recompense for what I'm denied.

So, each in our own way, we wait.

The harvest is in now, and Morgan has overseen the severing of the last sheaf. There is a nip in the air in the early morning, and often a knot of folk round the kilns where the corn is drying. We stop to warm ourselves as we pass, a good place for gossip.

I pass through the back of the hall, enjoying a bit of bread and honey, and Morgan's there, dressed for riding. Her horses are tacked and ready before the mist has lifted. She names some of her people. Her eye rests on me and I feel an unreasonable terror thrill through me. Because she wants me? Because she might not want me? I guess where she's going. Somewhere like old Caer Wenloe, dark fortress of Gwendoleu that ruled over the Solway before Urien got it. Certainly some secret place that never knew the hand of Rome. I have been with her before. I know what they will do. She names someone else. I am released for today. I am never sure, as she cannot be sure of me. I am too changeable. I hymn the praise of the Trinity in Urien's hall; I know the secrets of Ceridwen. She uses me sometimes, but she does not trust me. She is wise.

I see whom she's chosen to ride with her. Not Tegau Goldbreast. So I'm right. This must be the Mothers' business then. Morgan is curiously tender to the conscience of Christians. I've heard she was schooled in a convent. She never forces Tegau, though she compels others. Me, sometimes. She stands beside Urien in his chapel on feastdays, though she leaves before the sacrament.

Now she rides north with a dozen women and a

trusted escort, though they're hardly needed. Morgan the Healer has little to fear from anyone. I am a free man till suppertime.

An ordinary day in autumn. The bracken brown and the apples ripening red.

And then he comes, without warning. Beyond my wildest expectations, Arthur the King, to the court of Morgan of Rheged, and I am there. And when he comes it is all gold and rubies, and the shouting of the hoarsest voice seems like larksong.

They are a noisy lot, too, the crowd of men at his back. You can tell they come fresh from battle. Hard, eager warriors, thighs gripping the horses' flanks, hands firm on bridle and sword. Eyes flashing on all they see. You can tell they have ridden to death and back again, and all the world seems dearer to them now.

And the Pendragon, laughing at the head of them. The High King himself. All through my childhood they have sung me to sleep with tales of Arthur, his battles, and his feasting, and his hunts. Giants slain, great boars pursued, treasures snatched. But not, oh not, the songs I could have made myself. And now he is here before me. Like a golden oak tree firm in a gale. Like a river falling straight and roaring. Like an eagle above its prey. A mighty warrior. A king above kings. And the width of his smile gathers me in with all the others. My hands ache for my harp. How long must I wait till supper? I shall sing him such a praise-song as has never been made before. Arthur must remember Taliesin.

Urien's eyes are brighter blue than I have ever seen them. He's a proud man today. He and Arthur hug each other like schoolboys. I feel the High King's not been in Carlisle for a long while.

Owain and his brothers fall on their father with great shouts and armclasps. I'm scanning the ranks of faces behind Arthur. These are the names out of legend. Gawain, Cei, Bedwyr! I am longing to compose an englyn for each one of them, but I have not come face to face with their particular genius yet. It is hard to contain my patience and not get drunk with their fame. Oh, why didn't I ride with Owain, to see their long-legged, corn-fed horses in the onrush of battle? These heroes are Arthur's comrades, known and loved, daring in war, faithful when the shields hang quiet. Other quests have scattered the allies of Badon long since. These few stay loyal even before his horn sounds.

In the middle of all this row one quiet man stands closer to the king than all the others, like a son at his father's shoulder, modestly laughing. Arthur takes his hand and joins it to Urien's with a flourish. 'So, brother, since this young man claims no other father, take back your foster-son safe and sound. Look, not a mark on him, though he's presented me with a score of heads. You have taught him well. By the Trinity, I wish that Gwenhyvar had given me a son of my own so brave, so canny, and such good company.'

Urien and Morgan's foster-son? The only one of the litter I never dared ask about. So that's all it is. I don't mind telling you I'd supposed something more scandalous. Too highly-coloured an imagination, Taliesin, that's your trouble. All the same, a grown man and still at the court of his foster-parents? That's odd. Whose is he really, then? It seems his history may be closer to mine than I thought. I kept a prudent silence about my own mother. And the old thought won't go away. I guess what Morgan is doing

now at the raven-haunts of Caer Wenloe, or some
apple-grove of the Liddel, or a sacred well. I know
how we worship the Mothers.

The men are all jesting about each other's deeds
and boasting of their own, except Modred. All
tongues speak well of Modred.

Word flies fast. Carlisle is being inundated. It seems
as if all the housebound elders of Rheged are coming
galloping up to greet him. But the smile is fading from
Arthur's lips. He scans the thronging courtyard. We
all guess whom he's looking for. Urien's face is
darkening at this imagined slight. She should have
been here long before this. The High King of Britain!
Half the nobility of Rheged in her courtyard. And
where is Morgan? There are new arrivals every
minute, dust-clouds on every road. The Queen of
Rheged does not come.

The king's own sister. Queen of half the North.
Already the horses are being led to the stables and the
cup of the hospitality of Rheged has not yet been
offered. If I had been Arthur's sister, I would have run
to him with a spilling goblet of red wine. I would have
seized him by the hand and taken him to the softest
bed. With my own hands I would have drawn off his
muddied boots, unlatched his armour, dressed him in
a gorgeous mantle. But Morgan does not appear. I
watch Arthur's eyes searching in vain for her.

'The men of the North are quick with their
welcome, Urien Rheged. But your women insult me
still, it seems.'

'The Queen did not know of your coming today.'

'Morgan the Wise? Is there anything she does not
know?'

Here comes Tegau Goldbreast hurrying, kneeling

to the royal guest, offering up a brimming horn of welcome, a plate of bread and salt. A little late, and the wine trickles over her fingers. She is flushed with more than haste. But it is gracefully done. Her skirt sweeps the stones and pearls gleam in her bowed hair as bright as those that stud the rim of the drinking-horn.

Her voice is soft. 'In the name of my mistress, I give you Queen Morgan's welcome. She rode with her ladies today to a holy place above the Liddel. There is a spring, sacred from ancient times to those of her persuasion. Not a day has passed but your sister has prayed to some god for your safety, and her sons', as we do to the Trinity. She bid me tell you if you ever came in her absence, that her poor house stands ready to be made rich by your entrance.'

Arthur smiles like daybreak then at this pretty speech, and more at the pretty face. He drinks from the horn and passes it to Cei behind him. Tegau gets a far warmer kiss than she'd have permitted from any other man. There's jesting all round me. With cheers a warm-faced warrior is pushed forward to help her to her feet. Her eyes are bright for him above her companionable blushes. Caradawc Strong-Arm's a luckier man than I am, by the look of it. She leads the way. Modred himself attends the king to the best guest-chamber. On the threshold of the palace Arthur turns and lifts his eyes to the haze of hills beyond the Firth. His smile has vanished again. He looks like a child bereft of his toy.

And I? The moment he's gone I have forgotten Morgan. Am I in good voice? Will the harp be in tune? What shall I wear? What should I sing? Sweet angels and all the goddesses of Britain, what must I sing?

Chapter Six

I'm sitting in the windowseat overlooking the courtyard and trying over a hundred airs on the harp, none of them right, when I see her come. I do not realise at first it is Morgan. Her head droops like her horse's. Her dress is soiled. The women are spent too, the guard respectful, sober.

But when I see it is the queen I do not stop to wonder where they have been, what they have done. Better not enquire too deeply. I have news that must come before everything. The yard is as busy as a feast-day, but she doesn't seem to have noticed. I am not sure if I should yell it from the window or dash for the door. Too late. Someone is coming across the yard to greet her, limping a little; he's taken a leg-wound. Owain. She's dismounted now, swaying a little as she lets go of her horse, looking at her eldest son striding towards her. She puts her hand to her eyes as if to clear a mist. Then his arms are wide and she's enfolded in them.

I'm perched like a wren on a windowledge, watching them. This must be the moment when he tells her who is here. I see her start, step back. Her look flies to the walls of the guest-chambers. She starts to hasten for that door. Then I see her stop, falter with indecision.

Indecision. Morgan? That all-wise queen whose every gesture strikes with the sharp edge of authority.

My heart aches with a sudden tenderness for her, and just the merest touch of self-congratulation; the young and vigorous shoot for the flower that has bloomed past fullness. She is tired, her hair dishevelled, her skirt dusty. Take twenty years away and it would not matter. She could laugh off her careless disarray, the sweet tangle of the wayside briar rose. But the years are more unforgiving now. Arthur is here in her court, sudden, unexpected, after long absence. And she is not as she would like him to behold her.

She's taken charge of the situation, hurrying towards her own rooms, calling to bring the servants running to her and send them flying again in all directions, as if her stewards hadn't begun to prepare the feast hours before this. The doorway takes her from my sight.

I stand at a crossroads of the passageways. Urien's rooms or Morgan's? I haven't been bidden to either. But I cannot wait for evening. I cannot be left sitting on the margin of this day's events. I seem to feel the heat of Arthur from the men's side. So what takes my feet down the corridor that leads to Morgan's chamber? What do I think she wants me for now?

The shadows fox my eyes after the sunlight. A man is coming unevenly towards me, along the corridor trodden mostly by women. I recognise the limp again. Owain returning from his mother's room.

He checks at me, as I did at him, and peers in my face.

'Taliesin! Do you think my mother has time for

harpers now, when Arthur the king is waiting for her appearance?'

'I didn't know . . . I thought perhaps she would want . . .' Not she. I'm the one that wants to be noticed. Arthur's her brother. Do not forget your faithful Taliesin.

He takes my arm, not gently, and steers me back the way I've come.

'Listen, lad. You don't know the board. The stakes in this game are too high for you. We have had other smart young players before you. One bard got more from my father than a cup of gold.'

'Urien Rheged's a generous man!'

'Generous with his sword, when his honour's threatened. Have you heard of Tristvard?'

'No.'

'He won more from my mother than the rules allowed. My father killed him.'

Blood stops. It's more than shadows darkening my eyes. The air's terribly cold in this passage.

'Urien killed a *bard*! Because he and your mother . . .? But Morgan! What did she do then?'

Owain laughs, harsh as a crow.

'She would have slain Urien for it, with the same bloody sword. My sister Morfudd stopped her. Since then, my parents have come to an understanding. She agrees not to taint his honour. He allows her the rites of her kind, so she causes no scandal.'

I remember the smile on Urien's face. *'Morgan is not the woman to have married a fool.'*

And I thought that smile spoke sympathy!

Do not grow up, Taliesin, do not grow up. The rules of this game are stricter than you thought. Only a child is excused.

I shall not cease yearning
Unless I praise Urien.

I shall not cease yearning . . .

The words rattle in my head like loose teeth.

Morgan walks into the hall well before suppertime.
I'm there already, nervous as a bird with nestlings.
And when I see her, even I, Taliesin, gasp in wonder.
I thought by now I knew every strand of her hair,
every hollow of her flesh. But she is lovelier tonight
than I have ever dreamed. Gold embroidered on
purple. The finest jewels she possesses braided in her
hair. I think her face has been delicately tinted to
glow in the lamplight, a bloom of perfection, as
though the years were running backwards. Hours,
you might have thought her women would have
needed to prepare her like this. But it goes deeper
than that. Jewels can make a woman look hard. It
is more than bathing in scented oils and milk that has
softened her so. Her radiance comes from within.

I stand at Urien's elbow, bewitched, watching her
come up the long hall towards us. We're all the same.
Small hope that I, smart as I am, can catch anyone's
eye this evening, with every man and woman gaudy
as a kingfisher. But my time will come. Only I can
enchant their ears.

Morgan signs to the steward and the horn is
sounded. All faces are turned to the door now, all
the household readied.

There's a shout from the threshold, 'Peace, my
lords and ladies! Welcome Arthur, High King of all
the Britons!'

He knows how to make an entrance. He stands

40

four-square, feet widely planted, hands on hips to throw back the cloth-of-gold mantle and show off the sturdy strength of his figure, head tilted, laughing, and the torchlight from the doorway making golden flames of his hair.

Morgan moves. They are advancing to meet each other in the middle of the hall, their hands outstretched across the years that have separated them. Her reverence is queenly. Her jewelled head is bowed, her skirts sweep the floor. In no way does this diminish her dignity. In silence he raises her up and holds her by both hands.

Long they stand silent, looking into each other's faces, her white fingers hidden within his greater grasp. Too long for a brother with a sister.

At last her voice thrills. 'I am grieved beyond measure that my brother the king should honour my hall with his presence after all these years and another woman than I should offer him her cup.'

'A welcome as rich as this was worth waiting for, lady.' His eyes caress her body. The next words come oddly harsh. 'That purple gown becomes you. Did you fashion the embroidery on it with your own hands?'

Their fingers part suddenly. She stares at him, and the sudden swing of her black hair covers the anger flashing in her eyes. Urien comes forward to take Arthur by the arm and lead him to the highest seat. He must understand more than I do. Modred is quick to attend Morgan. And I, that thought I had conned a thousand scrolls of knowledge in my incarnations, from the court of the fair goddess Arianrhod to great Alexander, am busy shelving fresh sheets that no one ever showed me.

41

We've eaten well. It is time to pick up the harp. Now, more than any night in my life, the melody must ring true. I touch the first string, and the magic of my voice falls over them all. The drunken laughter hushes. The knives are still. I feel the power in my song binding them all.

I sing first of Christ in glory riding on the clouds. Then I rejoice at Arthur's coming to our feast. They are good songs, for a beginning. They please him, and he throws me a golden belt snatched, who knows, from the loins of some dying Saxon or Pict. The gold is nothing to me – well, nothing much – beside his smile. But I search his face for something more. Can he hear the great song inside me that is waiting to be born? Does he sense that I was created to hymn his highest deed?

The lesser bards are buzzing now. Tonight there is strong red wine to ease my throat. I gulp a long, cool cup and feel it turn my skin to fire. Someone is looking at me along the table. Modred. His eyes are shining too.

There is dancing tonight. Morgan grows rosy again as Arthur swings her down the line. Look, they're laughing together. All's well, surely?

She sits by the fire now, and Healer and I must play again. Music without words this time, expertly fingered. Arthur stands between us, horn in hand, leaning over her shoulder and murmuring to her. Only I can hear, beneath my playing, what he says.

'So it is true? You keep the old ways still.'

'My husband is a Christian lord. Rheged is Urien's kingdom.'

'Then, if the High King wanted wisdom, he must apply to its queen.'

She does not start, but her utter stillness speaks more than if she had.

'Arthur of Britain has his own wise woman.'

'The Lady of the Lake? Pah! Nimue and I fell out long ago. She thought because she had raised me, she could rule me, as she does everyone else. But the High King has grown beyond his nursemaid. She wanted to share power with Bishop Bytwini as my soul-friend, but there is room on the throne he worships for only one. There was a rare old row. She left in a temper.'

'And the Christian Church is not enough for Arthur now?'

He leans closer. 'The bishops speak to me of heaven. That is not what I want to hear. It is this world that is slipping away from me too fast.'

She lifts her face to stare at him. In wonder? Disbelief?

'What do you want? You would ask me to turn back time for you? To do still what we have not yet done?'

He raises his horn to her. His look is deadly serious, no flattery, no accusation now.

'Who else should help me, if not my wise sister?'

Did my fingers falter? The spell's not working. Cei roars with laughter at a jest of Owain's. The magic thread has snapped. Arthur looks round and finds his hosts too close for prudence.

The warband are shouting for more manly music, and I am only too glad to answer them. Now I make the shields on the walls ring with chants that have more to do with warriors than wooing. They roar applause.

Morgan's forgotten. This is the life for me. The circling wine jug. The wild tales of battle. The fair

and laughing women. Oh, to be a bard in Arthur's
court! To transmute his story into song. To ride
beside him – all right, behind him! – into battle and
come back singing of victory. To know on my death-
bed that all the verses I have made are echoing for
ever down the years!

But when I draw breath again and look round the
hall, I feel in my soul one thing is still missing. One
name that was always coupled with Arthur's in the
songs of his boyhood. How old would that face look
if we could see it now? A map of wrinkles. A magic
chart of lines that speaks him wiser even than his
years. Who knows of Merlyn the Enchanter now? His
loss gapes like a side missing from the figure that is
joined tonight in Morgan's hall. Arthur, the noblest
king of all the Britons. Morgan, the most potent of
wise queens. Taliesin, the sweetest bard that ever
sang. If Merlyn came, the square would be complete.

A shiver runs through me. Once upon a time,
Merlyn himself sang in this very hall. He went
disguised as Gwendoleu's bard, before Urien came
here.

So I sing a new song. I sing of Merlyn, who was the
greatest chief of magic among all the wise, who led
the victorious Pendragon to Ygerne's bed, who put
an enchanted sword in Arthur's hand and guided him
on the path to victory. Who sleeps – well, who
knows where? In some forest where the nightingale
keeps watch? Under a secret stone? What might
happen if that magic re-awoke? Could we snatch the
Island of the Mighty from our foes, like the fabled
spoils from the fairy fortress of Annwn? Will the
morning never break that brings great Merlyn back
to us?

The notes curl plaintively among the rafters. There, I say to myself, that should bring tears to their eyes. But what's the matter with them? Why is Tegau hiding her eyes behind her hands? Why are Arthur's warriors grinning like schoolboys when their teacher trips? What have I said? What's so funny about Merlyn? It's worse than that. The men of Morgan's branch are frowning blackly. Arthur looks angry. And when I turn for help to my lord and lady I find the sky has turned to thunder in Morgan's face.

I see it now, ass that I've been! All this time I've been singing of Arthur's coming, and I never thought what it meant. When Merlyn enchanted Uther Pendragon to Ygerne's chamber, it was Morgan's father that had to be killed, Morgan's mother who was appropriated.

I've made a fool of myself again. It seems they taught me all the wrong things in Powys.

But Urien is a Christian king, and courteous. He gives me a dagger to add to Arthur's belt and cover my confusion. He is always generous.

> Until my life ages,
> And death claims his wages,
> I shall not cease yearning
> Unless I praise Urien.

Chapter Seven

There's no room in Morgan's bed tonight, even for so slight a lad as Taliesin. I have angered her. The spectre of a red-eyed wolf has reared its grinning mouth above her hearth, and at my summoning. Merlyn. And I'd thought it was a name of benediction. Still, to be honest, she wouldn't have been interested in me even if I hadn't crossed her. Not on such a night. She had decked herself like the Queen of Araby for Arthur, not for me.

After Owain's warning I find it a relief. Carlisle is too full of the presence of Pendragon and his men.

But the morning is a new day, the mist creeping up from the river and the promise of sunshine beyond.

They are all astir for the hunting, those men that have come with Arthur, and plenty of our ladies with them. It's what I wanted to believe, that life, that zest. All their lives these men have been fighting. They could never sit still in Celliwig or Caerleon. The great battles are over, but there is always some other quest. It has thinned their ranks. Harrying, hunting through the hills, friends dying, maimed. You'd think they'd begin to tire of the sight of blood by now, the older ones at least. But these are Arthur's warband. They have lived another summer. They are alive, whole, most of them, anyway, and reckless with the joy of it. Why should I want them to stop living before their brief lives end? What would I sing of, if they were not as they are? He draws the young men by the magic of his name. The older ones lost their hearts to him long ago. He does not need Merlyn to bewitch them. Like me, they hope to live in legends still untold.

At first, we are all a little heavy-headed, and the beer tastes sour and the chill clutches at our bowels. But we are men. We are alive, aren't we? We laugh and jest all the louder to shout down the goblins on our shoulders. Soon it will be Samain, Winter's Eve. But not yet.

Men, goblins. In the damp before sunrise I cannot hold off the black invaders of last night. I come on Arthur's warriors crowding about the stables, and even in the mist some shapes stand out from the rest, harder-edged. Arthur's sisters' sons. In all the knotted web of kinship, no bond should be more sacred to a man than that. They are many. I name them over to myself. Great Gawain himself, Agravain, Gaheris, Gareth. And from Morgan's body, Owain, Pasgen, Rhiwallawn, Rhun. Sons of Arthur's sisters. No, half-sisters. One mother, Ygerne, that bore three girls and then Arthur, but not to the same man. His father, Uther; theirs, Gorlois. The slayer and the slain. The spoil, their mother. My heart shivers in the dawn as I recall how Morgan looked when I sang of Merlyn, who brought it about.

And now my bard's training brings names strumming through memory. Young Arthur felled Saxons and Angles: Flame-Bearer, Blood-Axe, Raven-Hold. But other names come softer on the

48

tongue and bitterer to the taste. British names, kings
that opposed Arthur in that dawn. There were
Cymric spears levelled against the upstart boy.
Gwendoleu, here in Solway. Lot of Lothian and
Nentres of Garlot, kings who married Morgan's elder
sisters. So that's the current I cannot help but feel.
There has been treachery here in the North. Urien
Rheged? No, never Urien. Urien was always true to
Arthur. The bards sing him brave and constant to his
High King. So where does Morgan stand? Merlyn is
not loved here, that's plain. Is Arthur?

I have seen her gaze locked in his.

I should have turned my eyes to other faces than
hers. What might I have read then in the looks of
these sisters' sons? For a bard, I've been curiously
careless about their genealogy. These are Gorlois's
grandsons. How have they been bred? Whose
warriors are they really, Arthur's, or their mothers'?
How dearly do they love this royal uncle they have
sworn to serve?

No! You're a too-wise fool, Taliesin. You see riddles
where there are none. Tintagel's an old grief, long
buried. Look, Gawain is nearly as old as Arthur. A
lifetime's loyalty there, for all his father fell fighting
the young Pendragon. And these others are Urien's
sons as much as Morgan's. They've risked their life's
blood for their uncle already this summer. The sun's
up and the mist is fleeing. You're a silly boy and no
true bard. You play 'Blerwm, blerwm', upon your
lips, and make the world a nonsense-song.

They've looked out a hunting-pony for me to ride.
It's not the sober cob that carried me sedately from
Powys, with rounded sides and feet like platters. I
wish it was. Surely Urien knows I'm no horseman.

I'm a horse-owner, yes. I have droves of them, farms, serfs, back in Powys. They make a handsome form of wealth. I don't have to ride them.

I study this grey mare from a respectful distance. A nasty-looking brute. Lively. I don't like the way she rolls her eye at me. I'm a bard, not one of these wild men of Arthur's that ride as if they grew from the saddle.

But here is Morgan among us. She's not dressed for hunting, that's plain. She is dark today, her jewels gone. Black robed, black-hooded, gold bands crossed upon her chest like a druid priestess. Why? Morgan does nothing without calculation. All eyes fly to her and the racket hushes. I see the hope in Arthur's face. He is not hungry for her body today. Can she offer him something else?

She carries a silver cup of wine, gently steaming. She walks through the press of men and beasts to the centre. The hounds wag their tails. Even the horses stand still for her, though she has said no word. She stops before Arthur's roan and pours the first drops of wine upon the earth, moving her left hand and pronouncing the age-old words. There is a murmur all round. Christians like Urien sit stiff-lipped, others mutter the response. I am one of them. The hunt's a dangerous game. And Arthur? His lips move soundlessly. He watches her intently.

She holds the cup up to him now to drink to his own success. His eyes cannot leave hers as he takes it, and all that I thought I understood last night is not enough. The new day turns dark and the apples fall from the trees like blood.

I have seen fear in Arthur's eyes.

He turns. Bedwyr puts out a hand as if to taste the

wine for him first. An insult, surely, in his sister's house! But Arthur's look falls on me, and he gives a curious grin. And I, fool that I am, blush like a girl. It's not ugly doubt after all. He's giving me the first sip as a mark of high favour for my songs.

There is an odd stillness. Arthur's men watching us, Urien's people grimly silent. I was right, the first time. I sense the tension of mistrust. Why are they all looking at this cup and then at Morgan?

There are black flies before my face. I'm going to fall. The king's taster! Why me?

Indignantly I turn to Morgan's face and find its features still, her deep eyes unreadable. Poison? Would she do that to me? To Taliesin? But no, she's not the one who is holding out the cup to me. It's Arthur. I am a trifle to him, Morgan's bard. His golden belt last night has paid for all my songs. He owes me nothing. All the magic of my singing, all the splendour of my praises, cannot buy one more hour of life from him. God, what a waste of talent!

I reach my hand to take the cup. The wine smells spiced. Time crawls as in a dream. From the anger all around me I feel I am reliving an old scene. In some past life of mine? No. The pain's here. A festering wound reopening. It is they who are remembering, not I. The silver's warm from his grasp. My stomach heaves.

Then Arthur snatches the cup back from me, spattering the ground, his horse, my tunic in a mad baptism. With a roar of laughter he drains the wine to the last drop and tosses the empty goblet for me to catch.

'If that is your price! See how well I will trust my beloved sister!'

But she is angered.

'Do you still doubt what I have to offer? Can you not forget? Will you never believe I have done you no harm?'

'No harm? I recall a woman dreadfully dying here, in a poisoned cloak you made for me.'

'That was not my doing.'

'It was not her death you intended, certainly.'

'I am Morgan the Healer!'

'Yes! It was you who stole my scabbard of healing from me. You keep it yet.'

A stillness seizes her. I am a bard. I know the power of a dramatic pause. But the line that follows is not the true revelation. Something has been left unspoken here.

'You kept the sword that wounds.'

'I am the king!'

'And I am . . .?'

'I have drunk your cup today. What more do you want from me?'

That steady gaze for answer.

Colour dark as the wine rises in Arthur's face. Gawain snatches the hunting-horn hung on his belt by a golden chain. He blows wild notes that set the hounds belling and the huntsmen running to whip them in and bring back order. But blood is up, the horses tossing their heads, the riders impatient. Old griefs and old revenge ebb, leaving those two in an island of animosity and spilled wine.

Modred is ordering the stewards to hand round drink to all the rest. They toss it down with shouting and laughter. The hunt's moving off.

I'm at the tail of the field. The sun shines out, but I'm still cold. There is more here than I knew. Was he right to trust her? What does she want from him, and what has she taken already?

Fly higher, little dragonfly, the water is too deep beneath you.

Chapter Eight

But now the hunt is on. I'm afraid of horses. In Morgan's circle they worship mares. But in Powys we danced the dragon, and nobody ever asked me to ride one of those. Give me my own two feet on the ground every time, and my harp strapped to my back. I wouldn't bring her here, my precious Healer. I wouldn't risk the fine maplewood cracked on the ground and crushed under cutting hooves. So why do I hazard the brittle bones of Taliesin, the fragile fingers that should pluck the harp? I must be mad. I wince even to think about what a fall could cost.

Still, I'm a poet, with a soul tuned to glory, a warrior on the frontier of song. I am too young, too talented, too bold to spend my life harping of high halls and apple orchards and contented kine. I was thrice-born for something greater than that. Today I am close to Arthur. Even I can catch the wonder of it, though I'm near to screaming and I'm slipping off the mare.

Three notes on the horn. The third strikes deep and low. I know what that means. The hounds have put up a boar. Just my luck. No tall magnificent stag today. A short-legged, snuffling, small-eyed, mean, vicious, snaggle-toothed, devil of a wild he-pig. Begging your pardon! Best not say that here. Don't

even think it. A pig's a sacred animal. The ivoried
divinity, the favoured flesh, the burrowing guide to
the mysteries of the underworld. Little pig, be
favourable to us. Sweet pig, lead a charmed path
through the dangers of your forest. Holy pig, sacrifice
yourself upon our spears. Can I look him in the face
on the high table, with the apple trapped between
his tusks?

The pounding hooves on the rotting floor of the
forest. The beech sprays stabbing for our faces as
we duck beneath them. The gleaming backsides of
the horses flying before me. Is this how it is to ride
into battle? Do the Saxons lurk in ambush like the
White-Handed Wraith of the Birch whose touch they
say brings madness? Do the Angles rear as straight
and unyielding across the path as black-tipped ash
trees?

And Arthur away in front of us all, like a god on
horseback. No one of his men can outride him, or
none of them dares to. He is one with his steed. I
have been with Morgan at the dances in the forest
where the bodies of men and women sprout
monstrous heads of beasts. But Arthur turns the old
world upside down. He is the chief in majesty, his
tribe's splendour, the head and shoulders of a man
knit to the polished quarters of a horse.

Modred rides just behind him, the constant guard
for Arthur's back. He is a better horseman than I
thought for one so young. Less reckless than Owain
and Gawain, cleverer. I think he whispers to his
horse as Morgan would. He scans the bushes on
either side. A touch too upright, though, with his
hand ready on his spear. He'd better watch his eyes
under that holly.

But the pace quickens as the hounds give tongue. They've seen him. I can't spare a look for anyone else now. I'm jolted to death. The mare is slippery with foam and sweat. I'm sliding off. Forget the reins. She doesn't seem to understand them, anyway. Hands knotted deep in the mane. Clinging on. Pray to Rhiannon, Mother of Foals, this brute can steer a safer course than I can. Tree-trunks rushing past. I shall fall off. Help me, somebody, please! They're out of sight. Oh, wait for me!

Terrible dilemma. I'm frightened to death of going faster, and scared out of my wits that I'll be left behind. I know what my body's telling me. Perhaps I could fall off, after all. Brave the wrath we have stirred in the battered forest behind me and limp home to Morgan. But even my weak blood is up. Ahead is Arthur, and the vanishing dream of my boyhood.

The distant horn keens on the wind. I was born too late. I shall never ride with him against the Saxons. I shall never witness him turn the tide back, like a cliff against the sea, like a strong gate under a siege. It's only a tale. But better than nothing is the wild boar, and Arthur's spear in its side, and I, Taliesin, there to see the bright blood. Then they will go, to Celliwig, Caerleon, Camelot. For me, it will be back to the hall of the stately women of the North, to courtly Urien, and danger-loving Owain. But not, oh not, the dream I could have sung.

I mustn't give up. I shall be paying for this for a week. With a backbone jarred and bruised, and my legs aching from the desperate grip on this slimy beast. But on, on. There is a press of warriors ahead, dismounted, broad backs bent over, arms raised. Men

57

shouting. Someone leaps aside with a curse and there's a roar of laughter.

My knees slacken. I tumble to the ground. Scrambling through mud on hands and knees, I see between their planted legs the hounds whipped off the prostrate boar bathed in gore. Arthur is smiling broadly. Morgan's forgotten. I have come too late. He's made his peace with the morning.

There's blood on Bedwyr's thigh. Torn cloth, ripped flesh, white bone. There seems to be a terrible pain in my own chest too. And all that way to ride back again. If I turn my head I know the mare will be grinning at me with yellow teeth.

I stagger upright, clutching a hazel stem. Arthur sees me and laughs aloud. He cuts off the boar's ear and gives it to me for a keepsake. This time it's a great honour. The prize will come spoiled to Morgan's table with a cropped head.

'No gold or silver here, bard! But a purse to hold what you have.'

I gasp my thanks and clutch my trophy. I want to believe he does this to apologise for scaring me and not to slight Morgan. I have it still. But two hours ago I could believe he would have watched me die.

I've bought that keepsake dearly. The twisted horsehair of the mane has cut my fingers. They'll be sore on the harp-strings tonight, no matter how I suck them. But I was there. I was there when Arthur killed the Great Striped Boar in the Forest of Rheged. Well, almost there.

I was right about the sore fingers. And I don't know whether it's going to be more painful standing up or sitting down. I'm so weary and aching I could sleep for a week and never mind the feast. But I am the watcher who may not sleep. I am the bard above all bards. I have balanced a million angels on the point of this well-trimmed fingernail. And what is a bard good for, if he cannot charm the huntsmen till the stars pale and the heavy heads fall sleeping on crooked arms, and the women droop and sigh? King Urien's still half-awake. Sing on, Taliesin. Safe now. Like a skylark between earth and heaven. So small, no one can see it, but its music fills the world. Sing on, and live.

> Until my life ages,
> And death claims his wages,
> I shall not cease yearning
> Unless I praise Urien.

He's asleep now. And Arthur sleeps. The king of all the Britons is dead to the world. Lay down the harp. Relax the tortured fingers. He cannot hear you.

Chapter Nine

Morgan sleeps little these nights. Go to her now, but softly. She is drawing you. She hungers for your youth. The dangerous magic Arthur asks of her she has never turned upon herself. The Mothers' rites she uses respect both waxing and waning. They will not stay the hurrying years or hold still for her the hope of what she's not yet had. Yet she feeds on me. I age a century each time, but see her softened, rosy, lovelier . . . and still unsatisfied.

Move carefully from the hall. Above all, do not disturb Owain.

Tonight I'm not in the mood. The base of my spine's been hammered so that I walk as if I had two wooden legs, and still it hurts. But the harp knows its duty. It tugs me to Morgan's chamber like a questing hound. My eyelids droop and I stumble against walls. Lucky my feet could find this way even in my sleep. They almost do.

I start suddenly alert. Is someone there, in the passage that leads to Arthur's chamber? Have I been seen? No. All's still again. Only the draught on a guttering torch.

Morgan has been waiting for me. I can see by the restless way she turns from the window with the moon on half her face. She's been to bed before this,

I think; the sheet's thrown back. But now she stands with a great green gown flung over her night-shift and her hair brushed loose. I see something else too. There'll be nothing wanted from me here tonight but music. I can tell by the women she has chosen to keep watch with her. Women? That Woman-who-is-not, squatting on the floor, sour because I have kept him from his sleep. The other, fair as he is ugly. Too fair, her bloom untouched, untouchably chaste, Tegau. Oh that a Christian maid, for maid she is, I do not doubt, should grow such breasts, such lips, such eyes. She is handfast to Caradawc Strong-Arm; they'll be married soon. There are others who sigh for that as I do. So young, and yet already a legend for constancy. Nothing for you there, boy, and you have weightier tasks. No need to swoon when her lids swoop down over those blue eyes and lift to flash you an April smile. Your May Day will never dawn with that one.

Aches or not, I think with a pucker of disappointment that I have come here only to give and not to get. For now I'm in her presence it sweeps over me that Morgan can be generous to men when she chooses. Superbly woman, as though one tide was rising to meet another, a second flood that threatens death and brings instead a re-creation. Shattering, and making new; exhausting, healing. I know now that Urien and I are not the only ones. Vain Taliesin. How could we two have contained her? Is she offering her womb to the gods, or punishing . . . someone?

But I am wrong again. Morgan can always surprise you. She sees the pain it costs me to sit, and the heaviness of the harp, and the pout I make as I shift on the stool at the end of my song. She ruffles my hair, as though I were just a little chap that had hardly learned to walk. Even Tegau smiles to see her so motherly. I want to catch Morgan's hand and hold it to my tired forehead, but I restrain myself.

'So you tried to ride with Arthur, and he has hurt you.'

'He gave me a token. The boar's ear.'

'Arthur is careless with gifts. He has left much behind him that he does not recognise.' Her voice is soft as cat's fur. Her hand strokes my head, not sensuously, but with another purpose. I feel myself relax.

'Woman,' she nods, 'the salve for aching joints.'

I am lying on Morgan's bed. The virgin Tegau helps undress me. There's irony. I allow myself to smile at my humiliation. Why not? Very skilled, these women. It is luxury to be in their hands. Even the big square paws of Woman, that should wield something less delicate, are no strangers to healing magic.

The ointment is cold at first, so that I laugh and jump. Then the warmth creeps into the muscles and the glow spreads and it is Morgan singing over me, and not I to her. What if Urien found us now? Well, no harm. No harm, much good, to me at least. I am rocking like a baby in a cradle, like a ship on a gentle sea, as though this bed could carry me to Paradise. Tonight, Paradise is not ecstasy but sleep without pain.

'What's in this salve?' I murmur.

'Primrose and wormwood,' she croons, 'bruised and boiled in butter. Mixed with old lard and yellow wax, and the suet from a he-goat and a sheep.'

'It must be the he-goat's fat that's making me randy,' I smile.

Just words. None of that seems important now. I know it's not the wormwood or the primrose making me whole, but the touch of Morgan's hands, the constant application of her spirit that will leave me rested and her tired. The bitter and sweet of her that is my healing . . . All our healings . . . All our deaths . . .

Tegau touches me on the shoulder. I start awake. The room is dark, save for one candle. I am alone in Morgan's bed. The queen kneels with her back to us. Praying? I dress and stumble from the room, and almost forget the harp. I feel sleepy but well, and I have paid her poorly. Outside the door I almost trip over Woman, settling to sleep across the threshold. For the first time I am caught by a warmth of friendship towards him. Whatever he did, he has accepted her bitter punishment. He guards her well, though I think it brings him little joy.

I follow him next day, Woman, walking slowly as though his skirts are hung with lead and he's forgotten how to stride. I know where he'll be going. A place I've been aware of for months, and kept away from. I've had enough of that kind of bewitchment. Morgan's high ceremonies are more than sufficient. I was once potboy to the cauldron of Ceridwen, and it nearly cost me my life; now I'd rather sing golden hymns to the Trinity in the hall of Urien. Well, I can tune my voice to tell of magic or miracles. I use neither of them. I carry my own enchantment with me. It is not for nothing that my harp is called Healer.

I feel the touch of darkness on my skin as I step

through the shadows into the little court. No Romans built this. They're a public people. Big squares, long open porches, rooms in regular rows, that's them. Everything predictable, orderly, no space for secrets in those barrack-room minds. This court is native work. Built? It feels more as if it had grown. A mould on a cast-off army boot. A toadstool sprouting from a block of crumbling masonry. Wattle, clay, thatch, turning their backs on prying eyes. A farmyard sound of clucking hens. A pen of black sheep. I pass a rainwater-barrel and glance in, expecting to see a placid mirror reflecting the sky and my own handsome face, and find its surface alive with eels.

Morgan's Woman has disappeared into one of the huts. I hear a squeal and wince. I've a delicate stomach. I wonder if he saw me coming and is doing it to spite me.

He comes out carrying a small brass cauldron in one fist and a live hare by the other. Long legs scrabbling against the air, long ears twisting as he fights, and screaming nonstop. A hare's a magical animal. He can't save himself, though. Woman sets the cauldron down in the centre of the court and takes a hatchet from his belt. He fixes his eyes on me and not on the hare as he says the words that need to be said. It makes my own neck feel uncomfortably tender. Just a flick of his gaze from mine, a practised jerk of the wrist and the head is off and the dark blood drumming into the pot. I watch him bleed and then skin the beast and remove the organs, wrapping each piece in dock leaves and setting it aside. When it is all done, he puts the parts back in the store-house, and shuts the door. All this time he's muttered plenty to the gods, but not a word to me.

Now he faces me. 'Well, bard? Are you still so green you need lessons in drawing a hare?'

'It's a lesson in courtesy I need to be practising. I've come to say thank you. I've hardly an ache or a bruise to trouble me this morning.'

Smile, Taliesin. Speak fair. Soft words open more doors than heavy blows.

'Why hang around me? It was Morgan's doing.'

'Morgan's my mistress. I give her the service of song I am bound to, and she in turn provides the care which is my entitlement. Thanks to her are but the gilt ink on that contract. You owed me nothing, so I am in your debt.'

'You might have been, if my service was freely given.'

'You're not a slave.'

He shoots such a bitter look at me then I take a step back.

'Slave? No! Worse than that. Woman!'

'Does all the court here know that you are not?'

'Who bothers to look at a whiskery crone? And if they do, who's going to question Morgan?'

'Was this her doing?' What I mean is, 'Why?'

'Yes, boy. You're scared you'll end up the same way, aren't you? Even though you're in and out of her bed like a flea.'

I wait. Silence is a powerful invitation to a lonely man.

'I was Smith. Teilo Smith of Way Bank. A great lord of magic. Near as high as her ladyship herself, though she would never allow it. I planned to set my power alongside hers. Not over her, mind you. A sort of partnership, I thought. She wouldn't have it. Look what she's brought me to!'

'So her power was greater than yours, after all?'

'She got her come-uppance, though, didn't she? There's others can shut doors in people's faces, besides her. He didn't need magic, either.'

This time he waits. I raise my eyebrows.

'Arthur?'

'Aye. That's the one. That's all she ever cared about. The rest of you are nothing.'

I know, but still I wince.

'But he's her . . . brother.'

He laughs, scornful of my sensibility. 'What's that, among kings and queens like them? But it's more than bedding him she wants. We're talking about his kind of power now. She wouldn't want to be his little plaything, like Gwenhyvar. She's the same as I was, though she'd curse me to the black deeps of Uffern if she heard me saying so. She thought the two of them could join hands. Brother to sister. His sword, her sheath. The right and the left hand of Britain, you might say. Noon and night. He wouldn't have it, though. He's a man, isn't he? He thought he'd keep the whole of it to himself.'

'And so he has, hasn't he? Arthur's the High King, and Morgan's just Queen of Rheged.'

He spits and grins with black-gapped gums. 'High King of what, though? Britain? He's only got the half of it, hasn't he? He's kept the sword, but she took his scabbard from him. I haven't gone twenty years in a woman's skirt and not learned something from her. She could have given him all he dreamed of, but he couldn't see it. He wouldn't pay her price. Or not till now, when he sees his time is running out.'

'It's not too late to mend? They're a proud pair.'

He whistles knowingly. 'You're thinking she might

still be a dangerous loser. Aye. You're right. Lightning like hers must come to earth somewhere. There's more than love between them. Best keep your head down when those two are around.'

The cup in my hand. The muttering round me. A tale of past treachery.

'There was something about a purple cloak.'

'You heard that, did you? Well, there was once another here like me. A different sort of half-woman. She'd been a nun. Morgan sewed a cloak for Arthur. You never saw such a mantle. I should know. It was my hands helped to work the magic in it. We brought it to him, that nun and I. Only Arthur made the woman try it on in front of him. Here, in Carlisle. It did her horribly to death.'

'And that was Morgan's doing? Her gift to murder Arthur?'

'He believes it was.'

'Don't you?'

'I'm not telling what I know to every chatterbox.'

What about me? Which one of them will it be more dangerous to believe?

'Arthur's a sacred king. He must be well-protected.'

'Swords! Any smith could tell you there needs to be more to them than a fine-ground blade. Arthur's never had time for magic, more fool him. He's lost two soul-friends that had a deal of power. Merlyn first, and now Nimue, by the sound of it.'

'Would that have been an even match? The Lady of the Lake against Morgan?'

I can see I am giving him pleasure. I've rewarded him for his trouble more richly than I thought. To talk man with man. To know secrets that even wise

Taliesin, pearl of bards, child of the cauldron of inspiration of Ceridwen, did not guess. That's a rare treat indeed.

'It might have been, if it had been one to one, and not one against three. And now Nimue's left him, has she? Seen off by the bishops!'

'He has their power of prayer to keep him.'

Woman would give no more answer to that than grin at me and wipe his bloody hands on his apron.

Chapter Ten

And I thought I knew it all when I came to Rheged, fool that I was. Sucking the thumb of knowledge, I, Taliesin, the marvellous boy. And I couldn't even see the questions I should have been asking.

Teilo knew. Oh, yes, he must have known, crouched like a surly dog at Morgan's feet all these years. But he wouldn't help me to the knowledge I most needed. Knowledge is power. He hugged that secret close under his apron. He hated me. To be fair, if I'd been him, I'd have hated pretty Taliesin, too.

So they all left me, innocent as a newborn lamb, to my first meeting with Margawse.

Arthur has gone. He stood for the last time beside the gateway, his great sword Caliburn strapped ostentatiously to his side. Morgan was cold.

'A safe journey, and the peace of your years be on you when you reach home.'

'There is more life in me yet, whether you help me or not!'

'I could have given you more of life than you imagine. But you yourself will not let go and trust.'

The king's hand flew to his sword-hilt. You'd think it was he who was protecting the weapon, not the other way round.

'You have taken enough from me already. You shall not have this.'

'Cling to your man's power then, like your father before you. See if that can restore your waning fire. It is yourself you have robbed.'

So he hasn't got what he came for. Proud, these two, unyielding, righteous. They hurt themselves.

He leaves, and she will not stop him, back to Camelot and Gwenhyvar, and the winter court. Once all the young stallions of Britain must have been jostling for a place in his paddock. As Arthur's warband they would win their fame, impress their women, inspire the bards. Even in peacetime, his would be the feasts, the hunts, the games not to be missed. Now only Gawain and the older men ride with him. The younger ones choose to stay with us and hope for another war.

Hard on his heels, Morgan's sister comes.

She rides into the castle like autumn on the hills, all flame and fruit, bringing her sons' wives behind her and a train of comely lasses. Red as bracken is her hair, and never mind the silver. I part her cloak with my eyes and find that the flesh is warm and yielding.

She pouts at first when she hears that Arthur has gone. Then her look swings around appraising the rest of us.

And there am I, gaping like a fish, as pretty a youth as ever rode out of Powys, and very good at two things, only one of which is singing. What chance did I have?

I have a weakness for green-eyed women. But these eyes are different. Morgan's are like the wild cat's, animal, dangerous. And Margawse? All vegetation. Like a wood in a rainy summer, heavy with blossom, perfumed, feeding on the bodies of men. And oh, she can twine her roots round my foundation any time she chooses, for all she must be older than Morgan.

But softly. That's a dangerous thought. I have been in Morgan's bed, burned by her ice, opening under her moon. And could the same Taliesin lie in the poppied noonday of her sister?

I have no choice. I went to Morgan willingly, not for myself, though you may not believe that. It was a small service I could do for her I worship. I gave myself to her loneliness and longing. But Margawse. Greedy Margawse. She has no shame. She doesn't need me. But she devours every man in sight.

So I find myself lying on tartan wool in the leaping firelight, watching it make roses on Margawse's creamy skin. And I look at her and laugh, for I know I have made her happy. No tears with Margawse. She laughs easily, from the belly, as though the world were one great joke to her. We laugh, lying together in Morgan's castle, and we laugh.

God, it makes me cold, just to think of it. I see it now. She is the destroyer, more than Morgan. Looking back, I am far more scared now than I had sense to be then. I might have died that very night for what we did. They let me live, those two great queens, only because I seemed a boy. I amused them. And because I did what I did extremely well. But if I had been a man. Like Arthur . . .

'He was even younger than you are,' she says, leaning on her elbow and letting the tip of her finger thrill along my breastbone. 'What did you say your name was? Taliesin? You are a jewel of a boy, a perfect youth. It's a long time since I had a lad like you.'

She rolls away from me and lies smiling at the rafters, arms crossed behind her hair.

'But he was man even then. And what a man! Come fresh from victory. Like the great horned one in the depth of the forest. He thought he had proved his right to all the does of the herd by the shock of his antlers. I shall never feel his like in me again.'

Then she laughs and reaches out to pat my flanks indulgently.

'Never mind, Taliesin. You did very well. You're a clever boy. And after all, what is Arthur now? Husband to Gwenhyvar. Father of one skinny stripling, Anir, though he must have a train of lusty bastards scattered across the country. Gwenhyvar? What good to him is a simpering sweetheart like her? She wasn't worth the horses' sweat that brought her up from Cornwall. No, if he wanted a mate fit for a king like himself, he could have cut a richer gem from Cornish mines than that!'

I lie still, hearing the rhythms of her voice sing on. Feeling sick. It takes a lot to shock me. I am the Puck, the mischievous magic boy, in and out of the bed of queens, and still laughing and living. Yet I am nothing in myself. I am not important. It is only my song that matters.

But, Arthur! The greatest king of the Island of the Mighty. A legend in the hearts of all his people. With his own sister? *This* sister!

And she is still laughing over it, after all these years, her whole yielding body at ease across the bed, fruiting with self-satisfaction.

My stomach heaves as she humps herself over me.

Very sure of herself, she is, this red-haired, sun-warm queen.

'It is a pity I am past the age of bearing children. We could have made a sweet infant, you and I. What do you imagine? A green-eyed daughter, that could sing magic, like a Cornish mermaid? Something merrier than Modred, anyway, for all I'm his mother that says so.'

Words without sense. Blood stopped. I do not want to believe what I have heard.

'Modred?' I ask faintly, wanting to be wrong. '*Your* child?'

'The son Arthur got upon me that day. What did you think?'

Modred. The boy without a father. The grave smiling, courteous, thoughtful prince. Bold and bitter in battle, by all accounts, yet as skilful in Morgan's councils as in Urien's stables, charming to commoner and nobleman alike. Her favourite, fostered son. No whiff of scandal about him, only a mystery. And yet I thought I'd guessed. Of course, I had not been sure, seeing he is so unlike Owain and the rest. Only, whose else should he have been, black-browed like her as he is? She wouldn't have been the first wise queen of her sort to have gone into the forest and come back with more than she took. Who his father might have been had showed no more to me than the shadow of the stag under the branches. The god disguised, most likely. Yet *Arthur*? His dawning gold with the sunset red of Margawse to make the dark night of Modred?

I slide out from the bed away from those too-open legs.

'I thought he was Morgan's.'

'Oh, Morgan, Morgan! False aunt and foster-mother! She never told you? She let you think he was hers? A lie as dangerous to Modred as the truth! No. I made him, Taliesin. I forged the weapon that will bring Arthur down when I opened my legs and let Modred into the world. The eldest of us, Elaine, restored him when our hopes seemed lost. And then we put him in Morgan's hand. She was always the man among us. Modred has had two births. When he comes to the third, it is she who will strike the final blow.'

I want to shout her down for saying that. Morgan is the exaltation of womanhood to me. Goddess, virgin. No matter that I have entered her many times. She comes to me always new, like the crescent moon out of the dark of the month. But I see the truth of what she is saying. Margawse is all woman, nothing more. But Morgan uses her womanhood like a warrior who seizes the nearest weapon to her hand. She could have matched Arthur, strength for strength. Instead, she is the converse of his shape, the darkness to his light. She fills the space he cannot. Because he is a man, she is a woman.

Yet it was Margawse with Arthur. She who devours men, laughing at me so sweetly over the blanket. I have found more comfort in Morgan's tears, more love in her unflinching condemnation. I stumble out of the room.

Margawse's voice follows me. 'Beware, Taliesin. Modred is a trap, set and ready to fall. You are not so small you cannot be caught in its jaws. Stopper up well that quicksilver voice. This is one tale you must not sing yet.'

The hall is full. Urien and Owain. Agravain and

Gareth, tall sons of Margawse, and one more that I must now add with difficulty to that list.

Margawse has followed me, still tidying her hair. More radiant than ever.

Supper is over now. Morgan has Modred by the hand. They are smiling at each other. Together they are leading the long dance, like the wild reel they leap the night before battle, the sacred struggle acted to please the Old Ones, the light and darkness at the heart of Britain. Their kin clap and stamp. And who is there now, since Merlyn, to watch over the tents of Arthur?

Urien looks at me long. He knows that I have played him false with his wife. But does he know now I have played his wife false with her sister? Would he forgive me that, if he knew? My hands are unsteady over the strings. Urien says nothing. I have come into great danger today.

> Until my life ages,
> And death claims his wages,
> I shall not cease yearning
> Unless I praise Urien.

Chapter Eleven

I suppose I must have stared at Modred too long. He noticed. Come to think of it, there isn't much Modred doesn't see. And I don't mean just those things that concern himself. We've all got sharp enough eyes for that. At suppertime when everybody else is full of drink and having a good time, Modred's eyes will be going round the hall. If he sees a serving-man with a bit of a fever and wiping his runny nose on his sleeve, as like as not Modred will get up and have a quiet word with the steward and get the man excused to his bed. I've come across him in the woods, sitting on a tree-stump and chatting to the foresters as easily as if they'd forgotten he was the king's foster-son. I've even, if you'll believe me, seen him take a full bucket from a pregnant slave-girl and carry it across the yard for her, and not demand the price of a kiss and a cuddle at the end of it, either. They tell him things. There's not much going on in Rheged that Modred doesn't know.

He let it pass that evening, though more than once he looked up and caught my eye on his. All the same, he never put a foot wrong in the dance or lost the thread of his conversation. He's a true courtier already. When he came to swing Margawse they smiled at each other, but hardly spoke. I was the one who plucked a wrong note or slopped my wine. And those are two things it's not like nimble Taliesin to do.

Arthur's son, Margawse's child. The one so natural, now I know the truth of it, the other so amazing. Yes, now I come to think of it, there is a kingliness about Modred. He conducts himself like a young man born to rule. He may even be more like a king than Arthur himself was at the same age. I've heard stories about that one that would shock some of you; he was a wild lad. What would Arthur think if he knew that Modred was his own?

Margawse's though; that sticks in the gullet. I cannot swallow the lump of incredulity in my throat. If he had been Morgan's now, it would have been different. Surely, surely, he should have been Morgan's son? Incest or not, anyone can see the rightness of it. Two great pillars, evenly raised. Two halves of a universal symmetry. Fling in all the clichés of male and female, sun and moon, day and night, and they are not enough. They speak of greater and less, of borrowed light. They make the one inferior to the other. I sing of strengths rooted in separate soils, growing together to embrace and uphold each other. A marriage and a coronation of equals.

It didn't happen. Modred, who should have been their son, is not. What is he then? The child of treachery. Arthur's theft of the womb of another man's wife. Careful, Taliesin! You've gone that road yourself. Margawse's trick, to cheat both Arthur and Morgan. There's an unpleasant beginning to shape so noble a courtier. All men speak well of Modred. All women too, though there's never a breath of scandal about his name. Margawse has warned me not to spill what I've learned. But I cannot hide my knowledge from Modred.

So next day I'm sitting on the edge of the fishpond shaking a stone out of my boot, and it isn't as much of a shock as it might have been when he speaks just by my elbow, though I didn't hear him coming up behind me.

'Can I tempt you to take a walk with me?' he asks.

Modred's like Morgan. For all his courtesy, when he asks you to do something it is not, properly speaking, an invitation.

I glance at the sky. It's a mild October day, with a blue sky deep enough to set off the brilliant reds and yellows of the trees, and not enough wisps of clouds to threaten a drenching for a few hours.

'Yes,' I say, 'if you'd like the company.'

We walk down the hill to the river and on to the shining sands. The wind blows cooler off the sea and the legs of the cockle-women are purple as they fish in the mud. We wrap our cloaks about us and walk on north round the shore of the Solway Firth, paying a boatman to row us across the River Esk. Modred chats lightly, asking me about the merits of wire or gut for the harpstrings, discussing the treatment for galls on a horse, asking my opinion of rebuilding the fort at Caer Wenloe. I know this was not what he has brought me here for. Once he stops, and stands gazing at a little beach on the opposite shore. A few clumps of sad grey willows on either side, no sign of fishing-boats on it, though it looks a good landing. He stands very still and silent. When I look back from that beach to his face I see to my astonishment there are tears on his cheeks. He sees me staring and gives a brisk laugh and points to a heron gliding over the water.

'He has a long memory, the heron. Let him discover you have a pool of fish and he'll strip it bare, and ever afterwards he will remember. If he finds you think he has forgotten and have restocked it, he will be back to swallow the rest.'

We watch the heron land on the beach and wade in the shallows, dissatisfied.

Presently I see where we are coming to. A huge round boulder that has fallen out of the sky. Well, no other explanation, is there? It stands on its own in those bare fields above the mudflats. Just the one house nearby. Not poor, a decent, clean-looking place. A bit more prosperous than you'd expect for a lone fisherman. Still, I wouldn't care to live so close to that stone.

I am wrong. I often have been, where this family's concerned. They flow like an underground river and come out where you're not expecting. It isn't the stone we are heading for, though it's plain enough that it's a sacred marker. Modred walks up to the cottage and whistles merrily, like a robin. A woman comes almost running round the corner of the house. Getting on in years, she is, but still strong and nimble. Modred sweeps her into a great hug and kisses her. He's not usually so free with women.

'Let me look at you,' she orders, pushing him back. 'Aye. You get more of a man every time you come. You'll do.'

'A man like my father?'

She frowns in my direction. I'm startled too. How much does each of us know?

'Not too like, I'd say.'

82

So she holds his secret. It is clear these two are old friends, though she is no noblewoman.

Modred draws a parcel out of the pouch he has slung on his shoulder. He shakes it out. A good wool gown. He has an eye for what will please a woman. A deep plain blue, and embroidered round the hem with crimson flowers. Rich and warm. Not too showy for one like her, but a dress she can be proud of wearing. She colours like a young girl when he holds it up against her with his hands on her shoulders.

'Be sure and let me know when the next grandchild's arrived,' he says. 'I've a silver gift put by ready for the naming-day, whether it's boy or girl.'

'Hush now.' She puts a scolding finger on his lips. 'Let be until it's safely born. Don't let the Fair Folk hear you making so bold with the future. It's bad luck.'

He swings her round with his hand on her waist to face me.

'I've brought you something else. The cleverest bard in Britain. He's come without his harp, but he can sing a pretty poem unaccompanied. You shall be royally entertained, as you deserve. Taliesin, this is my wet-nurse, Fencha. And more than that. Midwife, you might say, to my second birthing. I owe my life to her and her man.'

Again I see that quick, troubled look the woman Fencha shoots at him, as though this was a thing that should not have been spoken. But he squeezes her lovingly and tells me to sing, which I do, I, the Chief Bard of Rheged, there in the apple-yard of a fisherman's cottage, with only the two of them and a few fine-looking cattle to listen to me. All the time my eye is roving over the trim woodwork of the house, the well-kept beasts, the smart stout cart and the harness with bells on it hanging in the shed. It is more than the salmon of the Esk has paid for all this. Besides, I haven't seen her husband. He could be dead by now. It is clear this house stands closely with the palace at Carlisle, though it's a long walk between them.

'Will you come in and break some noonday bread with me?' she asks when I've finished.

I'm about to say 'yes', for it was thirsty walking, even before the song. But Modred puts his hand out and touches her arm.

'Forgive us a little while,' he says, smiling to soften her disappointment. 'Give us bread and cheese and a pitcher of milk to drink. I have a tale of my own to tell to Taliesin, and the Stone is the rightful place to do it. We'll come back for a gossip when it's done. We shall have need of good news of farms and families and festivals to take the taste of bitterness off our tongues.'

'Aye,' she says, the smile leaving her face. 'Your story makes hard hearing.'

'Except that I am alive to tell it. All it contains of happiness has been your doing.'

'It's a pity, then, I cannot have a hand in its ending.'

He doesn't answer that.

Chapter Twelve

We walk down to the Stone and bow to it. Well,
you'd have to, a thing like that. Modred offers some
milk and bread and speaks the reverence. He's gone
further than I have along Morgan's path. Still, it's
me flinches and not him when he puts out his hand
and actually touches the thing. Taller than him, it
is, and rounded. It could easily have rolled over and
crushed him.

'Do you know what they call this?' he asks.

'I can guess. There'll be nothing else like it along
this coast. It must be the Mabon Stone, isn't it?'

'Yes,' he says, and lets his hand fall back quick to
his side as if the rock has burnt him after all. 'Mabon,
the Son. Born of Modron, the Mother. This should
have been my Stone.'

A shiver of goosepimples runs all over me as he says
that. I know he is right, of course, half of it anyway.
It's clear whose son he should have been. Only there
is a darkness comes down over my mind when I try
to think about the other half of what he is saying.
What does that make Morgan, then? I think I know.
I think I've always known. And I have lain with her.

'And whose is it instead?' he shouts, whipping
round with his hand lifted so sudden I don't know
if it's me or the Stone he is going to strike.

'Owain's?' I get it in fast, skipping out of the way at the same time. Well, if Morgan is Modron, it doesn't take much working out, does it?

'Owain!' He slumps down and leans back against the Stone, as if he doesn't care if it has power to hurt him. 'Yes, there's more to Owain Enemy-Reaper than horses and dogs and cattle-raids. Be sure of that! Before Urien, Gwendoleu was king here in Solway. He kept a deadly set of chess. Few there were that could face him across that dangerous board. Gwendoleu of the Chained Ravens, that ate two corpses for their dinner and two for their supper. He left no son, or daughter either, to follow him. Urien got this kingdom after he fell. But Urien's a Christian. It was Owain inherited the chessboard and paints black ravens on his shield.'

'And you would have . . .'

He swings round on me with those dark haunted eyes. 'Do you believe Gwendoleu was a traitor? He made a league with the Angles.'

'To arm the Old against the New? Pagan against Christian?'

Modred stands with the light from the sea in his eyes, staring west. 'Do you not see them? The Irish over the water. The Picts in the North. Angles and Saxons along the eastern shore. The Britons in Strathclyde, Dyfed, Dumnonia. What if we were to join forces, all of us? Both Christian and pagan. Unite these islands in all their diversity.'

'That's a dangerous dream!' I remind him. 'That's how all our troubles began, isn't it? King Vortigern brought Hengest and Horsa here from Saxony and thought he had done a smart deal to buy their swords. Look what happened! They seized the land for themselves and more of their keels came flooding over to join them. Then they slew our best men of the Council in the Night of the Long Knives. Give the English an inch, and they'll be swarming all over us. They'll want to be masters from Land's End to the Orkney Isles! Arthur wanted to drive the Saxons out of Britain. Would you make peace with them?'

'You know he's my father?'

I nod, cautious.

'Arthur Pendragon lies when he rallies us to fight for Britain. He calls us to defend a country that never was. The Cymry were always at war with each other. It is a Roman province that Arthur is fighting for. And the mind of Rome has always despised the British soul.'

'Still, Arthur's son fights with his father now. Bravely too, if half what I've heard is true. How are we bards to make an honest living if you sheathe your swords and seal a peace between the lot of you?'

'Yes! I have fought for Rome and the Christian Church and Arthur.' There's a world of bitterness in his voice for one so young.

'But Morgan's son would have chosen another way?' Silly question. I should have thought before I spoke.

'Why ask me that?'

'Sorry,' I say. 'Tactless, me.' I sit myself down on the grass, a respectful distance from the Stone and put the bread and cheese between us. Might as well make myself comfortable.

'No, Morgan's not my mother, though I find it difficult to give another queen that name.'

'She's a wonderful woman.' I let the praise hang

in the air. Let him take it which way he likes. They are both true.

'Margawse! When she gave birth to me, she expelled more than she knew.'

Wait, Taliesin. Beneath the soft speech, the self-control, the courtesy and honour, there has been a great abscess of anger swelling to bursting. You're a harper, not a surgeon. Let him lance it himself if he chooses.

'When she lay with her brother it was not for love but for revenge. Ever since his birth she had waited for that chance, to trick him as Uther Pendragon tricked her mother, having killed her father first. I am her justice, the vengeance for my grandparents.'

'It's not all bad, though. She enjoyed it, didn't she? And what about Arthur? It takes two to make a child. Wouldn't there have been love and laughter on his side too?'

'Sixteen, and already a general. Hot from his first great victory, they say. It was his own fame he was in love with, not my mother. He dreamed of becoming another Roman Imperator. He wanted power over Britain, and with it, every woman in her. Love? He didn't even ask who she was! Laughter? Not once he knew. I was the burning beam that threatened Arthur's palace. I was the bear fighting his dragon in the sky. I was his Nemesis.

'Do you know what he did when he heard I was born and Margawse had hidden me? He went through those three sisters' lands gathering up all the babies born at Maytime. You saw that beach where the heron was? The local people avoid it. They say it's haunted, and well it should be. A warband stood on that beach, all those great names out of song and story: Arthur, Cei, Bedwyr, Merlyn. They put the babies in a boat and pushed it out to sea. And I, yes, I was one of them. His son, his firstborn. More than that; his sister's son, that we hold dearer to a man than his own wife's child. The boat was wrecked, here, just below where we're sitting. All those little children were drowned, or eaten by gulls. Only one came safe to shore, still living. Fencha's husband, Gavran, discovered me on the sand. He took me home. Fencha put me to her own breast, hid me from strangers and friends alike, kept me till the hunt had died away and Morgan's sister Elaine told her by second-sight where to find me.'

'So now? Which of them will you serve?'

'I do not know. How can I? I was misbegotten. I should have been Morgan's dream. The land made whole through her and Arthur. Instead, I am Merlyn's nightmare.'

I sit silent. You may think I am a chatterer. There are some themes too dark even for my tongue. She makes good cheese, does Fencha, but I've lost my appetite.

'I can see why you told me,' I say presently. 'Funny old world, isn't it? We're two of a kind, really. The selfsame thing happened to me. You, drifting down the Solway to be picked up on the sands. Me, thrown into the water in a satchel and found hanging on a fishing-weir. Cheer up, man. We go back a long way, our sort. Take Moses, now. The myths are full of babies in bulrushes. They can't keep us down, can they? We'll pop up somewhere where we're least expected. We're too valuable to be destroyed, you see. The gods have work for us.'

'What dark god singled me out, and left the rest

to die? The crucified Christ's Father? Teutates, who waits for his victims by wells and pools? And for what purpose? No, it is not the same with me. Moses' mother set him adrift in hope that Pharaoh's daughter would find him. Even Ceridwen in her fury fell in love with your face and could not bear to kill you. She gave you one slight chance. Your mothers consigned you to the waters, loving you. It was my father cast me out, in anger. I am not lovable.'

Never has the prince of poetry needed to choose his words more carefully. I am an entertainer, an inspirer, a strengthener. I know all the tricks to make a man feel more highly about himself than the sober prose of truth might suggest. That's what they want to hear. But how to tell this man he is better than he wishes to believe? I cannot flatter Modred. I wish I had my harp in my hands to show him what words cannot.

'Steady, now. Arthur's known for a handy man with a sword. He could have taken that blade to your neck and sent your little head rolling on the floor. All over. Oh, sorry! Too late now. But he was no Herod. He gave you the same chance that Ceridwen gave me. Was there not some pity in his heart too?'

'Fear! He dared not slay his sister's son. That would have brought a curse down on his head. If he did not know that, then Merlyn would surely have told him. The waves he pushed me into washed his own hands clean. He could blame the waters for my death and keep his blade pure.'

'Might he still not have hoped? His son, his firstborn. What if he knew now you had come back from the dead?'

'Merlyn warned my father he must kill me before I destroyed him.'

'Merlyn is gone.'

'And I remain. The seed of treachery. Even if Arthur were to welcome me with open arms, nothing can change that.'

'You have freewill,' I say. 'You could break the circle. You could be reborn.'

'How? When I know my birth has already shaped all our endings.'

'In Christ,' I try, looking up at the Mabon Stone and crossing myself, 'there was a new creation.'

But he is sitting in the shadow of the Stone.

Chapter Thirteen

Samain's past, and now it is all cheer. We are to go
to Lothian to celebrate the New Year with Morgan's
sisters. There is even a rumour that Arthur and
Gwenhyvar may be there to hold court. Do I observe
a flash of jealousy in Morgan's eyes when she hears
that news?

'What does he hope to win from Margawse that he
could not have had from me? Does he think her price
will be easier to pay?'

It's a thrill of another sort runs through me when
I think what a fire-feast in Red Margawse's court may
be like, with all that family gathered. I polish up my
harp and pack my smartest clothes.

'Will he come?' is almost the first question Morgan
asks Margawse, as she steps into the fire-warmth of
Din Eidyn out of the raw wind.

Margawse gives that flick of her head that makes
her hair leap like the flames themselves.

'How do I know? I am not the one with the second
sight. Still, you know our brother. Arthur must
always get what he wants. You have disappointed
him. So he must try a woman with a warmer
welcome and see if she can give him what all men
long for.'

She enjoys teasing Morgan.

After Christmas, the third sister arrives, Elaine the Fair. You can guess I've been curious about this one, knowing the glories of her younger sisters. The black and the red, and now . . . My tongue's hanging out for a sight of the firstborn of these three queens. Elaine the Fair! Imagination makes wild forays and heaps in my poet's lap treasures of gold and crystal, daffodils and roses, fragrance and light.

Elaine uncloaks in the hall. Pale, mountainous; hooded eyes; grey hair under a discreet caul. I see at once there is nothing here for a lad like me. She is the oldest Mother. I could climb on the hills of those knees and lay my head on the vast field of her bosom. But if I slept there, when and where would I wake?

All day she heaps herself by the fire, and her fat fingers endlessly braid wool, red and black and silver. I do not know what she is weaving, but I find I cannot easily tear my gaze from the spiralling strands.

We are all on edge. Will he come? Through so much wrong and bitterness can they still hack a way towards each other? Can the wounds be closed?

It seems they may, when the gatekeeper gives a great shout and all the dogs break into barking. Morgan and Margawse and all their sons are on their feet. Even Elaine lifts her head to listen; her fingers pause. Only a moment. Then she falls to weaving again, more rapidly, as though the time is short.

Time dulls old wounds, but they can still ache when the wind blows cold. I am there close to the doorway when Margawse greets Arthur. A smile of triumph flashes in her face. Her hands reach out. Then, at the last moment, the fire goes out in her eyes. Too much has happened since the night they lay together. He thinks he's cancelled out that past. Now he wants something more from her.

It's the only time I've seen her cold with a man. And he is stiff to her. He does not easily beg, and he is here as a suitor. Yet both of them I have seen more lusty with the flame of life than all their courts. Hard to believe now, the two of them in bed together. Hard to imagine, Arthur setting out to destroy Margawse's son.

Courtesy is a blessed discipline. There are greetings given, gifts exchanged, thanks rehearsed, drink offered and accepted. Such customs grease difficult joints.

And there behind him is Gwenhyvar. All that I looked for in Elaine and didn't find. Ash blonde and rosy, smiling sweet gratitude at all the nephews of Arthur's family who crowd around her. Gawain was already in attendance. It's clear there's a knot here, some privileged band. These are the queen's knights. There's a surprise! I thought it would only be the power of Arthur's name that drew them. Gwenhyvar? Pretty enough, yet after my first smile of pleasure, nothing more. I can't tell what they see in her from here, I, who have stroked Morgan's flesh, been overpowered by Margawse. Is there some magic in her I'm missing?

There's a young lady with her. Like a magic mirror to Morgan that turns time back. Both darkness and warmth in the same lovable person. Morfudd, twin sister to Owain. Gwenhyvar's woman. Here's joy for all of us.

A pale boy stumbles over the doorstep behind them. I hardly notice him.

I'm a guest in Din Eidyn. My duties are lighter, but

there's less chance to impress. Still, I stun them at
supper. Gwenhyvar claps as hard as anyone. She
looks delighted. I know what she's hoping. Next time
around it will not be Arthur that I praise. Let her
have what she wants. I shall be a richer man by the
end of the evening.

Next day is seems the same. I've sung my best. I
down a cup of mead and the hall spins headily.
Gwenhyvar is laughing with Agravain and Gaheris.
Beside the High Queen someone else is looking at me
across the table. I start, like a swordsman that has
dropped his shield. I should have noticed this lady
before. When did she arrive? How could the ready
eye and the wise thumb of Taliesin have passed
unnoticing over a woman of such beauty, such
warmth? Could the blazing sun of Arthur have so
blinded me, the radiant moon of Morgan so
bewitched me, that I would not have stopped at this?
A young-old face, like a very knowing child, heart-
shaped, to stir more than just a man's heart. Hair
golden as catkins, that are the first flowering of the
hazel nuts of wisdom. And I am made unwise as she
takes the jug from the serving-man and leans across
the table to fill my cup to the brim.

'Taliesin of Pure Song,' and her voice shivers with
laughter on that word 'pure'. 'You have sung of God
and man. Can you also turn your lay to a lady's
service?'

Queen Gwenhyvar, or herself? And how will this
one reward me?

'What lady needs the tongue of Taliesin to tell this
hall what all the world can see?'

There are many measures of beauty. A dewdrop
caught in a rose. Sunset purple in a sky of thunder.

The curl of hair upon a woman's temple. What kind is this? I sense a maze of charms confuse me. My thumb warns that I will see whatever she chooses to show me. A blushing milkmaid met behind the shippen, or a naked priestess with the knife.

'All Britain knows your name, Taliesin Radiant-Brow. Can it be that you have never heard of Nimue, the Lady of the Lake?'

Oh, yes, I've heard.

What is she doing here? Hasn't she fallen out with Arthur?

My eyes scan the high table for help. I read their faces freshly. Gwenhyvar is smiling confidently. Arthur looks defiant. The sisters are like watchful wolfhound bitches, bristling around their jewelled collars.

Nimue's fingers brush the inside of my wrist. The long table dissolves into a running river. The shouting beats like surf. Her blue eyes widen in a smile and I am drowning. I do not know how long has passed.

Silence falls like a rope thrown to rescue me, or like a lash. All heads have turned my way. As I grab the shore of reality I catch Morgan's face, and by her look I see the bank may be as dangerous as the river. Too late to slide my hand away unseen. I daren't look at any of their faces, but I sense Nimue has turned that merry smile on Morgan. Slowly, too slowly, she releases me.

I am on my feet. I clutch the harp for security. Gwenhyvar will have to wait this evening. I will only praise Urien. Nothing else is safe.

I'm not the only one disturbed. A voice booms from close to Arthur. Bishop Cyndeyrn of Penn Ryoned is riding into battle.

'Why is that witch here? You swore, my lord, you would cleanse your court of all such fiendish persons. Will you imperil your immortal soul to entertain that kind of counsellor again?'

Nimue smiles, angelically. Margawse looks dangerous. She knows this insult is meant for the sisters too.

'Is the world so full of wisdom I can afford to slight it?' Arthur asks.

'The Lord of Life is a strong tower enough, our shield and spear, arms for our comfort, word for our wisdom, salve for our sin.'

'Work me a miracle yourself, then!'

Arthur's fist crashes down on the table. Then he stares around. All ears are listening. Even the house-slaves are gaping. What is it that he wants so much? What is it that Arthur still needs? What is it that even the High King lacks? I know, I, that have been born anew so many talented times. I, Taliesin, lapped still in the lusty bloom of youth. I know what drives him so urgently to the wise women, Morgan, Margawse, Nimue, only to watch their smiles turn tenderly on me instead. I have what he lacks, haven't I? Better not make it too obvious, though. I feel for him, this waning daystar, and I am afraid.

Arthur's not the victor of Badon for nothing. He grabs the falling standard. His followers must not doubt him. They must not guess he is beginning to doubt himself. He slips a garnet ring on the bishop's finger with a laugh to cover it.

'A miracle? There! Transmute that into bread for the poor, if you don't want it yourself.'

There's applause for that, and the talk and the music and the storytelling flow around us once more.

But my eyes are open, as though a cloak of invisibility had fallen from the world. I feel much older than my years.

The wounds are not all on one side. Arthur and Gwenhyvar, they seem the perfect couple. He, the great golden king, hero of a string of battles, honoured in legend. She, silver-haired, so blonde you'd be hard put to say whether Time had added a thread or two of his own. She has what all women want – well, nearly all – a handsome, famous, loving husband. Both of them years younger than my Morgan. But the dream will not endure for ever, even for them. He feels the power fading in his veins, a vision uncompleted, a truce, but not a victory, a country half-delivered. Now the most famous band of warriors in the world is drifting away from him, declining, dying. His famous bastard, Llacheu of Great Renown, fearless among warriors, has been slain before him. And what has Gwenhyvar given him?

There he is, far down the table. One son of her own, Anir, just come to warrior's age. Unblooded in battle yet, I should think. Not much to look at. Hair flopping over his face, and at that stage when a boy's limbs seem to grow longer every day, and he can't get the hang of using them without knocking things over. He flushes and apologises, and I don't know whether it's pain or impatience that makes Arthur growl every time he looks at him. Both, most likely. Poor lad. It must be a heavy burden, being Arthur of Britain's only legitimate offspring. Funny that. The Pendragon's left a trail of base-born bastards across the Island, yet just this one runt from Gwenhyvar. You'd have thought there'd have been powerful magic made for such a marriage-bed, not to mention the prayers of the Church to bless their holy union. If Arthur should fail, all the weight of the Cymry's hopes, our expectations of a dream fulfilled, will rest on Anir's hunched shoulders. It's no wonder he's stooped with embarrassment and clumsy.

The harp is magic. It can scar with satire or it can turn a timid man brave. Sing of the warrior's glory on the eve of battle and you armour the heart better than any vest of mail; your song is more stiffening than leather binding on the forearm; you intoxicate more thoroughly than a vat of royal mead. So I sing of young Anir and tomorrow's hunt. I make him blush a deeper red than ever.

Chapter Fourteen

No space for me in Margawse's bed now. Morgan has
reclaimed her property. No space in my black queen's
either, not in another queen's capital, with Arthur
here. I know the rules. That's a relief. I've enough on
my plate as it is. At eighteen, I'm beginning to feel like
an old man. Well, all right, not all the time. Margawse
keeps plenty of lively lasses around Din Eidyn. Still,
I'm more careful than I used to be. Urien likes to keep
a name for a Christian household, on his side at least,
and it's not just his free way with gold that makes me
want to stand well in Urien's eyes. There's only one
king I'd rather have for my patron.

But tonight I'm terrified of Nimue. At bedtime I'm
genuinely glad to play the virtuous Christian and
scuttle away from any further closeness that might
wet me with her waves. Self-preservation. It's not
just fear; I've enough difficulties for a prudent man
to handle already. Doesn't do me any good though,
does it, this chaste circumspection?

To be an enchantress is not a matter of concocting
the correct ingredients in a cauldron, like a
housewife cooking a stew. It is more than scanning
the heavens to trace the wished-for movements of
the stars; a ship's pilot venturing by night does that
much. Little can be achieved merely by the pupil's

faithful recitation of the runes. High magic is the application of colossal will. That is why even I, Taliesin, famed throughout Britain, am straw to both Morgan and Nimue.

So what's the good? Shore up the bank of a brimming river in one place, and it is bound to break through where you're not expecting it.

I thought I'd escaped when I woke and found myself alone in my own cold bed, just the snoring of men around me in the straw. Too much strong wine, though. I'll have to get up.

Only the ghost of grey light, and bitterly cold. I pull on my shoes and skip outside to relieve myself, whistling to scare off any unpleasant shadows. Quick, now; back inside before my nest in the blankets gets chilled. I'm shivering already.

I've turned and taken a step in the starlight, and there she is, waiting between me and the inner door, Nimue, bright and flickering, like the reflections thrown by water on a wall. Is this a woman or illusion? In this half-light she seems to carry a glow around her, like phosphorescence on a marsh. I find myself turning Christian now in earnest. She brought up Arthur, and he paints a cross upon his shield, but the bishop is right. She's a dangerous lady.

'St Michael and all the archangels, defend me!

'I acknowledge my guilt and my sin is ever before me.

'If thou, O God, shouldst mark iniquities, who could stand it?'

I've been a bad boy. Hell waits for me at the end of the corridor, with smiles and ringlets. I ought to run, and cannot.

'Do not be afraid, Taliesin. I have no quarrel with Urien's bard.'

That's true; I'm Urien's bard, not Morgan's, officially at least. Hang on to that.

'King Urien likes his household to behave honourably. So goodnight, lady. Let me pass.'

Deliver me from the tempter. Shield me, my lord!

'King Arthur only lives for honour.'

She leans towards me, but beneath the softness I sense a tougher fibre now. She means to coax something different from me this time. I feel reprieved but wary. Her voice twines round me like the stems of water-lilies.

'You know that Morgan cannot give him what he wants.'

'What's that?'

I know what Morgan wants. And she would give it back a thousand times over. But what does Arthur want from Morgan? What is honour? Youth renewed? The strength to lead us back to war and fight the final battle? Could she work that?

Nimue shakes her head impatiently. I think she'd like to shake me too. Strange that a woman should seem to promise such wooing in the evening and the wind change so suddenly at midnight.

'Morgan has only one thing Arthur lacks.' She hesitates. Should she hand me the advantage of shared knowledge? Morgan could have it out of me in a moment. 'Well, it's no secret. She stole the scabbard for Arthur's sword. She, or her sisters, keep it still.'

'For Caliburn?'

The sword of old magic. I have seen it on Arthur's thigh, the talisman that got him all his victories.

'I armed him at his manhood with both sword and sheath, as I was charged to. She who entrusted them to me taught that the healing scabbard was worth ten times the sword, and so I warned him. When Arthur was young he would not believe that. Better a sword to slaughter Saxons and win him a shining name in song, better to die on the battlefield if that would win him enduring fame. What did he care for closing wounds? When Morgan stole them both, he begged me above all else to get back the sword, and so I did.'

I see it all now.

'And Arthur has survived beyond his wars? Now age is catching up with him. Could the scabbard really renew him? Make him young again?'

That glint of anger ripples across her waters. Then calm steadies the surface once more.

'He does not understand what he is asking her. Think, Taliesin, think what that would mean. Why is a scabbard offered but to sheathe the sword? Imagine Arthur and Morgan, reconciled. She holds the scabbard, he the sword. They both mean power. She will not let it go, will she? To have it, he must take her too. She is Morgan the Wise. Tenfold, her power of enchantment would smother his. Do you think that he would ever draw that sword again? Where is Arthur the warrior then? Think, Taliesin, Chief of Bards.'

I smell the nearness of Nimue's perfume, but it's not my body she's disturbing now. My poet's soul exclaims in pain at this threatened violation.

'But Arthur's the High King, our battle-leader! Victor against the Saxons. War's what he lives for. It's all the reason we made him what he is.'

'You understand! I saw in your face you were a

wise boy. Where is the place for poets in a pallid
peace? You must sing, Taliesin, must you not? A
thousand years from now your songs will still be
ringing. Make your greatest song for Arthur! He must
be more than a mention in the margin of history. You
too have power. You feel it, don't you? It is the bards
who shall recreate him, not the scabbard, so that for
all ages he shall be known as the greatest king that
ever was. He must fight again. His finest battles are
yet to be. Turn him from Morgan. She offers him
nothing but obscurity.'

Her white hand's rising to me and the floor is
rippling.

'Praise Arthur! When men speak of kingship, let
the very word mean him. Shut your ears to Morgan's
wiles. She was always jealous. Chant your great song
for Arthur, and you and he will live on to eternity.
Scorn Morgan's ways.'

Oh, excellent tempter. She lures me with my life's
ambition. Easy then to say, yes. Immortality for me
as well as him. I nearly said I'd give my right arm
for it, but what's the use of a one-armed harper? And
a bonus payment in this life, by the way she's smiling
now, her lilies opening. Still, there's more to life than
lust. That's just my sideline.

'You said yourself I'm Urien's bard, and Morgan
is Urien's queen. Can't I serve both of them? Arthur
and Morgan.'

'And let them come together? You know what
follows. The bold warriors will not shout, nor the
bright spears shake. The warhorses will not gallop
long-legged into battle. The light of pride will grow
dim in women's eyes. Are not the greatest tales
sparkling with the clash of conflict, ruddy with blood

spilt, loud with the cry of good victorious and evil slaughtered?'

'Yes,' I admit. 'Brave battle makes the best song.'

That, and the rain on the graves of heroes, and women weeping.

'Then sing it,' her whisper coaxes me. 'Sing how Arthur triumphed over his enemies. Make it come true once more.'

She lets me go, like a trout down a river. Her hand has not even touched my flesh. She has raped me another way.

Chapter Fifteen

Forgive me, Morgan. I'm not so green I can't see where Nimue's own interest lies. Yet the sense of what she has said rings true in my head as a bishop's bell.

I sing of Arthur. I excel myself. Even as my fingers work their magic I can see the spell's gone home for one at least. Candlelight catches the pale face of Anir, his chin thrust forward, his elbows in the slops of wine, soup down his tunic. His eyes are shining with the glory of the father I hold up before him. The enchantment's strong. For the first time he dreams he might be such a young man.

Snow falls, and melts a little, then freezes again. Even in this weather there are lambs being born, small signs of hope. Come thaw or ice, there is hunting, either on horseback or on foot. These men are like giants with magic boots. They can run up mountains as fast as my fingers can skip a scale on the harp, and still be boasting and swaggering at the end of the day, the young ones, anyway. I fancy Arthur lowers himself a bit more carefully on to his couch. Gwenhyvar strokes his hair. Then she turns away, and there's a circle of young men round her. Owain, Rhiwallawn, Pasgen, Agravain, Gaheris, Gareth . . . and Modred. The flower of her retinue.

The pride of his pack. In that shift of light I have seen that Arthur and his sisters are ageing. Their children are full-grown now. Well, Anir almost.

Modred is unacknowledged. Arthur thinks he has settled that score. Hush! That's a dark tale to set folk whispering in corners. Sing instead of Lindsey and Badon and the beaten heathen, and a king to surpass all kings. When the last verse ends we're all safe, sitting by the fire roasting apples.

Gwenhyvar is not so unchaste as to flirt with her escort. She rewards them with a pretty, queenly smile and gives them each a green scarf to wear for her.

It is Arthur who lures them. When he calls for the hounds there's not one of the pack would refuse to follow him. Nimue herself can draw a skilful bow. Urien teases me, and I venture my valuable person on the ice and rocks a couple of times. We chase the stag over the bare cold hills. No kill. It doesn't improve my playing. Where does Margawse draw her fire from in a country like this?

But today I have seen Morgan, Margawse and Elaine with their heads together, looking my way. I will go hunting again, I decide. I need the exercise. A slim handsome young bard gets more valuable gifts than a lazy minstrel who has let himself run to fat. No, I deceive you. I have looked in Elaine's face. I need fresher air to blow away dark thoughts. For once, I prefer pain.

It is too treacherous for horses, and little chance of picking up a scent on the frozen ground, but there are tracks in the snow that a man can follow almost as fast as a dog. Some men, anyway. Not me. Not young Anir, either. He's slithering over the stones beside me trying to catch up with them.

I grin at him in fellowship. I'll make a praise-song for him tonight.

'Don't wait for me!' I say.

I hop along in the rear, happy to be out of doors under a blue sky, and watch the spray of snow at their heels turn into gems every colour of a jewel chest.

Against all expectations the hounds put up a hare. You should just hear the row! You'd think he was a stag of seven tines. The dogs are floundering about and slipping all over the place. The men let out a yell and fan across the mountainside. They're going pell-mell to head the poor beast off whichever way he turns. There are bows levelled and spears raised. All for a scrap of brown fur and a pair of long ears and two bulging eyes.

Arthur's in the middle of the front rank, as ever, laughing and running as hard as the young men. I see my great golden king so full of speed and strength. I think he cannot die. This moment hangs outside of history. The sunlight and the spears. I fix it in my mind. My song shall be my spear, to pin this day to earth and hold it. No! I shiver as my foot goes through the ice into black bog. That's not the metaphor, to kill this day like a trapped hare, or to let it escape up the mountain scree. A song should hold life. Beyond the grave these men shall live, because of me.

Something has dimmed the bright day. The sun still shines, but there is a chill blueness on the snow. The shouts have altered. Why are the men standing on the ridge to my left, looking down? A horn checks the hounds. Baffled, they bark their indignation, and come to a noisy, jostling halt. The hare bolts on for freedom, zigzagging still up over untouched snow towards the peak. The other huntsmen are turning now, stumbling in drifts, skidding on icy rocks to see what's up. I pick my way more prudently through the stiff, scratching heather to where that row of black sentinels stoops against the skyline. Someone's starting to climb down. Gawain. The others yell caution to him.

Only at the last moment can we who have straggled up late see over the edge. The ground falls in a corrie with bare sunless walls. A gravelled hollow, an icy tarn, a few white rocks. One splash of colour sprawls with twisted neck among the stones. A dark green tunic embroidered with crimson. A red and black cloak. Even from here we know those colours: Anir.

Others are clambering down after Gawain, risking their lives at speed for a prince already beyond anyone's help. It doesn't need the shake of Gawain's head to tell us that. But his gesture breaks the stunned silence and all the men are keening now. One voice bursts out above all the rest like the roar of a stag. Fury and grief. Inconsolable rage at the theft of hope.

Anir has made his final stumble, gone clumsily wrongfooted to his death, not gloriously on an enemy's spear or a boar's tusk. Vainly outstretching himself to please his father, he has disappointed Arthur for the last time.

You can read the consternation in their faces. Not for a comrade dead. Men fall in battle or the hunt. It's common enough. But for the death of a dream. The last Pendragon. He hadn't been much of a future, Anir. But he was all they had. After Arthur, what? There are great men beside him; Cei, Bedwyr, Urien. But they are all within a year or two of Arthur. Among the younger generation, who could lift up such a sword as his?

Take the boy up gently in a hammock of cloak and spears. They will carry him home by the low road while we wind sadly down the hill with the chastened hounds. Modred and Bedwyr support Arthur. There are tears on all our cheeks.

Still, I am a bard, and my mind's already inspired with the rhymes of the lament I must be making this night. Rest now, young Anir. Never shall grief for a prince be sung like yours. While the ship of the dead carries you to the islands of Paradise, my harp shall mourn you with an immortal magic. Your grave, and Taliesin's awen, will be remembered.

It's a pity it couldn't have been something bigger than a hare.

It's worse going downhill over the ice. Madness, to go hunting on such a day. Would he have held back if he'd known? The king, with his spear restless in his hand and the Saxons quiet. Is that what Nimue feared? Would I have wanted him to sit at home? Is not this the Arthur we all cheer for, the mad, bold, boyish chieftain of our dreams? Death-dealing Caliburn, made mortal flesh.

I am last as usual. I see the tableau from far off. The sad procession, the women hurrying out of doors, the hunting-party closing in. I run the last furlong to catch up. This is high tragedy, not to be missed. Lucky they have strewn this highway with straw and grit.

Arthur's voice carries in the clear air, sonorous

with grief and accusation. It is Margawse he's addressing.

'This is your doing! Vengeful witch! Have you not done me enough harm already?'

'My doing! Did I call out the hounds with the ice hard on every loch? Did I charge up the braes and make every man of the court follow me, whether he would or no? Did I make a fool of myself to prove the man was still a boy, and force your boy to prove himself a man? Arthur Pendragon should look nearer home for his son's executioner.'

Hands are on daggers then, spears raised. Comrades are turning on each other, Arthur's folk, against Margawse's.

Nimue speaks; very white she is. Her pointing finger finds Morgan.

'You! You call yourself the Healer. Can you do nothing for him?'

No flash of triumph in Morgan's face, though Nimue owns that he herself is powerless. She wrings her hands and shakes her head, and seems to struggle for speech. 'You come to me too late. All that I have, all that I know, I would freely have given. I cannot restore his broken neck, or call back the soul you left behind in the glen. What is done must stand.'

'The scabbard!' shouts Arthur. 'You have Caliburn's scabbard. If ever I needed healing, it is now. Restore it! Use it yourselves! I will give you anything you ask in return. You can have the sword itself, if that will save him.'

Does he really mean that?

The blood is dark in Morgan's cheeks and brow and neck. She stands immobile. The whole court is hushed now, waiting for her response.

'I cannot.' Only a whisper, like ice cracking.

'For God's sake, do not deny me!'

'I cannot give you back the scabbard.'

'You hate me that much? The lad lies broken at your feet, and you refuse?'

She shakes her head through a slow eternity of regret.

'When you sent my woman Luned back to me dead, wrapped in the cloak I made for you, my hope was finished. I knew the sword would never come to meet the scabbard. I saw that you and I would never be reconciled. I drowned the scabbard.'

'You did what!'

'It came from the waters. To the waters it has returned. To her who made it.'

'Where? Where did you do this? For God's sake, tell me how far I must go to get it back!'

'You cannot. Her hand has taken it deeper than restitution. Neither of us can ever have it again. I have ritually destroyed that healing.'

'It was not yours. You had no right!'

'No. No right. No right to father's life, or mother's honour. No right to liberty. No right to love. When I, the Healer, destroyed the scabbard, I sacrificed the only power I ever held. I waited for you with empty hands. Since you would not accept equality of strength with me, I offered you the sharing of my powerlessness. And still you kept the sword.'

'They were both mine. Given to me at my manhood. Mine, not yours. I am the king!'

'Exactly. And I am nothing. How could this nothing help you?'

'I offered you the sword today!'

'It was too late.'

113

'You have killed my son.'

She bows her head in silence.

Elaine moves forward, very slow, and gathers up poor Anir in her arms. He isn't a big lad, but for all her size she must be stronger than she looks to lift him like that, as effortlessly as if he was a baby.

She smiles on him lovingly and rocks him gently. 'Sleep, little one. Fair women will attend your wounds and wine-cups wait you. The harps of the Summer Land shall soothe your slumber. In the morning, all shall be well.' Her soft lips kiss his cold brow.

Arthur glares at her, but finds no words.

There is a disturbance in the crowd. A little late, Gwenhyvar comes tumbling through, hair dishevelled, and throws herself on Anir's body. Her mother's keening splits the sky and all the women wail louder with her. Elaine stands motionless as Gwenhyvar sinks in a graceful heap on the cobbles, weeping. Then she walks slowly towards the hall bearing her burden, leaving Modred to kneel and comfort the queen.

Morgan watches this. Her eyes return to Arthur's.

'Yet what if I were indeed to restore your son to you?'

He starts. A gleam of hope is overshadowed by doubt. He backs away, and crosses himself.

'The boy is beyond help. You said so.'

'But how if I gave you a son back from the dead? I brought both sword and scabbard to your gate at Celliwig once, and you turned me away. I sent you a precious cloak and you put it on another. What would you do if I offered you your son again?'

Modred, raising Gwenhyvar, watches intently.

Arthur shouts, 'Murderess! A stolen sword! A poisoned cloak! Everything you promise me is tainted, woman!'

'No. You would not accept him, would you?'

She sighs and nods to her women.

'Prepare a sleeping draught for Gwenhyvar. And, Taliesin, warm your hands at the fire and tune your harp. It is your healing the High Queen will need as much as mine.'

I look to Arthur for permission, but he is stalking off indoors. It is Modred and Gareth who help Gwenhyvar to her chamber.

On the dais in the hall Elaine is laying the boy out on his bier.

Chapter Sixteen

They have taken Anir's body south, a cold departing. Miserable for me, to see the miles lengthening between Taliesin and the High King. No invitation for me now to sing at Arthur's court.

'I suppose that's the end of it,' I say to Woman. 'He won't want to see his sisters after this.'

'You, a learned bard! You can't see further than a blind kitten, can you?' He snorts contempt. 'They're like the seasons, those four. Spring, summer, autumn, winter, and then spring again. They'll come round. He can't escape them.'

'Do you think it was Margawse's doing?'

Her land, her mountain. Was it her hare? After all, he tried to kill *her* son.

Woman looks at me craftily under his veil. It's been long since he stood upright or gazed directly at another man.

'Who's to say which way the wind blows? Did you know her first husband, Lot, fell fighting Arthur's folk? She swore her sons to vengeance, though it wasn't Pendragon himself that killed him. Well, look at them now. Swarming around him like wasps on a ripe plum.'

I'm not sure what he's trying to tell me. That Margawse would make peace with Arthur? Or something darker?

'Can't he trust his own nephews?' Alarm now. I find Arthur's safety touches me too closely for comfort. Nimue's shaft has taken root.

'It would be a wise man who knew which side that lot are on. Margawse has never played the faithful wife, or widow afterwards. She's had other husbands since, and more that weren't. None of them lasted long.' He grins. He knows where I've been. I think the whole court knows.

Turn it off with a laugh, boy. 'I'm not surprised. It would take a mighty log to outlast her flame.'

'She'd better watch out it's not her that feels the edge of the axe, then. It's more than the women of this family that are dangerous. Avenge their father? They might well do that. They think their mother shames them. If I was her, and warm in bed, I'd want a great gold torque round my pretty white throat, just in case.'

The wind blows terribly cold in Din Eidyn.

The court of Lothian is in mourning, no heart for hunting. I'm not sorry. I'd rather stay snug by the fire and polish up a new lament on the harp. A Chief Bard is his own man, once he has fulfilled his duties. This weather I'd sooner be Gwion Bach tending the flames than bold Taliesin braving the burn.

What's up with the queens, though? Why are Morgan and Margawse coming into the hall cloaked, furred and booted, a glinting adventure in their eyes? Who is the stranger with them, this massive mound of wraps and capes? Elaine the Fair, who never rides or walks abroad, who seldom stirs from the side of the fire! Dressed for travel, in this bitter cold?

The queens' eyes scan the faces turned to them. They name their escort. This time I suck my thumb

118

and try to hide my face. No chance. Morgan's voice orders, 'Taliesin.'

I could protest. I'm Urien's bard, not hers. Even the king has no right to compel me outside my terms of contract. Idle words. We both know I won't waste breath on them.

Woman, her surly watchdog, is named of course. Not Tegau, though. Sweet, true, brave Tegau, that guards her Christian faith like a clear candle. Morgan respects that. I'm a Christian too, aren't I? When Urien's around, anyway. But Morgan knows there's too much of the blood of Ceridwen in me. I'm helpless before her.

Stark January. There isn't cloak and hood thick enough to keep out this cold. And the ruts are frozen into hard ridges under my boots. I slip and slide and worry about breaking my wrist. Hard climbing now. We follow a path up a bare, grim glen where the burn is frozen almost into stillness. At last I hear it sing. It chimes pure chords as it drops into a pool from stone to ice. These rocks are streaked with red. We enter the cave with care, for the stones are slippery. Reluctantly I help Elaine puff and heave herself up over the ledge. I know the signs inside, the stone table, the objects the women are setting out.

'Be thou my soul's shelter, thou my high tower!

'Forgive us our trespasses.

'Deliver me from the tempter.'

The Christian half of me babbles. I am not brave enough. Tegau is a more valiant warrior than I.

At least there should be a fire.

After all, there's nothing terrible done. What's the harm in offering a token to the god of the territory

119

at the beginning of the year? Corn, wine, a kid roasted with herbs. Just a modest dinner with a few friends.

That's not all we've come for. I didn't think it would be.

They stand, we stand, our fingertips upon the table. The knot is made, and hallowed.

'He will keep Caliburn now.' Morgan makes this a truth heavy with grief.

'You destroyed the scabbard without our consent.' Margawse's accusation.

Too slow, the third voice. We wait. All our eyes go to her, Elaine. She does not speak, but her plump hands fumble for a while in the heavy folds of her clothes. Something snakes into the winter light. She spreads it on the tabletop. I have seen it before, this woollen plait of red and black and white. All week she has sat and woven its strands, even while Arthur was watching her. It is braided now through a black and ancient leather, silver-clasped. I see what it is now. An old, old belt, frail with hard use, made newly bright and serviceable. A harness to hang on a warrior's hip. A strap to span his shoulder. The rings and clips that would hold a scabbard secure. A sword-belt.

Too late, isn't it?

'It is little enough. But it is well I have kept it. It is all the power Morgan has left us. It will have to serve.'

'For what?'

'Why now? Why did you not say you had this sooner? This is the bond that would have held them both together!'

'What is the use of showing the belt now we have

lost both sword and scabbard?' Margawse cries bitterly.

The younger sisters storm at her. Elaine, impassive, waits for their understanding.

'The line that measures out and cries "Enough"?'

'A last rope thrown to save a drowning man?'

'A noose to hang him?'

I should have stayed at home.

Chapter Seventeen

Their magic knot binds surer than I thought. The buckle tightens, though it seems at first as if I've slipped through the clasp.

Arthur will ride his frontier forts. Nimue, and my songs, have done their work. There's a new restlessness on him, by all accounts. Well, what is a king without warfare, without red blood on the sword, and playing football with heads, and speckled horses spattered with the rush of combat? What is a king if he cannot give gifts? Where is he to get the heaping gold, the corn-fed steeds, the rich-furred mantles, if they're not snatched from the palefaced Saxons, as they seize treasures from us? It's a brisk form of trading. You do not ask the bellowing cattle where they were bred, how many borders they've been driven over, how many times. I finger a brooch of gold and garnets on my tunic and wonder what British, Saxon, Irish, Pictish breasts have warmed its cool metal curlicues before it nestled here. On second thoughts, I wish I hadn't imagined that. Tremors of terror thrill through me. I see yet one more pair of hands rip it from this anchoring cloth. The nest grows cold, Taliesin is . . .

No! Back to Arthur, boy. Picture him in the summer dawn when the first long light comes

striding down the hills. He and all his warriors of
legend stand high as bardic imagination on the
moors. There is a line marked in both British and
Saxon minds. The rules are understood. Those
ramparts of the border forts, where our High King
stands higher still, are not there to repel flesh and
steel, but to hold off the advance of ambitious
thoughts. There must be fighting, now and then, of
course. If there were not, we might wonder if we still
needed a High King. But not so much as to upset the
truce.

You are right, Nimue. It is not enough. What is a
poet without warfare?

This time, it's different. He calls the older men to
ride with him. Cador, Nentres, Urien. It is the
youngest that he leaves behind to guard Gwenhyvar,
against the custom. We understand his message. King
Arthur is not finished yet. He is a king without a son
because he needs no son. Age, like the Saxons,
cannot encroach upon him.

I wonder if Urien of Rheged will decline the call.
But now obedience and temptation march side by
side. There is little enough of youth left to any of
them, and he's still in love with Arthur. They will
show their sons the meaning of valour.

This time he's going to take me! I shall have my
chance, I shall see Arthur in the glory of battle. No
matter what petty skirmish comes my way, my
bardic craft can raise it to the realm of high
adventure. My voice will be authentic. I was there!

My eyes are shining like Urien's.

'My lord! You will not be sorry. Nimue charged me
to sing for Arthur, to rouse him to war. There will
be deeds done this summer that shall ring round the

world and set the seas shaking on the farthest shores. Your fame will— '

'Nimue?' he interrupts me. 'This campaign is Nimue's doing? She asked your help?'

I flush with indignation. 'What else are we for, the druids, bards, the learned men and women? We are your inspiration. The Christian priests will thunder their psalms over the army too. You live by our poems and our prayers.'

'He banished Nimue once, for being too ambitious. Better that she had stayed by her lake.'

Too free with my tongue, wasn't I? In the morning, Urien's changed his mind. He will not take me. I plead. I remind him of Anir. What if this campaign is his last? What if Arthur's Llamrei were to put her hoof down a foxhole and the High King end his days with a broken head in the heather? Worse, what if this is the year when the settled pattern breaks, when the turgid blood of the British rises like the ninth wave and the last battle sweeps across the strand of history, and I not there to sing of it?

Urien's mouth sets in a tighter line.

'You agreed with me to be Chief Bard to Rheged. Is that not enough fame?'

Even a fair-minded Christian king is not above jealousy, it seems. Do not fear, my lord. The fights of Catraeth, the hall at Lyvennet, the pastures of Erechwydd, the courage of Urien, and the grave of Owain, all these shall live in song, because of Taliesin.

Until my life ages . . .

You know the rest by now.

125

Only, can't you see I was born for something more than this? Already the short spring day is dying. The light is reddening on the frontier forts.

I am left with the women.

Someone else is discontented with her lot. Gwenhyvar is fair, and Gwenhyvar is chaste, and Gwenhyvar is rather bored. Again she waits alone in Camelot. Well, not alone. Arthur has left her well guarded, rather too well, you might say, this time. Young lords that might have been raising the mead-horn on the eve of adventure, bearing the ash-shaft in battle, goading steaming horses into combat, must now confine themselves to rustic sports while their fathers earn praise as warriors.

In spite of them, the queen craves feminine company. She must hold her court. What is the use of this bevy of young gallants attending her if there are no older ladies to see and envy? She is young yet; and beautiful, isn't she? She could be Margawse's daughter.

They come, obedient to her royal summons, Elaine, Margawse, Morgan, and their households. Reluctant and curious. Does she have no fear of them now? What liquid has Nimue dropped in her ear that makes Gwenhyvar so sure of her own strength? It's been a long time since the three were invited to Camelot. A private enmity, a public loyalty. Arthur is still High King, and they are his sisters. Statecraft decrees he needs their kingdoms' support. Their family honour demands they must not diminish his. Where is the space for love, humanity, the meeting of hearts? These are not common folk. They are the prisoners of their position.

I ride with Morgan, across blue passes, down long green leafy lanes that lead us south, over ringing highroads the Romans left, along the old straight ridgeways that were the spines of a now fleshless past.

We come by the last high track to Somerset, and on our right a maze of meres and marshes tricks the eye with a net of shimmering light, level and liquid to the far-off Severn Channel. Or not quite level. No, not at all. Look, there emerging in the midst under a noonday moon Leviathan rises, a dragon of an island. Beyond its low ridged back a head rears proud and sudden to butt the sky. From miles around it draws the eye and holds it, a great eruption in that watery wilderness.

Morgan reins in her horse abruptly. I do not need her to tell me this is a fairy fortress. The evidence is plain.

'Ynys Witrin.'

The Glass Island. Glastonbury.

Nothing more to say, is there? Its presence follows us, though we turn our heads and move on. It's a powerful place, even at this distance.

'There is an abbey there,' says Tegau presently, looking over her shoulder. 'They have a holy thorn, sprung from the staff of Joseph of Arimathea. They even say the Lord Jesus was here as a child. And that the vessel that caught his blood . . .'

Morgan snorts, not too unlike her horse.

I believe Tegau. I could believe anything of that island.

Ahead of us is high Camelot at last. Against the bright sky its palisades stand silhouetted. Clean stonework flashes on its mighty banks. An old fort rebuilt by Arthur for new wars; a lonely, warlike place to leave a queen all summer.

When we come under its shadow, Morgan looks up. I cannot read her face. I think she does not wish to be here. She doubts the reason for this summons. Is Gwenhyvar as shallow as we have supposed?

A stream winds about the base of the fort through woodland. We climb, under the eye of sentries. Then, halfway up, the wind takes word of who we are and everything changes. Someone is running to meet us. Gareth. Morgan's own daughter Morfudd is close behind him, merry with greeting. We're inside the walls and the grim hard shell cracks open to reveal a sweet kernel of welcome. Gwenhyvar herself is kissing Morgan. You'd think there was common cause on the distaff side.

What a kingly hall! I haven't seen anything to touch it outside Roman cities. He'd like to have built this in masonry, Artorius Imperator. But the plastered wattle becomes Morgan better. Tonight the fire will leap on these painted walls and birds will croon to us from the thatch and we will gather in a circle and tell old stories.

Elaine was here before us, and now Margawse arrives. Agravain and Gaheris embrace her, though not too warmly. Her sons have a prickly northern sense of dignity. I remember Teilo's warning. If I were her, I'd tread carefully with Gwenhyvar's young men. They've a great capacity for hurting each other, this family.

A kingly hall, but a queen's court. There are games and riding and picnics and picking flowers. If Gwenhyvar still grieves for Anir, she covers it well. She teases Arthur's nephews more like a sister than an aunt. Sometimes we row in coracles on the river. 'We could make an expedition to Glastonbury,' says

Gwenhyvar. My thumbs are pricking with anticipation, but we do not go.

There's less wine drunk at Gwenhyvar's table. My head is clearer than I'm used to. It makes me oddly uncertain about my actions. The women have retired already. I stroll down the lane that separates the guest-chambers from the royal rooms. I settle my harp in its bag on my shoulder for reassurance. I'm not sure if I'll be wanted tonight.

It is not quite dark, but I see or hear no movement till a man speaks.

'Where are you going, Taliesin?'

Modred? Here, in the shadow between Morgan's house and Gwenhyvar's.

Don't stop walking. A check means guilt. Your harp is the passport. Just Taliesin, going about his job. Thank your stars it's not Owain. He was thought man enough to be away with Arthur.

Modred is barring my way. Not ostentatiously. I hear his hand loosen the knife in its sheath and let it go again. No more than a hint. He stands at ease, motionless, a man fulfilling his duty.

'You think I come too late?'

'Too late for what?'

'To bring Morgan sweet rest.'

'Morgan of Tintagel? You come nineteen years too late for that.'

Nineteen years. There's a nice calculation. The lifetime of both of us.

I don't feel like arguing. These men are jealous of their ladies' honour. Still, I thought Modred understood.

I shrug and turn for my own stall in the men's quarters. An early night and plenty of room without

the warband. I shan't have to pick my way over a
fuddle of drunken warriors.

When I reach the corner, Modred hasn't moved.
His shadow still stands at the crossroads between
Urien's and Arthur's queen.

Chapter Eighteen

Next day it's gone clean out of my head. Arthur's back, and half his army! Some lords will have gone home to find their ladies have flown the coop. His warband trot their horses through the hollow twisting way up the big hill, while we look down on them and cheer. Tegau has gone bright red. She's screaming as loud as any of them. Caradawc Strong-Arm's there, and all her virginal water has turned to wifely wine. Oh, unassailable, true Tegau Goldbreast. They'll be married this month.

The standards nod. The high horns cry out to us. The warriors have decked themselves with more jewellery than they went away with. They've found somebody foolish enough to fight with them. That will please him. Kill another calf and count the wine jars. There'll be a rare old feast tonight. Is the harp feeling up to it? It's been singing softer songs lately.

They are nearer now. It's not only the living faces that are lifted to us. There are heads swinging from the horses' necks. That must be a chieftain or two, gracing Arthur's harness. But not too many. Mustn't upset the diplomatic balance. It wasn't Badon, but it will have to do.

They're grinning at the thought of clean clothes, warm baths, good food. And now women! Our ladies waving on the walls don't cheer as loud as the roar of the warriors once they've seen who's waiting for them.

Women? There's a shock, as if I had looked at my own reflection in water and seen a stranger peering over my shoulder. I thought we were the female party welcoming back our fighting men. That's not the whole truth, though. So the tales are true. Arthur has women with him, on his side. Not many, a small tight band of warriors. They're muscled enough, but definitely not men. In kilted tunics, chequered cloaks thrown over the shoulder, braided hair, as rich in ornament of gold and bronze as any man. But weaponed, proud of themselves, defiant, and not without scars by the look of it. The men leave a respectful – resentful? – space between them.

And leading them, in a wicker chariot, with a golden breastplate that moulds itself over her flowing robes, Nimue. She grasps a silvery spear and looks up, smiling triumph.

The world is full of dangerous reverses. Be careful, Taliesin. The Lady of the Lake, that smiles so sweetly from a field of waterlilies, can be the angry storm that races down the loch. Remember Merlyn. Morgan is not the only woman with power.

Arthur dismounts. He's seen his sisters waiting to welcome him. This was clearly not by his knowledge. He glares at Gwenhyvar.

'Is a man not safe in his own home? Do they rob me of my son and come to devour Camelot as well?'

'They came to honour me as queen. May I not brighten Camelot in your absence?'

'You'd hold a court without me? Are you growing so high and mighty, madam?'

132

'Great victors need great courts to celebrate their homecoming.'

'Victory? A handful of heads and a lame horse!'

Then he bursts out laughing and hugs them all strongly, sisters included. He's in a good temper. It's gone well. I see his golden beard caught in the tide of Morgan's black hair flowing over his shoulder. I catch their laughing faces. I think I shall never understand them.

Nimue's the only one who sulks at the sight of reconciliation. I grab hold of Owain.

'Is it true? Did she really fight? Did she use that weapon?'

'She stood in her chariot on a hill and she shook her spear. She cursed our enemies and howled on us to slaughter them.' He grins like a hound. 'Once it was monks and bishops who did that for him. Nimue's better at it.'

Morgan laughs merrier now Arthur's come.

At supper I sing my poor thin songs of battles I have not seen. I mourn the fall of heroes I cannot remember meeting. They'd have to be heroes, wouldn't they, since they died? I make it sound as thought this was the high summer in the fortunes of Britain. Some of the silver they have taken comes my way. I'm a rich man already. Does nobody but me hear the poverty in my songs, see the lays that swell in me like a pregnant woman past her time? Taliesin, in Camelot, at Arthur's board – and nothing much to sing about.

The very next day they're off hunting. There's a lust in these men to kill, and in me to tell of it. They need the fame I give them, I need the deeds they do. And not a few women ride with them under the leafy oaks. Morgan, who's lost ten years at least in the fresh wind that blows in with Arthur. Margawse, Nimue. Not Elaine, of course, or Gwenhyvar.

Now, in the spring weather of Somerset, I don't need to be bullied. I'll risk horses and horns and branches and breaks to be at Arthur's heels while I can. For a week the sun shines as never before, and our days are full of sport and the nights of pleasure. Tegau Goldbreast is wed to Caradawc Strong-Arm amid great celebration. The women smile and the men sigh.

Only a week. Tomorrow they ride back to the border. The hounds of age are after Arthur. He dare not stop running.

Hope, Taliesin. His recklessness could provoke the last great conflict yet.

Our final hunt is over. The stag is trussed, and the merriment has faded. I find myself riding back by the mere with Morgan. Our mounts pace softly under the trees. We are neither of us as hard as those we have hunted with.

'Taliesin?'

For once, her voice does not command; it pleads. Be the more careful, boy. Wait, listen.

'You are a light lad. You find a welcome in many rooms. Would you get something for me?'

'What can Taliesin bring you, that my queen herself could not command?'

'Something of Arthur's.'

'What, my lady?'

'It does not matter. Only . . . not spoils of war, a treasure made by craftsmen only for him to bestow again as a gift. Some possession more personal to him. A thing that is truly his, and no other's.'

'Whom shall I ask for this? Arthur himself, or Gwenhyvar?'

She laughs then, and her eyes dance like emeralds in the flickering leaf-light. Very appealing, that smile.

'You need not beg from either of them. You wanted to ride with Urien on this raiding-party. Now I appoint you Morgan's reaver!'

'I'd ask you why, except that I know you wouldn't tell me.'

'Suck your thumb of knowledge and see if it gives you inspiration.'

We joke. We both know this is no laughing matter. Morgan asks nothing lightly from anyone, nor do they refuse her.

Serious, then. Taliesin's to be a thief again. Oh, dear, I remember Gwion Bach, and what it cost last time. Shake that thought off. But I do not play my best this last evening.

I sit down and take the horn of wine they pass me. Everyone seems to be smiling but me. Me and Morgan. Her eyes have gone dark now, like the shadows under a yew tree. Perhaps she too can feel that the day is turning too far. I have arrived too late and she has delayed too long. So little chance remains to both of us. Our dreams must be delivered soon. Her eyes beseech me to remember what she asked.

I force a smile for her. Haven't I seen her laughing, held on Arthur's breast? The men are home and safe, most of them. Everyone's merry. Pity about Anir, but the men are toasting Gwenhyvar. The corn is springing. There's meat on the spits for the poets of Christendom. All's well.

All's well? I'm sorry, Morgan. Nimue looks radiant. She is the one who will goad Arthur to war.

The High King will be late to bed. The men are carousing. Tomorrow the long road east, damp tents, deserted forts, uncertain food. Tonight they will fill themselves to the brim with good meat and mead. The women go earlier to bed, hoping for something else before their heroes are felled by drink.

A lesser talent than me is Chief Bard in Camelot. I leave him twanging. I have other duties.

It is growing late, and half of us are in our chambers. Well, I'm in Morgan's, as it happens. She has come to that age when women flush and thirst and cannot sleep. For a young man I've learned a good deal about the needs of women. I am the hand that strums softly while the castle sleeps, the voice that murmurs poems at the wakeful midnight. It's not a Chief Bard's job. But nobody can charm the restless pillow of my queen more tenderly than I can. I have been discreet. No sentinel challenged me this time. Besides, all the corners of Camelot have been full of sweet laughter and hushings these seven nights.

Her ladies are gathered round. The younger ones are yawning. Such sweet soft faces need their sleep. At last she sends them away, all except Tegau and Woman. Tegau looks soulful. She is wakeful for someone else, this three-days' bride. Beside her blossom we make a poor pair, Woman and I. The one too manly for a dame, the other too maidenish a man to be a battle-poet.

But now Morgan has a task for me behind the enemy lines. Her hand grasps my wrist, hot and dry. She is thirsty for something more than I can give her.

I feel how fragile the bond that ties Arthur to her. It has been a sunlit week. A sudden storm could separate them for ever. Like her, I know a desolate ache for something to remember Arthur by. For me, one last heroic deed; for her, this keepsake. I nod. Trust Taliesin.

The air is sweet outside. There's still deep-throated singing from the hall. The Pendragon sleeps in a fine house opposite this one, when he's finished drinking, that is; the royal chambers. I tiptoe across the path in the April gloaming, fearful I'll set the guard dogs baying for my throat and bring the warhost running. Does Morgan realise what I'm risking for her?

The lamps are all out but one. Pray that Gwenhyvar and all her ladies are asleep by now. Push the door gently. Close darkness inside. Stupid to come like a thief in the middle of the night.

When else should a thief come?

Taliesin's a thief. And what he is stealing he does not understand.

Cold feet now. Cold in my stomach, too. I'm backing out. Not that I'd say no to Morgan, mind you. I wouldn't dare. But better ways than this, better times, better light.

Too late. Someone's awake! No maiden, either. The hiss of steel, the fumble of an urgent hand and then a sure grip on my wrist. The edge of the blade to my throat. He sees me better than I see him.

'Your name, and business in the queen's house in the middle of the night? And if the name you speak fails to match your face when I get you outside, I'll separate your head from your heart by the same distance.'

'Taliesin,' I squeak.

I feel him check. The warlike certainty's gone out of his grip.

'Taliesin? In Gwenhyvar's rooms?' He speaks louder and less guardedly. I know the voice for Gareth's.

'Silly me! Got the wrong door in the dark, haven't I?'

'That mistake could have cost you your life.' But he lowers the blade. Still, he's not satisfied. 'You didn't think to cheat my aunt Morgan with Arthur's queen, did you?'

Not, would I cheat Arthur, you notice, though the king's his uncle too. Very devious, this kindred.

'Not me! I've a tricky enough boat to row, as it is.' He chuckles a bit.

'Look over your shoulder, then, and watch where you're steering. The queen's not so lonely she needs the likes of you.'

'Don't worry,' I promise him. 'It wasn't her I was after.'

I back out, trembling like a dog in a thunderstorm.

Gwenhyvar is fair, and Gwenhyvar is chaste, and Gwenhyvar is closely guarded.

Chapter Nineteen

Arthur's gone again, like a dust storm through our camp. Does he feel, as Morgan does, that the days are oddly short, though the year is moving towards May Day?

It's beautiful weather, and the whole court rides out to cheer them on their way. The women are brightly dressed. They've threaded their hair with ribbons and jewels, to fix a picture of themselves in their menfolk's memories. Tegau's eyes are bright but brave. The young men of Gwenhyvar's guard are showing off before their older relatives. Their pride is hurt because Arthur is denying their manhood. They do not need to spare their own horses; they will be stabled back in Camelot all too soon. They prance and race, circle and gallop round the pacing column of warriors and war-gear.

I let them go, watching them for a while from the ramparts. I haven't the heart for this outing. I'm no horseman. Arthur is leaving us.

Besides, I have other plans. This is a better time for thieving, broad daylight, plenty of people about. People? You thought they'd all of them ridden out with Arthur? Servants. As invisible to the nobility as common flies, that are only noticed when they settle where they shouldn't. But in the life before this I was Gwion Bach. I've sweated over cauldrons too.

Give them a good day and smile at them, then, as you cross the yard. Put a spring in your step and hold your head high. Don't sneak this time. Walk like a man who knows where he's going and has every right. To Arthur's chambers. Whistle a bit. It's a lovely morning. No more difficult, this, than the spell you lay on the host after supper's over, to make them believe tales that will suit your fortune.

Open the door and step inside. Easier in daylight. No warrior with a drawn dagger, this time. No one at all. Not even a slave with an armful of rushes. Makes me feel guilty again, somehow, this emptiness. No harm, though, is there? I know Morgan loves her brother. I have felt myself transformed inside her. I hear the name she cannot help but cry.

No difficulty this morning, knowing which way to turn. A great bear carved on the right, leaping dolphins painted on the left. I listen for a murmur of voices behind Gwenhyvar's door. Nothing. Too nice a day. Her serving-women will have found themselves work outside to enjoy the sunshine. Right, then. Here goes.

A kingly room. The bed's big. Nothing to cramp his style here. Rich hangings to keep out the draughts. Painted wood and cunning carvings. The great hall itself is not more colourfully decorated than this. Scarlet and gold seem to be his favourites.

It's a shame it's not royally kept, though. The bed's unmade. There are dirty clothes in a heap on the floor. Great Arthur should be better served than this. If I were Gwenhyvar, I'd drill a smarter army to attend my king. Still, such untidiness suits my purpose. I look around, judiciously. What should I choose for Morgan? I try not to hurry, though I don't want to linger. It must be done right. This is important to her. She does not easily beg.

I walk to the middle of the room and turn, considering. And then I see it. My heart gives a great bound as if I had peered through the branches of the forest and seen the face of a wolf, not a yard away from me. It is lying on the coffer at the foot of the bed, beside me, a magnificent sword. A name leaps to my mind and fills me with amazement. It can't be, can it? Arthur's great weapon, Caliburn? No sword in all the world to match that. This hilt is heavy with gems. I search for the pair of fire-breathing dragons and find them, and yet . . . I marvel that a soldier could grasp this handily in earnest battle. Jewels are not the true worth of Caliburn. All Britain knows it is his talisman of victory. Would he leave it behind when he rode to war?

The scabbard is richly crusted too, but the poet in me plucks a note of sadness. The true cover for Caliburn is long since lost. Teilo has told me. Ancient black and silver, it was, not much to look at, but wonderful to touch, precious with healing. On a black day, Morgan drowned that scabbard, ritually casting it into a bottomless lake. He thinks she killed herself that day. I will not believe it. I am too young to bury hope. I have seen them laughing.

Caliburn survives alone, dangerously unmatched, the killing tool. They both came to us from the water. The first has already gone home. The sword must follow one day. Not yet! Not yet! With all Taliesin's great song still unsung.

I cannot take this sword for Morgan. I'm not that

daft. All the same . . . my hands close round the sparkling hilt and find the metal cold, the gems sharp. Puzzled, I try to draw its unhandy weight.

'No, boy. That isn't Caliburn. She took that once before. She will not get the chance again. It nearly cost Britain his life the first time.'

Guilt floods my cheeks. Gwenhyvar! Back so soon, and alone? She halts in the doorway, her face flushed with distress and streaked with tears. Parting has been too much for her, it seems. Still, though she's not a tall woman she stands straight and imperious now, as if she's forgotten already what she was weeping for.

I try to smile. 'I didn't think it could be.'

She looks at me, considering. I am Taliesin, the finest bard that has ever sung in Camelot, and a limber young lad for a lady. I see she knows that. But she wants only half of what I can offer. I have sung her praises. I will have gold, horses, fine tunics from her, land, even. But I am Morgan's. She does not trust me. I read all that in her face.

What do I care? Why should I want skimmed milk? I, that have tasted wine and blood?

'Didn't you know Arthur had two great swords? Caliburn, his weapon of war, that Nimue armed him with when he came to manhood, and this, the sword of Britain's government, put in his hand by Bishop Dubric at his coronation, on his most sacred oath to guard her peace.'

She takes the regal sword away from me. I'm not sorry. It was a heavy thing to hold.

'I didn't know. Too young for his coronation, me.'

Tactless, that. It was her coronation too. I watch her face change, and I'm trying to cobble together some compliment to cover myself. But she smiles suddenly, and there's a gleam in her eyes as if she's thought of a sudden purpose.

'Wait there, bard!'

She darts across to her own room. I hear the lid of a chest thrown back, the sounds of search. Gwenhyvar returns. In her hands she bears something reverently. At first I think it might be a distaff, but it holds no thread. A shaft of polished greenstone, weighty, valuable. The top is carved into the semblance of birds' heads, fourfold, looking all ways with garnet eyes. From its lower tip three human heads gaze upwards.

'Do you know what this is? Do the bards sing of this?'

I shake my head.

'I did not think so. It is the queen's sceptre,' she explains. 'My staff of office, given to me when Arthur received his sword, in a separate coronation, in another church, before the witness of women.'

Curious. Morgan never told me of that. No, not curious. Morgan speaks very little of Gwenhyvar.

She lays her sceptre beside his sword, and we both stand looking at them. I'm not sure what she's trying to tell me.

'I always thought Arthur got his real power from Merlyn.'

'Merlyn?' Her laugh is light and yet so scornful. 'The bards praise him, don't they? No. It was Nimue who gave him the arms of war, and the Church that entrusted Arthur with this sword of peace. The Lady of the Lake was wiser than Merlyn. Drop by drop she drained him of his secrets, and in the end he told her one too many. Where is Merlyn now? Mad, lost, buried in the forest? They went into the woods together, and Nimue came back alone, laughing at her own cleverness. Since then, she has sought to be the watcher over Arthur, the spirit that wakes when he sleeps, his shadow in the sun. Very powerful is the Lady of the Lake, but he will not trust her. There was only ever one woman in the world who could be to Arthur what Merlyn was.'

There is pain in her face. I have misjudged her, thinking her a shallow, pretty toy, but she is a hurt wife. She sees too much. Arthur and Morgan . . . And I shiver. I see through her eyes this is too dangerous a love for him. We must protect him, she and I.

And because I am sorry for her, I say without thinking whose service I am here on, 'Beware of Modred.'

'Modred? *Modred*?'

Her colour deepens and her eyes widen. Shock? Disbelief? Fascination? I should have known the moment of deep understanding between us had passed. I am back in the shallows of her mind. She thinks I am warning of danger to herself, not Arthur. Her world is once more as narrow as this bedchamber, and made for the same purpose, though a moment ago she was holding a queen's sceptre in her hand.

She crosses quickly to the window and stands looking out, gripping the frame. A vole, held by a stoat, would not have had a more single thought. Sickened, I turn to go. Have I been a traitor? To which side?

Something white, lying on the floor beside the bed. A shirt of Arthur's. Someone should have washed it. The mud of the hunt cakes it, a deep, red-brown, the colour of dried blood. It smells of his sweat.

144

Behind Gwenhyvar's back I gather it up. This of Arthur's for his sister-queen. Strange that she needs to seek such a keepsake after all these years. Can he really have given her nothing at all?

I push it under my tunic and I'm crossing the outer threshold when I bump into Modred. My turn to colour. Why did it have to be him? Well, somebody would have to be detailed to escort the queen home early, wouldn't they? Modred is always the willing courtier.

He asks sharply, 'Where were you?'

'Talking to Gwenhyvar,' I stammer. 'But I've done her no harm.' They know my reputation.

'With Gwenhyvar? And no harm?' And he throws back his head and laughs coarsely.

I tremble to the soles of my shoes. I have never heard Modred laugh loud and lewd like that. He's always a courteous, quiet-smiling man.

Then he is gone, in through the door of the royal chambers where I have left the sword of kingship.

Walk on, Taliesin. Don't look round.

Gwenhyvar is fair, Gwenhyvar is chaste, and Gwenhyvar is waiting by the window.

Chapter Twenty

I've put that shirt in Morgan's hands. I don't know if I've done right. She stared at it hungrily, but she didn't cover it in kisses, or me either.

The sisters are impatient to be home now. In Garlot and Lothian and Rheged the corn is sprouting. It will soon be May Day. There is work of more than one sort to be done for the success of herds and crops. While the men campaign, the women must oversee the growth.

Does Gwenhyvar ride her farms as Arthur rides his forts? Hard to imagine. The High King's not like other chieftains. The whole island's his estate. He's a pack-leader, not a sheepdog; a sacred symbol, not a working farmer. Morgan is rooted in the land, Urien's land, Rheged. The fishing banks of the Solway, the pleasant pastures of Erechwydd, the high fort of Lyvennet, and the moors all the way to Catraeth that overlook the Angles. She feeds the earth with what the gods demand. She is the steward of the soil. She heals Urien's people. She keeps their king safe and whole.

And Gwenhyvar? From Caerleon to Camelot or Celliwig, what is she but Arthur's camp-follower? Can her sceptre keep him, or Britain, from harm?

She rides a little way with us to set us on the road.

I see her now, her dappled mare standing at the edge of the trees, her skirts spread wide over the horse's flanks, medallions and bells winking on the coloured harness, smiling a little disappointedly. Smiling, because she knows she looks prettier so; sad to see us go. She fears these sisters, but she fears desertion more. It has been a lonely thing to be Arthur's queen.

I raise my hand and crinkle my eyes in a special smile to tell her I understand. No chance of a last song for her; the harp's packed in its bag. The daughters of Gorlois will not wait; there's a long road north for us. So I turn and see her figure dwindling, surrounded by her bright ladies like butterflies. We're leaving Tegau behind with her, wife of Caradawc now. A semicircle of horsemen guard Gwenhyvar. Their hands are lifted too. Half of them are our men. Agravain, Gareth, Modred.

Oh, salt-tide brother of mine, by the water that bore us both, will you guard your unknowing stepmother well for Arthur?

From the midland country the sisters go their separate ways. A few weeks pass. The feast of Beltaine is celebrated and over. Morgan moves contentedly amongst corn and herds. If she was a cat, she'd purr. The calves and lambs look strong. The increase is good.

And then it comes, like a flaming arrow in a sleeping camp. Gwenhyvar is taken.

News, rumour, argument, speculation! We're all milling about the exercise yard. We've forgotten the niceties of noble and commoner. He's rich, who seems to have more of the truth. So we grab each other and shout and question. Morgan comes, sweeping across the sward in a gown of green and gold. She looks angry and I think I know why. Where were the men who should have guarded Arthur's queen? They stand too close in blood to her. This touches her honour. Owain, her eldest, is not among them. He rode with Urien and Arthur. Rhun, the clerk, has remained to administer Carlisle. He stands behind her now in his long scholar's gown, tall, frowning, concerned. But the younger ones, Pasgen and Rhiwallawn, her nephews . . . her foster-son, Modred.

Morgan has no reason to love Gwenhyvar.

No! She's as upset as anyone, that's plain to see. She is not feigning, surely? Urien's priest leads us to pray for the High Queen in Carlisle's church, and Morgan is there. In Urien's absence, she takes his place. She knows the rules.

I picture Gwenhyvar, that vulnerable wife, standing in the disorder of Arthur's departure. Am I upset for her, or do I feel the burden of a fine romantic story coming on? Still, no use in a ballad without a satisfying ending. Somebody will have to rescue Gwenhyvar first.

Owain himself arrives. He and his men are haggard and weary. They have scoured the route from Camelot to Carlisle for news of Gwenhyvar. They arrive empty-handed.

Arthur has summoned them all, the women of his blood. I wonder what he wants, but Morgan believes she knows. She is not afraid, as I am. It is not the suspicion that Arthur's wrath may be turned on his sister that makes me nervous. It is my own suspicions. I do not want to part the bracken and see an adder's nest. Her eyes sparkle and she throws back her head and asks Owain, 'Can Nimue not find

149

his queen for him? Does he fall back once more on
our wisdom which he has so often scorned?'

'The Lady of the Lake is not far-seeing.'

We all know who in his family has the sight: Elaine.

So it's pack up our bags and trek all the way south
again, is it? And I thought I'd done with horses. The
harp weighs heavy on my back. There'll be few
presents for a poet till Gwenhyvar's found.

I'm wrong again. It's sailing weather now. We skim
the shores of Dyfed and come in on the vast tides
of the Severn Channel.

Camelot looms, darker already to me without its
graceful lady. Four ramparts to pass through, up the
steep hill. A narrow cutting, the great oak doors. Our
footsteps echo solemnly in the shadowed passage
under the great gate-tower. Arthur's not here to
meet us.

It is Morgan's daughter again, lovely winning
Morfudd, stricken now, who comes running to clasp
her mother, with Tegau behind her. There has been
no word of Gwenhyvar. The men are out beating the
countryside far and wide.

The story pours out. They have told it many times
before.

'It was May Morning, so we were all of us up before
dawn and dressed in green to go maying.'

'It was Gwenhyvar's wish. She chose ten of us
ladies to attend her.'

'And as many warriors, with Gareth leading them.'

'It was grey and misty beside the river, but we
thought no harm. This is Arthur's country, his
stronghold.'

'We were spread out among the hawthorn trees,
gathering flowers and boughs for the festival.'

'We did nothing shameful in our maying. Gwenhyvar is a Christian. She shuns the darker rites, but she likes to keep up any pretty custom.'

Only pretty custom, Tegau! The naked girls in the dew? The maypole? Steady. This is no time for teasing, boy.

'The men had their spears and they were watching the forest. We had not come for hunting, but we all felt it was that dawn stillness when deer might step out from the trees.'

'Then Gwenhyvar called to them, so they put down their spears and she filled their arms with the may-boughs we had gathered.'

'That's when they fell on us in a rush, like a storm of hail.'

'Riders, masked and helmeted.'

'Twenty at least. We never expected it, so near to Arthur's own fortress.'

'In a moment the blackest among them had snatched the queen on to his own horse and galloped away. We heard her shrieking. There was nothing we could do.'

'Our men fought desperately to reach their horses, but it was already too late.'

'The devils escaped, taking their wounded with them, even their dead. Not so much as a riderless horse was left to tell who they might have been.'

'Gareth is sorely wounded.'

Gareth, holding a dagger to my throat in the dark. Gwenhyvar is well guarded? Not closely enough. Poor lad! He'll carry the family's disgrace for this.

Nimue is here, icily furious. You can see whom she blames, no matter that Arthur's sisters were hundreds of miles away.

151

Could she be right?

Arthur comes back before nightfall, raging like a hound denied food. When brother and sister greet this time there's no laughing embrace. Still, he kisses her. Whatever dark thoughts he has, he needs her wisdom now.

Margawse is the next to arrive. She's come a long way in haste, but she's gleeful, and barely bothers to hide it. There's more bitterness than you'd think feeding her flame. She'd better be careful. Gareth's her youngest son – youngest, that is, of those she acknowledges; Modred's history is still a secret from the world. Arthur is looking for traitors, anything to earth the thunderbolt of his rage, though it shatters what it strikes. I hope Gareth's wound is deep enough to swallow suspicion.

Elaine takes her time. She never hurries. For me, I wouldn't mind if she dawdled so long she never got here. But she comes. Arthur stands by the heap of stones from the old pagan temple he has plundered to face his bulwarks. It has cost him something to ask his three sisters help him find Gwenhyvar. Bishop Bytwini pronounces it a punishment for backsliding from the promises he made to Christ, but Arthur daren't believe him. He's lost. He prays with Tegau and Urien and the rest of us Christians for his wife's safety. Then, like a child, he runs back to his Mothers. I know how he feels.

That evening I watch Elaine take that old black swordbelt from her travelling-bag, and pass it to Morgan. The new colours of her weaving glow clear in the dusk. Morgan looks at it for a long while, and then nods her head.

After all, it seems Elaine can tell Arthur nothing.

Chapter Twenty-one

I should have known. It's back to the saddle for me, isn't it? We're all summoned for this hunt, any man who's fit enough to get a leg across a saddle. At least they've found me a sweeter-tempered grey. The ladies are ordered to stay within the walls. Their lords won't risk being shamed by another rape. We leave them to their own kind of search. Not Nimue and her band, of course; they've gone already, more feared than feared for. Are those Lake-women hunting Gwenhyvar's captors now with their sharp spears? Or have they gone to work a more private magic?

I ride with Modred. There's a strange bond between us. We're two of a kind, rejected, dangerous. The descendants of Jacob, who stole Esau's birthright. Gifted with more than we were meant to have.

We are winnowing the woods, flailing the fields, combing the coasts. We search for a silver pin in the great tapestry of Britain. What wouldn't I give to be sitting in the women's rooms strumming a tune, while the needles flicker and the coloured threads dart in and out of the weave like birds through foliage?

Dappled leaves, throwing their hatched shadows

on uneven ground. Enough to dazzle the eye and give me a headache. My mind reels as I wonder at the number of trees in Britain. And every oak is a possible hiding place. We stand on the long ridges above the trees and the mist floats up from the valleys so that each line of hills becomes an island and there are fairylands hidden from sight under white waves. We ask. Everywhere we go, we ask. And it seems to me that the people's faces have a shuttered look. What was open and gossipy before has become secretive. I do not trust their smiles. I think that no one will ever find Gwenhyvar.

She is Creiddylad, maiden of most majesty, snatched by the king of deathless Annwn, Gwyn ap Nudd. And Arthur is Gwythyr, demanding her back to the lord of daylight as his right. On the top of Glastonbury Tor they fight for her, every May Day until the end of time.

I've lost count of how many times we've turned down some river valley till we meet the sea, how often we've climbed a cliff path to ride on the short starred turf, how many cottagers we've hailed with the same question, how many heads have shaken. Modred has wheeled me round so many times I haven't the least idea where we are. We could be at the farthest west of the land where ogres and mermaids live, or half a day's ride from Camelot. I'm losing interest. This ride's a dream, or it would be if it weren't so uncomfortable. I've left my harp at home. I'm even carrying sword and shield. I, Taliesin, like a butchering knight! Will we come back to find that Camelot is dead, her king long gone, only the wind wandering over the fallen ramparts, and my harp cracked and the strings rusted? My voice is cracked and rusty with the dust. We bump along. I'll never complain of being given a hard stool to sit on after this nag. If I can ever sit down again!

Modred is harder. Day after day he hunts Gwenhyvar with a sober, intent look on his face.

That's good news, isn't it? It ought to silence one suspicion.

'One of our family must find her. Arthur believes that we have cheated him.'

Well, is he right? I wouldn't dare say that out loud, of course. I look sideways at Modred under my eyelashes, and he catches the question. He gives me a grin, so sudden and charming that I see for an instant his father in him.

'And if I had? What good would it do me, riding the round of Dumnonia with you, instead of enjoying her? Unless I did it from spite.'

Silly wasn't it? And besides, she's his stepmother, as he well knows.

For days it rains, and the low clouds shroud all landmarks. We have come to a low, wet land. Then the sun pulls up a fog that makes a witching world between the puddles under our feet and the blue sky overhead. No birds sing. No little warblers and thrushes, anyway. Big bitterns boom, tall herons spear the pools, the curlews' cry circles mournfully in the mist. We've lost the friendly hares and squirrels of the woods. Slick, nameless creatures dart across our path and plop and dive into unseen water. The horses start and shudder. We dismounted long ago. We have to feel our way. I think we've lost the road. The water's come through my boots and when my horse tugs back on his bridle I think he's right. The hooves suck out of the saturated ground and leave fresh lakes behind us. It would be hard to turn round and go back.

'Do you know the way?' I ask, and my voice sounds more lost and dismal than I want it to.

I cannot hear what he answers. It might be the whoop of a swan.. But there is a way. Sometimes when the mere seems wettest all about us I find under my feet the slippery corrugations of bound timbers. I wonder where it's going. Modred's some way ahead. He seems to be hurrying. His horse trusts him more than mine does me. I envy the bond these warriors have with their steeds that will carry them even into death. Then I remember that Morgan speaks with animals too. I recall I have been a toad, I have been a wren, I have been a roebuck on the mountain. Past lives. Forgotten languages. As a drover, I'm a failure.

The blue is going out of the sky. The shimmering whiteness of water that was all around us closes into a dull, dark circle. The fog has roofed us over. The reeds seem to stand taller, but they make no sound. Modred's a shadow on the wall of vapour. Then he's gone.

'Modred!' I cry. Only a startled clucking and the beat of wings.

'Modred!' Silence. The fog begins to drip.

Terrible panic pounding in my chest. We've been paddling in this marsh for an hour or more, and all I've done is slop my way behind Modred. He's the man of action, prince, hunter. My genius is to record deeds, not to do them. I wasn't responsible. I only followed in his footsteps.

Now there are no steps but mine, no road unless I find it. Even as we stand still I feel myself begin to sink. The horse has suddenly become a friend, but he's as terrified as I am. I hug his neck for warmth and I find I'm nearly crying.

'Help! Modred!' He'll turn back soon. He'll come and save me.

A dark, damp, desolate dereliction. Where was he leading me, anyway? Go back, or on? Where's on, in the winding way that bends from bulrush clump to island of osiers, finds stone for seven steps, then wood in water? Every foot an act of faith, each pace a prayer.

'Holy Jesus, by thy road of sorrows, Gracious Father, creator out of water, Spirit of all our wisdom, get me home!'

One step at a time, and then another. Terror that I shall never find a third. Stooped like a hunchback, smelling the stench of rotting vegetation, peering. Is the fog thickening or the light fading? Bring back the sun! But this is a world without heaven. Is Hell like this, cold, clammy, featureless, without other human life? A fiery furnace would be almost welcome, even the shrieking of tortured fellow human beings. It would be easier if I didn't have to tow this recalcitrant bag of bones behind me. Sorry, old friend! Treacherous thought. Suppose I let go of the bridle? Saved myself. Every time I look round to tug him after me I lose sight of the way I was going.

No. An unhelpful horse is better than nobody. The thought of utter loneliness appals me. I'm weeping now.

Hope's sliding away with every stumble in the mud. It leaves in its place a kind of reckless abandon. As well drown now in this half-light as later, in the dark. Right, then. Splish, splosh, thump, stamp.

There's causeway, and sand, and peat, and stone, and . . . Aah! No! I'm up to my neck in foul water.

Humbled, I fumble for firm foothold, shivering with shock, chastened and chilled. I've lost the track; I've lost the horse; I've only my life, and that will leak away by morning. Where is the grave of Taliesin? A mystery.

On hands and knees now, the Chief Bard of Urien Rheged, whimpering like a baby.

And then the steady splash of oars.

Chapter Twenty-two

Never there where the action is, am I? Chief Bard to Britain? Maybe this is Ceridwen's revenge, that I should have the soul of poetry and lack the opportunity. Modred could have sung the story, but Modred is modest and discreet. If it had been Gawain, now, we'd never have heard the last of it, and a bit more ornament every time he told it. No, Modred may be storming fortresses single-handed, but no bard is by to celebrate his deeds. And where is Taliesin?

I'll tell you where. In a dark, damp, stinking, shuttered shed, in the middle of a marsh, only fit for frogs. A prisoner! I, Chief Bard of Rheged, that have made odes to Arthur. On a quest to deliver the fair queen Gwenhyvar. Bearing a sword and shield, on a hardy horse, but ready to pipe a praise-song too at the first opportunity. There's justice for you!

I don't hammer on the door or try too hard to break my bonds. I'm frightened. These are the Little People, aren't they? Black, straight-cropped hair, a darker skin. They move in a quick, secret way like hunted animals. They don't carry themselves upright and brag and swagger like good Celtic Britons; and yet perhaps they understand more of Britain than we do, as much at home in her waters as the brown trout, as used to the ways of her woods as the dappled deer. Were we the doom to them that the Saxons seem to us? What would I do if I captured a lone Saxon? What are they going to do to me?

These are the folk that make changelings of our children, that turn milk sour and shoot elf-bolts to cripple old men and women. They are different and dangerous. I can barely make out what they say.

Is it safe to eat what they give me? Or will I be goblin-ridden for the rest of my life, pining for fairy food I can never find again? In the end, I can't help myself. I'm starving. Milk and fish. I mutter a prayer to Saint Peter and wolf it down.

You can't go on being terrified for ever. It's like being in a house full of big spiders. Once the horrid novelty's worn off the nerves decline to jump. I'm bored.

I try my charms on the woman who brings me food. She's middle-aged, with dugs that hang like goatskin water-bags, and a skirt that doesn't seem to cover as much as it should. Older women have never been a problem to me. They usually gobble me up like a tasty sweetmeat. She doesn't understand the signals. Fine words are wasted on her untuned ear. I'm a failure.

I'm alive. But in which world? The door opens briefly as the woman leaves. I have a glimpse of pale, still water. Thick willows crowd low islets, closing us in. The fog has gone, but there is little to see. Four children and a dog run into the water, shattering its stillness. They are oddly silent. I don't hear them shout or laugh. The mirror's broken. The door shuts me in.

I remember a boat. Hardly more than a raft with

shallow sides. The small, dark, silent men and women that plucked me from my perilous roost among the reeds, and poled me here. Not talkative, these marsh people. Not friendly either, to feed and dry me and then tie me up. I tried singing to them. I thought that might impress them. But a man came and struck me on the mouth. They are a secret people.

This can't be the Blessed Isles, can it? Where are the fair women, the wine, the feasts and song? Too dingy for heavenly Jerusalem. A pallet of reeds for a crystal throne. A chink in the thatch instead of the radiant Lamb that needs no other sun. A muddy puddle at the door for the River of Life.

It's too uncomfortable to be anything but the world I was born into when Ceridwen's nine months were up and Taliesin shot into the midwife's hands to amaze all creation. I wasn't welcome then; I'm not here. Why are they keeping me a prisoner? Where is Modred?

There was a newt crawling over the planking this morning. I talked to him like a friend. I lie awake in the dark hearing all sorts of rustling slithers and pray that they are nothing worse. I've done a lot of praying lately. I've lost count of the days.

Days? Weeks, rather. Life creeps sluggish and slow, like the last blood leaking from a dead dog. Taliesin's dying. I'm not allowed to sing. I have no audience, no praise, no gifts. No women clap me with bright eyes. No men look at my youth, my talent, my face with envy. I'm wasting away. My skin is pale and puckered from the damp. I've sores where I sleep. The daylight is a stranger to me. I'm half-blind. Why do they bother to keep me alive?

Months. Midsummer passed us long ago. The days are shorter now, and the nights colder. I've a terrible cough. I think I know what I'm kept for now, like a prize boar in a pen. When the year turns, and all our strength is needed to haul back the sun . . . When the harvest is in, and the earth lies waiting to be renewed . . . When the gods are hungry for blood . . .

Urien, Tegau, Bytwini, Saint Michael and all the angels, pray for me!

. . . Pray for me, Morgan.

The door crashes open. There's red firelight outside. I've never seen such a glare in all the time I've been here. I hear the Little Folk yelp, an inhuman outcry, shocking even me who has grown used to their careful mutterings. Flames leap in the water.

A dark giant shape bursts through the reddened doorway, casting a swooping shadow as he stoops over me. I think I screamed. I can see the light on the blade, feel it touch my skin. Give me back my slimy solitude, the rats and worms! A heave that sends my bonds cutting into flesh. The knife scrapes wrists raw. A last jerk and I fall back jarringly. I'm not dead; I'm free.

Loosed, anyway. But for what fate? A hand hauls me to my feet. I stumble after. After all these days my legs have forgotten how to walk. I don't understand what's happening, but what use to argue? We are running now, down to the water's edge. Well, he's running and I'm staggering. He pushes me into a little coracle and we spin away. Not slaughter, then, but escape? There are figures leaping in front of the flames. It's all over in moments. We dodge between the islets, from flickering firelight to blinding darkness. I don't think they are following us. Modred settles to the oars.

Modred! When did I realise that? Well, who else should save me? Who else would have known where to find me? He laughs, low, warm and friendly. 'Welcome back to the land of the living, Taliesin. The dead return!'

I start and look around me. The night is lighter now, the mere is wider. The fire we have left is not the only one. On distant hills around us gold beacons jewel the sky like new-made stars. On lower eminences the bonfires redden the mere and sedge. Dark figures dance before the light and in the lake their shadows circle.

I have escaped from fear and plunged into terror. This is Samain night, when the frail walls of mortality are down! The dead return to us, and all else from beyond the grave. The fiends of Hell. The black hounds from the pit of Offern. Ghouls unimaginable, but not unguessed. The night when every Christian stays barred indoors and keeps a light firmly burning. No threshold of darkness to let in the Devil, no need for a flame rekindled while we have Christ's light, yet stay at home and seal the doors and windows well with prayer.

And where am I on the most dangerous night of the year? Adrift on unhallowed water with all the fires of evil raging round me.

'I'm tired,' says Modred, with a sigh. 'Could you take a turn at the oars? Steer by the bonfire on Glastonbury Tor.'

Chapter Twenty-three

Not fairyland? Not Hell! The sedges of Somerset. And Tegau said there was a blessed abbey at Glastonbury. Oh, bring me safe to those true men of God and I swear I'll never meddle with magic again.

The abbey's not all there is at Glastonbury, though. It was no monks that built that bonfire on the top of the Tor. As we pull nearer I can see explosions of sparks hurtling into the air. The din of hammering metal echoes over the water. Modred grins.

'Govannon's Smithy. He is shaping a weapon for the King of Annwn.'

Not safe then, here. Not safe in any place tonight. The King of the Otherworld comes back to claim his own. Tonight the monks stretch out in prayer in their little church. Their lifted hands hold back the dark in fragile fortresses of faith. Tomorrow the sun will shine upon their gardens, their cattle will graze the slopes of the Tor. But tonight, fire! The Smith of the gods beats out his monstrous challenge on the iron. Gwyn ap Nudd will rise to claim that sword, so mockingly near to Arthur's Camelot. Dawn will send his crew back into the hollow hill they came from. But that's no comfort. Dawn's far off. This night is theirs. I wonder who's dancing round that fire.

I was tied up a long time. My arms are stiff and

weak. I can hardly heave the oars through the
dragging water. Besides, it's not open mere. Streams
wander through the mud. Reeds lean and part.
Sometimes a bigger channel's been cut, straight and
shining. Then I've lost it, and I have to bend round
islands overhung with trees. And every time I look
over my shoulder, that fire leaps through the
branches at me and the noise terrifies me. I tell myself
it's meant to drive out evil. I don't know which is
worse: what's up there at the fire, or down here in
the dark. I want to be home in bed; in prison, even.

The oar catches on a root. I struggle feebly with
it. Modred is saying something. I feel his strong hands
taking over. I shift precariously to take his place.
Faster now. I can hear the water whispering along
the side. Where did he learn to manage an unhandy
craft like this? We're swinging round. The Tor's over
my right shoulder now. Modred is threading this
marsh like a skilled pilot. I must not ask the questions
that are surfacing in my mind like frogs. He rows
with a bared sword laid across his knees.

The fireglow is dying. The noise grows distant and
sweet as a church bell. We bump the bank. No
accident. Modred has found a landing in the
darkness. He holds the coracle steady while I stagger
out and fumble with the mooring rope.

'Where are we going?' I whisper.

But Modred silences me. We creep forward over
yielding ground. Again he stays me with a grip on
my arm. He goes on alone with a sword in his hand.
I'm left clinging to a clump of bushes. Don't leave
me in the dark!

A distant murmur of voices. I listen for a shout or
the clash of steel. A long stillness now. No human

sound, only the hidden noises of the marsh. Then, quite close to me, a whistle. 'Taliesin!'

I stumble forward, obedient and eager as a dog. Modred wants me.

I see the first pale light is beginning to fade the stars. Thanks be! I am alive, my soul shaken but unscathed. I tell you, I've come a good way nearer to the one true God this night. Only let me see the dawn, and I promise this time . . .

Modred is not alone. A small cloaked figure stands beside him, clinging, crying, a woman's noise. Her face is buried in his shoulder. He holds her gently, stroking her hair. She babbles of fear, distress, desertion.

'There,' he smiles. 'Hush, my sweet lady. I swore that I would return and take you to your king. Look, here's Taliesin come to chaperone us!'

I know already as she turns her face. Gwenhyvar. I feel amazement strike through me. Here, after all this hunt? Found. So many men, so many miles, so many months. Found here, so close to home. So close? But is it? Where have I been? Where has she been? Did we cross some threshold? Is this the unclaimed land between two worlds? Not truly earth or sea. Its water not truly fresh or salt. A time not wholly light or dark. The worlds collide at Samain. Only tonight could we come back to the living. I don't know where we've been.

I reach a daring hand and touch her sleeve. It's real.

Modred has saved us both. I'd like to cling to his hand myself. But Gwenhyvar's tears embarrass me. This is Arthur's High Queen. But she can't let go of Modred.

'Do not desert me. If he should blame me for this
. . . No matter what lechery he does himself, it would
be the fire for me. Do not allow him, Modred!'

'Be brave, my queen. Let your appearance speak
you wholly virtuous. These tears are suffering and
relief, not guilt. It is anger that has coloured your
cheeks, not stolen pleasure. You are a woman
wronged and righteous.'

'Uphold me, then, Modred. Be my witness. I am
afraid to return.'

'There will be nothing but joy at your appearance,
lady. The time is coming when we must restore to
Arthur all that is his.'

He leads us a little way on. A hut, dark, without
fire. Astonishingly there's a cart. A patient horse
waits in the shafts.

'What happened? How did you find her? How did
you find *me*?'

He shakes his head. 'Save that for Arthur. I shall
make a full account.'

So here we are, the secret son of Arthur, courtliest
of warriors, driving a cart like a peasant going to
market. And the Queen of Britain, squatting among
the straw with the Chief Bard of Rheged. No gilded
chariot, this. There's a strong smell of pigs.

I'm jolted about in the back like a sack of turnips.
Gwenhyvar is huddled in her cloak. She doesn't look
joyful at her rescue. Modred is whistling like a
ploughman. A chill strikes up from the ground as
morning grows. Faint shades of grey. The fires have
gone out with the stars, only on Glastonbury Tor
a dull glow of red, like a baleful eye. Yet, that's
where we're going. Wheels jolting on the causeway.
The bank towers over us. Modred calls to the

gatekeeper. We're on hallowed ground. Holy to whom?

No sun yet, to draw up the mist. But the shadows lighten and the world grows clearer. I rub tired eyes. That must be the abbey ahead. Not much to look at: wattle and daub, a few huts, a little church. It looks homely, safe as the hencoop when a fox is on the loose. From their oratory we can hear the sound of singing:

> God my Creator, God the Sustainer,
> Merciful Judge, loving and wonderful,
> Thy hand has protected me
> Through the dark waves.

Day. The monks are coming from their chapel, hollow-eyed and hoarse. It's a long hard night for praying men, the Eve of All Hallows.

Modred and I help Gwenhyvar down. Her dress is staled. Her hair's dishevelled. Her face is streaked with tears, but she tries to smile through them and clings to Modred's hand. Courteously, he disengages himself. Her lips tremble and her wet eyes plead. Well, I'm a bard. What should I think? Would he play Trystan to his king's Essylt? Nephew to aunt? No, it's closer than that, isn't it? But Modred's known for an honourable warrior, sword sworn to Arthur. All men speak well of Modred.

The youngest monks have the nimblest legs. They're crowding round us already. It's early in the day for pilgrim visitors. But before the abbot can reach us and hear our story, their heads are turning.

Others are coming slowly down the path that winds from the Tor past the dew-wet churchyard. Not secret devotees of Gwyn, who melt away in the November shadows. A noblewoman leads them.

There's another shock. *Morgan?* Here, on hallowed ground, All Hallows Day? Impeccably cloaked and gowned, but her eyes are heavy, her head bowed. It is clear she has been awake all night. But where? Involuntarily I twist my head and see the tall Tor towering over us, quiet now, her fires sunk down into her dragon belly. A wisp of smoke steals up into the pale blue air. The warfare's over. Gwyn's sleeping it off. The Church can hold this island in peace for another six months.

Trailing behind her is Teilo. He doesn't look so good. His nose is red. With fire or cold or drink? There are smudges of soot on his face too. I remember that Teilo was once a smith.

The abbot Congar starts too when he sees her. He hurries forward, calling to her.

'An awesome vigil, lady. You have passed the night unharmed, Saint Brigid be praised!'

She smiles and bows her head to get his blessing.

Would Urien's queen mock a Christian abbot? It is not like her.

'Let us trust that your prayers and mine for souls in peril will be answered, Father.'

But now the nearest monks have got wind of Gwenhyvar's name. There's excitement! The news is spreading. I've missed what Modred is telling them. Morgan's face holds me. She's stopped stock-still on the path, visibly startled. She is staring at Gwenhyvar as if she can't believe her eyes, and then at Modred and me.

Chapter Twenty-four

Gwenhyvar claims the sanctuary of the abbey. She will not go back to Camelot. She begs to be reunited with her husband here, under the benign justice of Abbot Congar's eye. I'm not surprised. Even from Ynys Witrin we can see the distant hillfort of Camelot, a stronghold walled for war, a place for fighting-men. In frontier society wives are treasure, possessions to be prized, stolen or spoiled. Here in Glastonbury, among poor, chaste monks, they are more dangerous but less endangered.

Arthur is sent for. I think of all those horsemen threading the maze of Britain in search of their queen. Some may never return to Camelot from that quest. We must wait.

That morning, Morgan beckons me. We leave the gentle abbey and its guesthouse. She leads me up a long and winding maze. It coils round the slumbering dragon of the Tor, climbing into the dull November sky. I do not want to be here. Why haven't I got the courage to refuse her? Still . . . haven't I seen her bowing for the abbot's blessing? I think I nurse a small vain hope that there is not a great divorce between two forces: Abbey and Tor, brother and sister, Arthur and Morgan. Arthur, spirited away by a wizard, emerging as the champion of Christendom;

Morgan, brought up in a convent, nursing the flame of the Old Faith between her hands. The Prince of Peace, armed with a sword; Morgan the Healer, who is also the Destroyer. Their shadows cross and mingle. What am I to believe? I fly for comfort to Urien. Sane, human, true. I want to clasp his warm hands, calloused with harness, heavy with rings. Take me back to you, Urien! Take me back. But Urien's not here, is he? I toil unwillingly to the summit.

Ash on open hearths, sodden with rain. Shelters of withered branches. Chewed bones of joints. I find a tiny bronze head – broken from what ritual vessel? His eyes stare at me redly; I drop it hurriedly. But Morgan picks her way among the detritus of festival as if it was nothing but old ground sand upon the beach. She stands, and I come beside her, looking out over the steely water, dark-twigged trees, to a cold sea.

She has something in her hands. I recognise it. The old belt from Arthur's scabbard again. Laced through the leather, the new braids of Elaine's weaving look dulled already in this lifeless light.

'I can give him what he wants,' she says quietly, 'even now. But if it comes from me, he will not accept it. Perhaps he is right. It might indeed destroy him.'

Does she suspect what I do?

Shamefacedly, I join my intercessions to hers. All right, I know I promised!

Later, I see her walking in the orchard with Modred. The wind bends the branches of the apple trees angrily. Modred comes away smiling.

I wonder how long it will take them to find

Gwenhyvar's husband. But he appears, riding hard, the very next day, with a stout warrior-band at his back, stern men, spears set, swords jangling on thighs, shields on shoulders. Morgan stands close beside Gwenhyvar, like a sister.

Gwenhyvar's tense, but I observe her grow in stature as she sees this escort. They have come for her. Their mailed might makes her High Queen again. She draws herself up to face them.

Arthur flings himself from his horse before all the rest. I wait for him to throw his arms wide and embrace her, but his face is dark with doubt and dignity defied. We hold our breath. Then he can't help himself. A great joyful grin dawns over his countenance. Gwenhyvar's lost to sight, crushed against his chain-mail shirt.

Not long, that happiness. He's got to find somebody to blame. He rounds upon Morgan.

'You, here! Is this your evil? Was it not enough to steal scabbard and son from me? Must you rob me of my queen all summer too? Why!'

'As always, you accuse me falsely. I came to this holy island with your knowledge and consent, to work what I could for Gwenhyvar's return. Is this my recompense for success?'

'Release is easy, for those who have held the key.' She will not drop her eyes.

'Ask Modred.'

There's dangerous. This is what I've been dying to hear. Yes, please, ask Modred! My fingers are itching already. Oh, why is the harp still in Camelot?

He tells it simply, modestly. A plainer tale by far than the one I'd like to listen to, but still full of marvels. How we were lost on the mere and

173

separated. How he was caught and imprisoned and believed me dead. How a maiden restored his sword in secret. How he fought free of his captors. How he barely splashed to safety with his life. How he stumbled on a grim fortress with a moat around it and a lone sentinel in a tower, hard to converse with. How he found a perilous bridge and crossed it. How a grisly gatekeeper repelled him and how Modred, angered, forced his way in and slew the guards. Not one remained alive to tell the tale. How, in a shameful prison, he found Arthur's lady, kept without light, without women, without honour.

A little moan escapes Gwenhyvar, and she moves involuntarily towards her saviour. Pain stabs through all of us. You can see it in Arthur's face. Is his bright jewel cracked?

So he must turn to Gwenhyvar herself for the truth of those dark days. She sobs, remembering. Our cheeks grow warm with rage and shame. The abbot leads her to a private chamber. Arthur follows. What she must tell him is not for us to hear.

It's uncomfortable waiting. Modred leans over the fire, as though he would kick a log. But he holds himself still, watchful. Then he gives a small smile in my direction and his boot stirs the flame.

They come back at last. Arthur's striding ahead of the rest. Morgan's arm is round Gwenhyvar. Abbot Congar is arguing.

'Sire! You do your lady wrong. You must take her back. No one else accuses her. She pleads her innocence. Where are the witnesses that it is other than as she says?'

'I am the king. I will not be mocked. Can a man not do what he wants with his own wife?'

'No, sire, you cannot. You are bound to her by the oaths you swore on your marriage-day.'

'Even if the brute has fouled her?'

'The Queen denies it.'

Arthur has halted. Modred is facing him. He is smiling a little. His voice is level, reasonable.

'Before he died, one of the fiends who guarded her let slip that the foulest deed of all was reserved for Samain Night. It seems I came just in time.'

Arthur is glaring at him. The log crackles in the silence and spits fire. Then there's that huge grin again that turns the storm to sunshine. His hand reaches out to clasp Modred round the shoulders. His cheeks are wet with tears.

'Ah, if only I'd had a son of my own like this! Family may fail me and friends come back with empty hands, but Modred, that has no father, has proved truer than all my kinsmen. And what a wife he has restored to me! Look at her, all of you, and honour Gwenhyvar. True to her king through threats and terror. Chaste as a virgin nun against vile advances.'

We cheer. This is the stuff that legends are made of: our queen abducted, castles assaulted, the lady delivered. But Modred is circumspect and modest, and Gwenhyvar is blushingly reluctant to speak. Nobody asks where Taliesin was, that should have been the one to sing this song. They've more interesting captivities to talk about.

He joins their hands in front of him and kisses both, Gwenhyvar and Modred, her small white paw in his darker grasp. Gwenhyvar colours. Modred smiles gravely. He lowers his eyes. His lips brush her hand. But no more than is fitting.

'Who will lead me where this monster lives? Modred has butchered his men; but Arthur himself must slay their master.'

Modred bows, obediently. 'I will try, my lord.'

'What was the traitor's name?' Arthur demands of Gwenhyvar. 'Where is his den?'

She whispers, 'I do not know, my lord. He came to me foully masked. I saw and heard nothing of who he might be.'

The Abbot Congar is no stranger to the powers of evil.

'There is a name. The local people speak it in whispers: Melwas. King Melwas of the Summer Land they call him, though no such authority has been given him by Church or Council. Likely he is not a man of mortal flesh. They say he has such a fortress as you describe, hidden from human eyes save for one night. From there he rules the Summer Land in secret and spreads his darkness on these marshes. Men disappear. The tale goes that none who have crossed his narrow bridge ever return, and mothers use his name to frighten children with. His brood defile even this blessed island of Ynys Witrin on the holy night the heathen call Samain. No Christian eyes dare look on what is done then, for their soul's sake.'

His look slides round to Morgan with wonder.

Action now. We must hunt the villain. We must excise this evil from Arthur's land. A sternly-armed warband sets out, and I am rattling in leather and mail like the rest of them. I'll be in at the climax this time. The last verse of this tale must be better told than the first.

Rain falls, as Modred leads us down the causeway into that wide, wet world. Difficult this time, the Tor at our back and the whole circle of the mere to choose from. We pick our way uncomfortably. No prints to guide us. The land's awash. The fires are out. The islands loom untenanted. No sign of huts. Paths lead us into mud and disappear. We cast about and find ourselves knee-deep in water. There is no one to ask. Our clothes are saturated and our spirits low. How can you lose such a fortress in the daylight? Not hard the answer: easily, if it was never raised by human hands. Nobody says it, but the thought is in all our hearts. Arthur looks keenly at Modred, but he shakes his head. Grim-faced, he tries another way. I trail behind. Hope of a heroic ending died long ago. We won't find what we're looking for in this meandering marsh. Why was Modred so sure by night, so pixie-led by day? False thought! Rain blots out the Tor, pimples the puddles, turns trackways into tarns. The fires were yesterday. There's no truth here.

Sullenly we stumble back to Glastonbury. Arthur is surly. His eyes still accuse Morgan, though nothing is said. Modred's the only one that comes out of this well.

In private, the king questions me. What can I tell him? I have been imprisoned, like Gwenhyvar, but in a place still more vile. Terrible water-serpents were my companions. Goblins, naked and toothless, brought me foul food. Fierce fires encircled my gloomy gaol. It was only Modred who rescued me.

Arthur's no fool. As I finish, I fear he's going to laugh and toss me a trinket for a hearth-tale well sung. But he sighs and frowns. Difficult to shake off, the dark hordes that haunt us from our childhood. They pursue even a Christian king. Angels and elves, boggarts and demons, people our world, whatever gods we name. He is not satisfied, but he dare not disbelieve.

Why then do I find myself curiously reticent on certain points? The raft that rescued me in twilight on the reeds. Why the Little Folk should keep me unharmed. How Modred found me. Why we were not pursued. That steady steering through the twisting channels, coming to Gwenhyvar's waiting-place like the centre of a maze. The cart, the voices, the half-heard murmurs of Gwenhyvar on Modred's shoulder. Peace, boy! That was a night out of time. Nothing is what it appears on Samain Eve. He saved your life, didn't he?

The queen's honour and the king's run parallel. She is escorted home in triumph and royally housed in Camelot again. Gwenhyvar goes back to her winter king, that was once our prince of summer. Fires leap now where they should, on the hearth of kings. All's well again.

Chapter Twenty-five

And they call this the Summer Land! We'll be here a long time, by the look of the roads. The whole land's a lake.

Arthur has savage moods now, like a boar that's been robbed of his sow, but even he takes no pleasure in hunting phantoms in the pouring rain. Inactivity grates on him, so we fill the days with board-games and gambling, wrestling and dancing. There's plenty of occupation for a nimble bard.

One question still hangs over us, low as the clouds.

Margawse's lip curls when she sees her brother's wife return. She's sorry now she didn't add her powers to Morgan's. Her sons are out of favour because of Gwenhyvar. Those green eyes linger reflectively on Modred. I force my mind to remember that this too is Margawse's child. It's no good. I can't make the connection. Only Elaine looks well content. She smiles and knits endlessly.

Arthur has started to build a church, here on the hilltop, to give thanks for Gwenhyvar's safe return. Cross-shaped, the latest thing, with a mighty tower in the centre; I've seen the plans. But the rain fills the trenches as fast as they dig them. Leave it for summer. Let's go indoors and play more games.

Let's pretend our honour's untarnished, our guards

not tricked, the Prince of Darkness doesn't roam the marshes unchecked. Arthur's High King. The singing's loud and the mead's strong and Arthur can still wrestle Cei to the ground.

As the waters swallow the land, the Lady of the Lake returns to us as she should, in a fine barge, swan-prowed, sailed by silky ropes. I didn't see it myself. It's a muddy walk to the river.

Still, I can watch her now, pausing at the foundations of Arthur's church between the gate and the hall. I note the signs her hands trace over it.

She carries no weapon this time, and she's beautiful even in a dripping cloak, but still smiling as coldly as when I saw her last. Arthur's not too pleased with her, either.

'What kind of counsellor is it who keeps away when there is evil magic to counter? All the wise women of Britain were here except you.'

Her eyes flicker maliciously over Arthur's sisters and then Bishop Bytwini.

'You swore the Church was all the strength you needed. My help was scorned. And then in extremity you run back to the women who have always betrayed you. What could I do for you now, that these cannot? It was for those who stole Gwenhyvar away to restore her to you. As I see they have.'

Arthur's rising out of his seat now. He doesn't trust these sisters either but they're his own blood. Pride wrestles with suspicion. He sinks back in his chair.

'If you believe you have the knowledge, if you can spy the seat of treachery better than they can, put it to the test. Do anything you have to do. But find me the villain.'

Her eyes flick up, alarmed. 'I never claimed to have the seeing. Your whole court knows who has the gift for that.'

All eyes turn to Elaine. Her fingers dart; the wool twists and dances. Save for those hands she sits impassively.

'She can tell me nothing.'

'Cannot, or dare not.'

Then Elaine moves, thrusting her needlework into Margawse's hands. She rises, ponderously, to her feet. Why does the least action of this woman carry a meaning greater than it appears, making us hush and watch her?

'A contest? You and I, to see whose net can catch the bird of truth.'

Nimue is afraid. Not all of Merlyn's spell-books could give that clarity of sight to one not born to it. She finds an unlikely ally. Bishop Bytwini upbraids his king.

'Sir! You swore to leave that way behind you at your baptism. How often must I warn you? Have no dealings with these witches.'

No dealings with witches, in a family like his! But Arthur is ready for him. 'Did not King Saul go to the witch at Endor and raise the prophet Samuel to show him the truth?'

'He did, my lord. But—'

'Am I forbidden what Israel's king is allowed?'

'You may ask what you will in the name of the Trinity, my lord. All else is devilish.'

Elaine smiles. 'Ask in whatever name you choose.'

'She mocks you,' Nimue counters. 'It was I brought you up to know both Christ and the Mothers. I put power in your right hand and your left. Bytwini's own hands have given me the holy sacrament, when he was nothing but your household chaplain.'

'And I have worked a heavy penance for it afterwards!'

Whom can Arthur trust? The marsh is here, even in Camelot. Bring us back to summer drought, and hard ground!

He chews his lip. I feel for him. Hard to shake off, the custom of centuries. He'll go to penance, make a good communion. But he must know the name.

So evening comes, and the hall is made ready, the circle drawn and a brazier lit. Arthur sits in a great chair, with Gwenhyvar beside him, holding his hand. She is pale and troubled. Well, what lady wouldn't be, after what she's suffered? Elaine lowers herself, to sit cross-legged within the circle. Nimue faces her. There is a set of ivory pieces before each of them, carved with the sacred alphabet. Morgan, Margawse and their women stand outside the circle, close-ranked, insulted. Packed round the walls are all the nobility of Arthur's court. His kinsmen, greying knights like Bedwyr, Bishop Bytwini, Tegau, lovely Morfudd. All tense and uneasy. In a game like this, you never know how the dice may fall. A pulse jumps in my throat. Elaine knows I was in the marsh a long time without witnesses. Does Nimue?

Arthur calls on the bishop to pray for truth in the name of the holy Trinity. Nimue listens, with a little smile of contempt. A long Amen rumbles around the room.

The test begins. Nimue casts a spray of willow on the flames, Elaine a sprig of gorse. At the first names Nimue conjures, the bishop stalks out of the room. Arthur turns his head uneasily to watch him go. He is in too deep. He wants the culprit too much.

The dice roll.

Smoke thickens. Elaine's voice deepens. We watch entranced. The pieces shift upon the floor, first one side, then the other. Patterns emerge, waver, break and re-form. Lines are lengthening, needles pointing. All of us feel the pressure to shift position, to break, to run. Will it be I? Will it be I? Arthur is leaning forward, peering down, like a hawk about to stoop.

Elaine's eyes are closed. She cannot see how the pieces move under her hand. A name mutters through her lips. In the same instant Nimue, wide-eyed, cries out to us.

'Modred defiled her.'

'. . . It was Morgan's doing!'

'No!' Two voices shriek in protest. Gwenhyvar's and Morgan's. The spell's broken. The smoke is clearing. Elaine slumps, asleep. Nimue looks worn out, a woman once pretty, now faded and spent, half sitting, half lying on the floor.

No one heeds them. Two names are ringing in our ears, and a third word: 'Defiled'. Arthur is on his feet, furious.

Then Morgan flies to her sister, scattering the circle, her nails raked to strike the unconscious face. 'You cheat! You cheat!'

No man dares stop her. It is Margawse who grips her wrists and wrestles her into silence.

Hot blood, darker than foxglove, suffuses Gwenhyvar's face, her neck, her ears. Sweat glistens on her brow. Her hands are clutching Arthur's shoulders.

'She lies! This is evil, my king. You should not have meddled in unholy ways. Modred it was who came and rescued me. Should I not have known if it had been the same hands that snatched me from my friends? The same shape that towered over me in the night? The same voice that promised me dishonour or death? Never was it Modred! Never!'

Doubt clouds the king's face. The whole hall's in an uproar. Only Modred stands unmoved. His face is pale and calm. His hand avoids his sword, hangs lightly by his side, though weapons are out all round him. Arthur is moving like an angry breaker to overwhelm his sister.

'You have deceived me again!'

Morgan has stopped before him, deathly pale.

'I will not waste breath to excuse myself, though I am falsely accused. You would never believe me, though Nimue knows she has no power of seeing. But this, more serious by far, you must believe. Modred it never could have been that fouled your queen. Modred, of all men, you have no need to fear. Listen to me, Arthur! Elaine is ageing. Her memory is dim and her powers are failing. If she had truly been the wise woman she once was, she could never have made so great a mistake. Not Modred. Never Modred!'

She holds her hand out to her foster-son, this work of half her life. Slowly, his eyes on hers, he comes and takes it in his own, steady where hers is shaking. She leads him closer to Arthur's throne. In her face is an intensity of joy, a task fulfilled. She lays his hand in Arthur's.

'Brother, I give you your own son.'

Chapter Twenty-six

There's matter for a song, for you. Can't complain now, can I?

Arthur's uncertain. He's sired enough boys up and down the kingdom, but whose is this?

It's Margawse's turn to cause an upset. Not like her to be the last of the three in coming forward. She's blushing like a maid, too, and laughing a bit to cover it. She falls on her knees before Arthur.

'Once, my brother, I bore you a son. You thought him dead in infancy.' Not laughter that makes her voice shake here. 'You did not know the Mothers had kept him from harm, loved him, brought him up to a noble manhood. Morgan has told you the truth.'

It's Morgan's turn again. She draws from the breast of her gown that buckled belt. How long has she nursed it there? I shiver to imagine the warmth in the leather as she slips it round Arthur's neck and then round Modred's sword-arm, binding them together in a loving clasp. It is very prettily done.

'I cannot give you back your scabbard. I buckle this to you instead.'

Arthur's nonplussed. He stands, Modred's hand locked to his. His eyes search Morgan's, looking for treachery, and seem to find none. Then he starts to smile, the sharing of a rare delight.

The threads draw together, the last knot twisting to its seal. I see how much these two have wanted to be reconciled to each other. Was it all for this? Uther's lust for Ygerne, the killing of Gorlois, Merlyn's theft of Arthur, Morgan's banishment, Margawse's incest, the babies drowned. All the sad shocks of history for this one night, a blazing fire on the hearth in Camelot, and a family now standing in front of it, the flames leaping on Arthur's grin, and Morgan's cheeks, and Modred's hand. You would have thought there should have been a simpler way to arrive at this point. Not so much pain.

He stoops and kisses her. The whole hall sighs. Silence for a few heartbeats, between the lightning and the thunderclap. Then Gwenhyvar screams. Well, why not? Certainly she's not Modred's mother.

Modred himself? He gives that rare, grave smile that has made the whole world honour him. It's too much for Arthur. A son, of noble blood, with a royal mother. Tears burst from his eyes, he throws his bear-arms wide and crushes Modred to him.

'Son, forgive me!'

Now there's consternation! Margawse's other offspring look furious. Whatever old tales they may have heard, it's clear they've never known who Modred was. The youngest of the litter, and Arthur's son? And for the rest of the court: the king and his own sister!

'Get that fool of a bishop back! What am I to do? I was a lad then that did not know his own family. I was young. I tried to drown an act of folly.'

Bytwini's here.

'Sire, you served penance for that sin long years ago. The past is paid for. The boy's alive. Once

186

Abraham mistook the Lord's intention and sired Ishmael. But God is merciful. He made that boy heir, not to the Promised Land itself, but to a great fortune. Praise God who has brought you a blessing out of evil.'

Well, there's a cheer to set the roof-posts rocking!

Nobody but me notices that Morgan is still staring at Gwenhyvar. At the queen's scream, her own hands have flown to her face. I see in her half-hidden eyes the horror dawning. Between cupped hands she cries, 'No, Arthur! No!'

Too late, now, isn't it? How could he hear her in all this cheering?

They're all flocking round.

'Welcome, lad!'

Cei and Bedwyr are clapping Modred on the shoulder, congratulating him. Tegau is kissing him.

Slowly Morgan turns, walking as if in a dream. She pauses where the Lady of the Lake still writhes, neglected on the floor. Nimue starts back from her. But Morgan's hand reaches down and pulls her to her feet.

'I should ask your pardon, Lady. You see more truly than you know.'

Bitter the anguish in that admission. And then she flees.

In all the rejoicing, there's one word Arthur can't shake off. His turn to look to Gwenhyvar now. Joy's replaced by dark suspicion, jealous rage, as swift as a March storm. Defiled?

Not defiled by Modred, though. He can't believe that now, can he? Not when he's been given the son he's longed for, noble, brave, as clever with the harp as good with hounds, as wise in judgment as deadly with the sword, and most of all, of royal blood, on his mother's side as well as his father's. Ygerne of Dumnonia's line, twice over. Pity about the incest, of course. Still, it looks as if the penance he'd done will serve for that, as well as for infanticide on a grand scale. I've a feeling the rules for kings aren't the same as for the rest of us. Easy to forgive Arthur. He has a famous smile.

But Gwenhyvar can see the other side of his coin. She's running for protection. Where? To Nimue. I wish I could hear what story she's sobbing on the Lady's shoulder!

Elaine's lids are lifting. Women guide her stooping, sleep-ridden, to slump on a bench beside the fire. Does she know what she's said?

Nimue's voice strives for authority.

'Morgan the Faithless has as good as admitted her guilt to me. You do not need me to tell her past treacheries. Remember her lover Accolon, to whom she gave your stolen sword, who would have killed you with it if I had not stopped it. Be certain this was some creature of hers that held your queen captive to spite you and sow the seed of mistrust between you and your wife.'

That's not the name he wants to hear, either. But Morgan's gone. The spell is broken. He glares at Nimue and then at Margawse. She's no friend of his, who tempted him into one dishonour, and then another. At Elaine, who has blackened both Gwenhyvar's name and Modred's. No doubt whose version he's going to believe, is there?

You were wrong, Morgan. Arthur has accepted your gift at last.

He holds out a generous hand to Gwenhyvar and

she takes it shyly. She still looks sick and agitated. Of course, that's not surprising, is it? Modred's not her son. Poor Anir's dead less than a year, and here's a replacement. I hope that's all that's the matter with her: a mother's jealousy. You've a dirty mind, Taliesin. This is the stuff of high romance. Still, she stares at Modred, fastens on Modred with eyes wide and helpless as a doe that has seen a fox enter her form.

Modred has not once looked in her direction. He has found his father. His arm is round Arthur. Modred is no longer the rejected child. He is tender with this grey-haired king as a mother with her infant. There are tears in quite a lot of eyes, mine included. Romantic, me, after all. Advent fast or not, we're going to lay on the biggest feast of the year tonight. The prodigal father is embraced by his son.

Morgan is back for the feast. Does nobody but me remark that she has a haunted look? It seems Arthur's in a mood to forgive anyone tonight. All the same, I notice he's pushed Margawse down the table. He'd rather pull the curtain over that side of it. Morgan's a different matter. She's given him his dearest desire. He wears the swordbelt she gave him over his heart, like a trophy, though Modred's unclasped now. Nimue's warning is soon disregarded, drowned deep as Merlyn's nightmare of a traitor son. Modred is seated between Arthur and Gwenhyvar. A happy family party.

Supper is over and I entertain them royally, while they sit around the fire. No need to sing of battles now.

Arthur's magnanimous. He takes Morgan's hand in his. So very thin and white it looks. So vulnerable.

'Sister!' I have never heard such warmth in the Pendragon's voice. Nimue hisses. I do not need to look at Gwenhyvar. I can imagine the hurt.

Arthur is a big man. He grows greater still, looking down on Morgan. And she is all woman before him, her head slightly bent. I grieve for Urien Rheged. We all feel the thrill that carries from her fingers held by his, along her singing nerves, to the heart.

'You have wronged me greatly before this, but today you have given me great joy. The time has come to lay our enmity to rest. For all the occasions I have spurned what you offered, I ask absolution. And all your old treachery to me I now forgive. Let Modred be the symbol of our union. After pain, hope. After bitterness, love. In place of denial, faith.' His other hand is on Modred's shoulder, holding them both to him.

'Symbol for symbol, emblem of oath. I have the belt. I lay my sword before you two.'

Caliburn, gorgeous and warlike. Two dragon-heads rear from the hilt, red-tongued, eager for battle, his royal weapon. He lifts his hand and holds it out to her. The blade is bare between them.

'You tell me you have destroyed the scabbard. We cannot call that back. But what if I now disarm myself? Let you and I give up our warring powers. Shall we make Modred our heir and give him Caliburn, and go down into a happy old age?

I turn for help and find that Nimue is furious. Modred is smiling. Gwenhyvar's . . . astonished?

And I? I feel the bottom falling out of my world. Arthur is giving up his sword. I am too late.

But Morgan is ageing before my eyes. Her cheeks

fall in; the warmth has left her face. Her eyes are bottomless lakes.

'No!' she says, pushing the sword aside so swiftly that it cuts her hand. 'No! No!'

She drags the belt off him. The ancient leather snaps.

The tears are flowing down her face. The whole hall looks, aghast. They think she hates him still. Am I the only one that hears her grief, screaming like a harpstring on the point of breaking? The words are torn from her, as though she would say anything but this.

'Do not trust Modred!'

Arthur has snatched Caliburn back. For a moment I think he will strike off her head.

The sword slips back into its false scabbard. He signals angrily to me. My shaking hands pick up the harp.

I sing of Arthur's wars.

Chapter Twenty-seven

We can't stay now, can we? Their hands have met for a moment; now the reel has flung them apart. Who will be partnering whom when the music ends? My last night in Camelot, then, and all that way north to travel at the foulest time of the year.

The ladies have left the hall, but the drinking's still going on. I've had enough to make me queasy.

I step outside, and find the sky is clearing. The air is crisp and the stars high and bright. I blink like a sentimental fool, looking up at beauty, clean, eternal. A waning moon tonight, and the eyes of angels looking down on me. Tear off the roof, smother the fire, put out the torches. See us as we really are in this cold blue light. Not paragons of chivalry, not potent witches. Men, women, muddled, loving, hurting. Foul before God, but all He has. Surely He must love us? There's no one else.

I wander towards the rampart. Cold tightens the flushed skin of my face. Careful, now! You nearly fell into that hole. What's this, then? The foundation-trench of Arthur's church, half-filled with water, a muddy ditch with a multitude of stars. He's abandoned it until the summer. Gratitude for Gwenhyvar's return is cooling now. Will it ever be built?

Time you were in bed. You can't carry the burden

of this turbulent family on your shoulders. But I am Taliesin. My original country is the region of the summer stars. I was with my Lord in the highest sphere on the fall of Lucifer to the depths of Hell. I have borne a banner before Alexander. Yes. But what did you do for any of them? Princes fell and princes won. You sang about it. Let the banner of song for Arthur and Morgan be richly woven. But they must make their own story.

Bed now for me. Which way in the dark? You've made that mistake before. No, I'm forgetting, it wasn't a mistake, was it, Gwenhyvar's house? Poor Gareth, he got it hot and strong the day he lost her. She'll be well guarded tonight. Or will she?

I know that whistle under the breath, the little cheerful tune. I've heard it, jolting in a cart out of a tricksy marsh, with will-o'-the-wisps dancing beside the path. Stars, weep now. Taliesin, you could stop this. One shout would rouse the guards.

Modred, my almost-brother. Modred, my soul-friend. Two babies abandoned, two princes found. The prince of poetry and now the premier prince of Britain. Is this the man who will make this Island one? Is he the hero who will lead the final battle? The son of Arthur, Modred? Have I found my great song, after all?

She won't open to him, will she? Not now she knows. Her husband's son, her stepson-nephew? Look how sickened she was in the hall.

Such a merry little tune he breathes, so confident. And the window opens, the shutter swings, revealing the darkness that waits within. Modred's leg is over the sill. Close the casement now. Shut out the stars. Modred is in, and Arthur's out.

I turn, skin prickling, as I have done sometimes and found a cat staring at me from the corner of the room. There's something pale in that doorway. A woman's face. Not Morgan, not Margawse, not Elaine. Nimue is watching this. Like me, she sees the truth. We hold the axe that could topple Arthur's palace or fell the traitor, that could cleave Arthur from Morgan for ever, the ruination or the salvation of Britain.

Our world's unmade. What shall I do? Tell Morgan? Warn Arthur? But Morgan's heart has cracked already with the knowledge of what she has bred, and Arthur will not allow himself to believe it.

The old king must die; the new one takes his place. And in his youthful mating the land revives. That's how it goes, isn't it? Perhaps . . . Shame on you, Taliesin. Arthur keeps a Christian kingdom. You swore to put all that behind you, didn't you? Keep your eye on the stars; don't look in the ditch.

It's too late at night for theology. I've got a headache.

The viper is snugly in Arthur's tent. Nimue knows. Hang on to that. Nimue is Arthur's guardian, and she knows.

Next morning, the king's like an old dog in love with a young master. He's almost fawning for a pat on the head from Modred. Nimue, Margawse, Morgan have given him what he wanted: a sword, a kingdom and a son. But he can't forgive the women. They have shamed him with this accusation of a double incest. It cuts too deep across old wounds.

The family's splitting. Gawain and Owain will be true to Arthur. Agravain takes the women's side. Gareth and Gaheris are wavering. Urien clasps

Arthur warmly. His duty calls him back to Rheged. His love for Morgan, his loyalty to Arthur, are both unquestioned.

Home to Carlisle then, turn my back on Camelot. Never be Arthur's Chief Bard now, will I? There was a time when I thought he might make me an offer. The greatest king we ever had in Britain, but a little lacking in judgment on the matter of music.

Goodbye, Modred. I can't help the lump in my throat as I grasp him by the hand for the last time. Only I wish he wasn't standing beside Gwenhyvar like a son with his mother. I can't look her in the eye now. Well, good luck, boy. You haven't had much till now. Not too late to sweeten the soul, is it? Only, don't wound him to the heart. He is the heart of all us, Arthur Pendragon.

Arthur and Morgan won't touch as they say farewell. There's too much pride.

Too stormy for ships, and miserable riding even on a Roman road. We're splashed to the shoulders. Sometimes a weary horse will founder, but we buy another and press on. The ground is hardening as we move north and there's an edge to the wind.

I'm caught wrong-footed again. At Chester, Morgan bids farewell to Urien. Not home, then? I look to Urien for advice. I'd rather be back in Carlisle, hot bathwater, thick walls, than wandering west in winter into unwelcome adventure. But Urien nods. I know what that means. Always in the queen's escort, me, never one of the men.

We come to the shores of the Menai strait on the coast of Gwynedd. A large, low island. Mon. So that's it, is it? The womb of wisdom. Once the greatest college of secret knowledge in all Europe. The last calamitous stand of the druids against Rome. I know the story: furious seers massed on the beaches armed with both sword of steel and staff of magic, black-clad women tearing their hair and shrieking imprecations, young boys and maidens, ready to die rather than see their sacred past, their spiritual future, trampled into ignominy under the boot of history. Just for a moment, even the legions faltered. Only a moment, before the end, and all their cherished weave of wisdom went down into oblivion, drowned deep as their gifts to the gods in the innermost lake.

All? Not quite. Some guardians returned. In caves and forest groves, at wells and cromlechs, some strive to bind the salvaged strands together. Morgan has come to keep faith with her mothers, and to ask something in return.

We are given welcome, in great simplicity, but with respect. The women are given a house apart, with many windows opening on the stars.

More women arrive. Women? I am ashamed of what I was expecting: old hags risen out of peat bogs, mermaids with blue skin combing their hair, kelpies with mares' faces? These are fresh girls, maidens every one of them, difficult to come by in the service of magic. Vowed virgins nowadays are mostly Christian. Those that have chosen to serve the other way are soon initiated. But the guardians of Mon have brought her what she asked for, nine pure May-Maidens, wise and whole.

Morgan will not even touch the work herself, though she directs it. I've never seen her so dedicated, so intense. The guards and I may not set foot inside their sky-lit house. For this, even Teilo doesn't get the name of Woman. We hear the girls singing at night as they weave.

A gown, white and silver as a shaft of moonlight. No dewhung spider's web on April morning shone with such sweet purity. It is finished, flawless, fairy-light.

Is this magic, or madness, in Morgan's mind?

'A gift most fitting for Tegau Goldbreast, Caradawc's wife, purest of virgins and now most constant of wives.' She entrusts it to one of the maidens with a challenge. 'Take this to Arthur's court, and give her this message. Make it known that every lady may try this gown, but only she who is true to her husband will the gown fit. It will shame an adulteress with a skirt above her knees. And this for Caradawc Strong-Arm,' laughing crazily now. 'A drinking-horn and a side of bacon! This one will spill the drink of a man not true to his wife, and a mouthful of the other will choke the philanderer.'

'She's out of her mind!' groans Teilo. 'He'll never allow Gwenhyvar to take that test from her. Morgan sent him a purple cloak once that had death stitched in every fold. Does she think he'd let his queen try that gown on, with her spells woven thick in it?'

Morgan's merry as a girl in love, though her eyes are as bright as a woman with fever.

'He is a warrior. He must accept my challenge. Gwenhyvar will be shamed if he refuses.'

'He will take nothing from you.'

'He has taken Modred!'

A cry of agony. All his life she has reared the boy for this. Yet it cannot be how she meant it.

Arthur and Gwenhyvar will celebrate Easter at Caerleon.

Chapter Twenty-eight

So home to Carlisle and wait. Grey skies in Rheged,
bitter cold. Nothing to do but harp by the fire and
sport on the wolfskinned bed, is there? We both need
cheering up. Only I never get the thong of my
breeches undone. I'm not even asked to her chamber.

'No, Taliesin. I am not for you now.'

What's up? What have I done wrong? I must have
looked as indignant as a pup that's had a bone
snatched off him by the bitch.

'I am Urien's queen.'

'Oh, yes? Since when did that trouble you? And
what am I? Only Chief Bard. Only the prince of poets.
A mere nobody. The snowflake on the cromlech. The
butterfly upon the mountain. I know, I know. Don't
tell me.'

She strokes my hair and smiles fondly. How close
must I stand to that perfumed breast?

'If you had truly been a prince I would never have
allowed you to enter my chamber to stir my
cauldron, Gwion Bach. You helped me make our
mysteries. You have served me well.'

She's changed. She doesn't give me my quittance
in gold, I'll give her that. She presses her lips upon
my head. I know what it means. Very final, that kiss.
This is a new Morgan.

A cloak of chastity has fallen on her too. The red blood has stopped running. Only Urien may come to her bed now, while she waits. I know her fire still burns; I feel it. But she must be worthy. The white mantle of Tegau Goldbreast will prove Gwenhyvar a whore and the sisters true. Arthur will cast out his adulterous queen soon.

How can Morgan the Wise so delude herself? I weep in my solitary bed, not for myself but for her.

His answer comes. It is Teilo who carries it unwillingly to her, a parcel like the one she sent to Caerleon, the same size, the same weight, the very wrapping. Her maiden-messenger speaks softly.

'King Arthur has commanded Tegau to reject your gift, Caradawc Strong-Arm to send back the horn and flitch.'

There is a letter.

'I want no magic meddling in my Christian court. I do not trust you. You sow dissension. Your gifts are curses that distort the truth they promise. Take back your mischief.'

But Modred was the most mischievous gift of all, and he is firm in Arthur's love, dearer than his wife now, dear as his sword, dear as his honour.

Morgan will not believe it. She stares at the unwrapped gown, the purity of white fouled with his black suspicion, the incontestable proof of magic thrown back in her face. We wait for her to rage, to weep. She calls for her workbox, very calmly, takes out a pair of scissors, heron-shaped. Suddenly, the storm is on her. She seizes, slashes, snaps. The scissors wreak a ragged devastation. The spell's in shreds. All purity, all faithfulness, all loving trust lie heaped in ruins round her. She won't stop there. There's something else.

The belt of Arthur's Caliburn. The last narrow binding that should link sword to scabbard. The colours that newly-furbished it are bloodstained now. She hacks at it savagely, forcing her fingers to drive the blades through the leather till the marks stand out as livid bruises on her hands. Black leather, white linen, both destroyed. Modred's unmade. I know, seeing the scattered pieces, even before she sweeps them up and casts them on the fire with curses.

I play my softest songs to soothe her. I am David to her furious Saul. It's very affecting. I'm weeping hard myself, but it won't put out the stench of that fire.

Nothing but the sword left now, is there?

I see her beauty start to age.

Since she spurned his offer, Arthur will no longer admit to growing old. While Caliburn's in his hand he's still the king. Don't slay me yet, he cries to us. There's still a deal of strength in me to nourish the land. He takes his sword and honour and army to Armorica, to fight for his cousin Howel. Modred he leaves behind as regent. Morgan was right. He must accept her challenge to Gwenhyvar's reputation. Caliburn he takes to war. The sword of government he trusts to his son. He leaves Britain with Modred. He leaves his wife with Modred.

Is this what Morgan wanted? Modred in Arthur's trust, Modred in Arthur's bed, Modred in Arthur's wife. She has tended this foster-son. She has fed him her pain. Is this how she imagined the fruit would taste? The bridge, that should have joined her side to Arthur's, becomes the inroad of treachery. This is her doing. All her life culminates in this. She has tried to warn Arthur. She has failed.

She stands dumbfounded at this outcome.

I wait for her to summon the wise, to work strong magic, to turn the supernatural universe upside down and shake some goodness out of it.

Nothing. She seems as helpless as the rest of us, haggard and haunted.

We wait for news. I listen for the cries of crows to call disaster.

The campaign is going well. Arthur has covered himself in glory. He's killed a giant.

Arthur's besieged. They won't be back for some time.

Cei is killed.

Gwenhyvar is divorcing Arthur.

Chapter Twenty-nine

Gwenhyvar! Soft-spoken bride to great Arthur, the decorative lady at his side, the sweetly smiling hostess to his warband. I didn't think she had such audacity in her.

Gwenhyvar divorces the king? We've underrated her.

That's roused some swans' nests up and down the country, I can tell you! Morgan is stung from her lethargy into sudden vigour. She's speechless with fury. I watch admiringly, the flinging jet-black hair, her cheeks like firelit windows in the snow. Eyes? Terrible the thrusts of them. And she is only one. Is this happening across the Island? Red Margawse, grey Elaine. Are passions rearing, muscles tensing, anger hardening in Lothian and Garlot and further still?

Gwenhyvar's accusing the king, and she's called a council! What's Modred doing? He's Arthur's regent. If she's not Arthur's wife, she's not the High Queen, is she?

She summons the Church and aristocracy to attend her at a great congress in York. All the noble ladies of Britain are specially bidden to appear.

They'd like to refuse, fling the summons back in her face. But curiosity rages like a forest fire. The kinswomen of Arthur must be there to hear this.

There'll be men too. Arthur has not left the country undefended. Urien rides with us, grim-faced. Always courteous to women, Urien, but there's no question of allowing this. Divorce Arthur? This goes beyond all chivalry. He must oppose her.

York's overflowing. You'd think it was a festal crown-wearing, except that Arthur's missing, and his famous warband. He's taken the young men this time. The flower of the Cymry are falling on foreign soil while Gwenhyvar stabs him from behind.

We crowd into a fine, stone palace with painted walls. I could be there on the floor with princes and dukes. The aristocrat of artists, me, the Chief Bard of Rheged; the harp ranks high as the sword. But I'm not very tall. I slip into a gallery above and crane over, the better to recount the scene. Packed here too with avid watchers; I hope these beams will bear us.

The bishops are gathered at the front of the chamber, croziers in hand, like a gang of shepherds watching out for the wolf. Abbots and abbesses from monastic cities, startling in white among secular riches. On the other side kings: Nentres, Urien, Mark of Cornwall, and still more queens, fiercely resplendent in their court dress. Gwenhyvar's call has roused two dragons, the white of the Church and the red of Britain's noble blood.

They're a terrifying sight, even from up here.

She can't succeed, can she? Why would any woman want to renounce Arthur Pendragon?

It's a pity there aren't more men here. Most of our young colts and our sturdy stallions are in Armorica with Arthur. What's left are old stale hacks. Sorry, I don't mean Urien, of course! Men like Cador the Duke, Gwenhyvar's own foster-father, and grey-faced Ulfin that once helped Uther Pendragon break into Tintagel. There are young toughs left in Britain, of course, guarding the Pennines, the Wall, the coasts. They can't all desert their duty, even though the kingdom is rotting at its centre. Those who can, have ridden in overnight from posts nearby. Agravain, son of Margawse, and a handful like him. Edgy, excited, alarmed, doubtful. Laughing too loudly and flashing their battle-torques.

But the noble women have come in their full splendour. From Gwynedd and Gwent, Clyde and Calchvynydd, from Elmet and Erechwydd. All their married lives their men have gone to war, whether it was Saxons or a neighbour's cattle herd they had their eyes on. When the lords canter off over the hills in the early morning, it is the women who tend the land through the long day. When our boys come home to nurse their knocks and fettle their war-gear, the pattern of seedtime and harvest, of calving and shearing, does not detain them long. We pretend that power is with the men; these ladies carry their stewardship tactfully. Gwenhyvar has broken the code.

The hall's a riot of noise, but the hush that falls as Gwenhyvar enters is like nothing that's ever greeted her before. She's still High Queen. She's wearing her golden crown and a purple robe that surrounds her with royalty. In her hand she carries that greenstone sceptre. The crowds lean to see her coming and then sway back. She walks through their ranks, slow and stately, with a sober retinue following. She does not incline her head to left or right. She doesn't smile. I think she's nervous. I'm not surprised.

Modred is just a pace behind her. Why doesn't he assert his right as regent? His eyes are modestly downcast. Then from time to time he raises them and flashes that rare swift smile at a man here, a lady there, and they nod back to him. Modred has many friends. He's a diplomatic man. Where others of that family are quick with their swords and make enemies, Modred has always offered an open hand, a listening ear, good counsel.

The churchmen part abruptly, sweeping their skirts away from Gwenhyvar more widely than courtesy allows. She ascends the dais, takes her seat in one royal chair, with another empty beside her. Modred stands behind her. Odd that he doesn't occupy Arthur's seat.

When the heralds have silenced us, Gwenhyvar stands to state her grievance. Her voice is small but clear.

'Ladies and lords, I come before you as High Queen, of equal majesty with Arthur . . . No, hear me out!

'Remember this. When Merlyn brought me from Cornwall to marry the Pendragon, it was not just for my beauty or for the hope of sons, though I had both. He chose me out of all Britain for my royal blood, for that most ancient line of the kings of the West. Arthur claims to be the son of Uther Pendragon, and I believed that true. But he came to us out of a childhood shrouded in mystery. Only Merlyn knew the truth of it, and Merlyn is with us no more. My birth is known; my childhood with Cador my foster-father was openly seen. I am no stranger to royalty.

'Then, and only then, was Arthur cried High King. It was my betrothal that legitimised him.'

'Vain woman!' Bishop Bytwini cries. 'What has that to do with repudiating Arthur?'

'The form of our coronation was agreed between Merlyn and the Church. Two separate celebrations, in different churches, one for Arthur before the men, one to crown Gwenhyvar before the women. Is that not so?'

The bishops nod, warily. There's a throb of assent from all the older ladies. Morgan and her sisters must have been there. Before my time, of course.

'In one church Archbishop Dubric of blessed memory placed the crown on Arthur's head and set in his hand the sword of the Island's government, while in the other you, Bishop Bytwini, in the same instant, by the ringing of the bell, gave me this sceptre and pronounced me Queen, not as his consort, not passing on a secondary glory, but in my own right, through my own bloodline, an independent coronation.'

Well, that's set poor Bytwini chattering like an indignant magpie.

'Madam! You distort events beyond all sense and decency! How can the woman be an equal to her lord? It was for convenience and modesty we separated you. One church could not contain so great a gathering of lords and ladies. Many had had to be shut out from your marriage ceremony. It was Dubric's consecration that was pre-eminent. His hand conveyed the true sovereignty of Britain. What I performed on you was the insubstantial mirror of your husband's crowning.'

'The same oil from Galilee. The very gold of our crowns from the same mine in Wales. Are your hands not flesh and blood, as Dubric's were? Are you not both true bishops in the line of Peter? Did you not say when you placed this sceptre in my hand you were giving me the power to rule?'

'A pretty rite for ladies. The dignity due to a loyal wife. How could you think that made you equal to Arthur? You are a woman!'

'And the women are my witnesses. Is not this true?'

A hesitation. Names pass through all our minds, the wheels of mighty chariots: Rigantona, Cartimandua, Boudicca. It's not been so long since, after all, and from the women, like a summer thunder, because they do not know where this may lead, a thrill of confirmation.

'Aye!'

'Then hear this.' Her voice shakes, but she steadies it. She's been well rehearsed. 'The High Queen Gwenhyvar accuses Arthur. Since that day I have played the part of a Christian wife. Obedient, self-effacing, faithful . . .'

I can't be the only one to gasp a protest, can I!

'I have neither used nor abused the power placed in my hand with this sceptre. Yet it is sovereignty, and it is rightly mine. My dignity is Britain's. Arthur has shamed my honour, and so yours. The royal seed that should have fertilised your High Queen has been wasted on other wombs.'

She looks hard at Margawse when she says that.

'He was neither our king nor your husband then,' Margawse cries out.

'And you were neither his first nor his last whore!'

That's foolish, Gwenhyvar. It wasn't in your text, was it? Oh, yes, he's hurt her. Still, she needs the sisters' support.

The Bishop tries to calm them down. 'The Church does not condone that sin. But men are frail. The foolishness of youth . . . Our Saviour teaches forgiveness, seventy times seven.'

'Would Arthur have forgiven me one single act of adultery?' One single act? Those wide blue eyes!

'Christ stopped a stoning for that very cause . . . But a woman's case is different. Your wombs are holy. We must know who is the father of our children. Besides, you do not have a man's desires.'

You can feel the prickle in the air, like unspent lightning. There are more ladies than lords in this hall.

Gwenhyvar's not one for histrionics. She's been nerving herself for a long time to say this. She won't be shifted from her complaint.

'No king may commit adultery against a sovereign queen.'

Oh sweetly grim, that pale frail face, that quiet voice, those periwinkle eyes. Gwenhyvar's going up in my estimation. I could be interested. Down boy, she's spoken for twice over.

Modred is listening to this like a patient shadow.

It's Abbot Congar's turn. 'Let old sins lie, your majesty. The blood of all of us runs slower now. Why shame great Arthur and yourself with this?'

'Not slow enough, my lord Abbot. It seems fresh rains can still stir up a foul flood. I bring sworn testimony. Not tavern-maids on long campaigns, not Saxon captives, not too-hospitable daughters of distant lords. The ladies of my own court, in my own house, this very year, while I lay waiting in my marriage-bed.'

Bytwini's brusque. 'We cannot hear this now. The king is not present to defend himself.'

'What possibility of defence is there, when those of my subjects he has compelled cry out against him? Which of you has Arthur made to lie with him?'

Her women have clustered beside the dais. At her appeal a field of hands, like slowly-sprouting flax, climbs skywards, some shy with shame, some spiky with indignation. So it's not only on the battlefield Arthur's been trying to relive his boyhood! Bytwini's blushing. It's not the thing itself – he knows about sin – but that she should speak about it openly. We all know it happens.

'You hypocrite! Answer for yourself. Adulteress!'

Morgan's voice shocks us with shrill accusation. Even Modred starts. But Gwenhyvar has not yet done. She holds the high estates of Britain in her power now. Princes of land, of art and intellect are listening to her. She feels the intoxication of an audience. She almost smiles.

'Yes, Morgan the Faithless, one woman defied him. Despite his threats to bind her silent she unfolded the tale to me, showed me her bruises, washed my feet with the tears of her wrath, to her great honour and his shame.'

Gwenhyvar's hand reaches out to the group of her ladies below. My cheeks grow hot with indignation. I fear who this must be. Does Arthur's lust run as red as that? Would he touch even Tegau Goldbreast?

Someone is separating from the throng, rosy with womanly warmth, bowing her head in injured confirmation. It's not Tegau. Oh, ye gods! Morfudd,

maiden most lovable, twin to Owain the Raven,
Morgan's own daughter.

I seem to hear a scream that makes the door-posts
tremble. The painted frescoes scatter in whirling
dust. The world is tumbling. Steady, Taliesin. No
one else has heard it but you. Morgan hasn't spoken.
Nobody sees the universe has shattered.

Chapter Thirty

I tear my eyes away from the flayed face of hope.

'We cannot judge this without the Pendragon.'

'Go to a convent if you're not content.'

Those men are Arthur's friends.

'A potent king may fructify us all,' a woman's voice dissents, while others hiss her.

'Potent!' Over the stiff skirt of court dress, Gwenhyvar's hands angle accusingly across her womb. 'One son in eighteen years, and he is dead. And now, nothing. Your king will not return from Armorica. His fighting arm is failing, like his wasted seed. He cannot give me an heir.'

That troubles them.

She says he's been too much of a lad, and yet he's past it. Well, inconsistency was never a stranger to political rhetoric.

'What need have I of further proof? Our royal marriage contract has been betrayed. If Arthur had caught me in adultery, he would have had me pulled to pieces between two horses. Yet now I bear the punishment of barrenness for his deeds.'

You could speak, Taliesin. Her women know! Why does Tegau stay silent?

'I, the High Queen of Britain, put Arthur away from me for this just cause. Your former king has left this land for wars that will not profit you. He leaves the Island without a father, husband, son. He may be dead already. I, Gwenhyvar, shall rule you myself, and with a truer service.'

That makes us gasp, the men louder than their women. That's not how we understood this divorce. We thought we were witnessing her abdication.

Bytwini tries to stop her. 'Madam you have no right! The High King was anointed. No one, not even I, can take away the grace that God has given him.'

'Your release will not be necessary. Arthur himself has passed his authority to another.'

The curtain sways and parts behind her. A fair lady robed in rippling gold and blue is flowing across the dais towards us. On her upraised hands she bears a splendid sword, more brilliant than Caliburn, no weapon of war. But all our eyes are fixed in incredulity on the lily-face above it. *The Lady of the Lake!* Arthur's soul-friend, Merlyn's successor. Taking Gwenhyvar's side?

The wind has changed upon the mere. Boats stagger in sudden danger. Where's the shore?

Nimue offers this sword, not to Gwenhyvar the High Queen, but to Modred the regent. My hands have held that priceless weapon, the symbol of Arthur's sovereignty, given into his grasp on the day of his coronation. Modred of Good Counsel kneels, as one who understands the worth of what he takes and his own unworthiness. His lips touch the blade, his fingers balance the hilt and tip.

'A precious trust. I was endowed with this power by Arthur, to use for Britain's good, without condition. That power, by this sword, on his own authority, I now surrender to its proper lady. My love and loyalty I pledge to Gwenhyvar, sole sovereign of the Isle of Britain. I call all men and women who love her name to serve her likewise.'

Bowing before her, darkly handsome, knightly virtuous, youthfully honourable.

Urien's weapon's half out and many others. The hall is loud with protest. But other lords are cheering. Modred's been working hard. They like his style.

The Chief Bishop rages. 'This Council cannot annul your marriage. It does not have that power. Only the Holy Father in Rome can do that.'

'Rome's gone,' smiles Nimue. 'Even Arthur could not restore it. The Church of Britain stands alone, with you at its head. Come, Bytwini, let you and I be allies.'

'Allies! While you debase the holy law of matrimony, raise women over men, deny all natural order.'

There's a whiteclad abbess or two that bridles at that. They have their own high ladies, this British Church.

Nimue persists, 'I am for Britain, not for Rome. I serve her children. It is to them that I appeal. How do you say? Will you have Gwenhyvar the High Queen over you?'

'No!' cries the Church, and 'No!' shout Urien, Ulfin and a stout rearguard like them. But Cador is Gwenhyvar's foster-father; he's torn. Mark of Cornwall has suffered bitter taunts since Trystan stole his queen Essylt; he has no love for Arthur's court. And the ladies of Britain? They are tasting the savour of an old power long lost.

The cries rise ragged, like the first waves breaching a sea wall. Then the bulwarks tumble and the flood is on us.

'Aye! Gwenhyvar!'

'Gwenhyvar of Britain!'

The nobility is bending its knees in homage.

One voice is momentously silent, though Margawse and Elaine have affirmed Modred's act, Morgan stands staring like a woman possessed. Nimue and Gwenhyvar have noticed. They watch. All hangs on this. Morfudd takes Morgan's hand, appealing to her. Her wise green eyes stare up into her mother's outraged face. As dangerous as Owain, this one.

The dark of the moon. A generation's gone. The king's eyes turn to the rising crescent of her daughter.

Modred, still kneeling, smiles.

One word, torn from the roots of Morgan's being. '*Aye.*'

I see her sway. I want to rush and hold her, but I can't move for the cheering press of bodies around me. Nimue's smile flashes, a fierce triumphant culmination of a lifetime's hope.

'The nobility of Britain has affirmed it! I show you Gwenhyvar the High Queen!'

This time the roar of cheering must crack the walls of York.

The bishops, abbots and abbesses are sweeping out. An equal pain in Urien's eyes. His hero and his daughter. He hesitates. His loves are tearing him apart. Then, 'Never!' he cries, and struggles to reach Modred.

Gwenhyvar's blushing, both regal and modest in her bearing. The silver braids tumble over Modred's bowed black hair as she bends to receive the symbol he offers her. She holds both sword and sceptre up to us. She faces us sweetly.

'I rule alone now, because I must. But this sword is a heavy burden for one woman. The land has wilted enough under a feeble grasp. You need a younger king.'

That's clever, Gwenhyvar. You've touched a deep nerve there. The Year-King's run his path and reached the dangerous springtime of another Beltaine. She kisses Modred, chastely, and motions him to rise. His arm supports her trembling majesty. It's been a long ordeal.

Now cries are ringing with delight. An old religion, new romance.

The gash is closing over already. New skin is forming.

Arthur, what battlefields, what beds, what pains, what pleasures, have kept you from this wife and son it seems you never knew? Why have you left us to this moment?

Morgan tears her eyes from Morfudd to gaze at Modred. What has she taught him all these years, walking together in the forest shadow? Was it of this? He turns to look at her again and bows respect.

The tears start to fall, silently, agonisingly, from Morgan's eyes. Oh, lad, you don't know the half of what's been done. You haven't seen the belt, that should have held both sword and scabbard, shredded and smoking on her fire.

Nimue's exultant. She thinks these are the tears of defeat on Morgan's face.

She does not know that Modred is already destroyed.

Chapter Thirty-one

I struggle down the stairs and push through the crowds. I can't find Morgan. Urien is arguing with Modred.

'You took service with Arthur, before he knew who you were, as I did in my youth. You let him comb your hair and shave your face. We pledged him our swords and hearts. Mine will never turn against him, though all the world betrays him.'

'It was not Arthur himself who took your loyalty; it was the Pendragon, the figure of Britain.'

I catch the pain of memory in Urien's face. Modred is wrong. Urien loves Arthur the man, more than he loves his dark-souled foster-son. Urien, who has helped to raise him with his own boisterous boys, knows that behind the smile there is more about Modred that he will never understand.

'I will not break my oath to my anointed king.'

'We are the soul of Britain now, Gwenhyvar and I. Your oath has passed to us.'

'I should kill you with my own hand, here.'

There's a guard around Modred already, but the young man sinks to his knees, very winningly for one who's the most powerful prince in Britain now. His neck is bared.

'No harm shall come to you in this court for those

rash words, my foster-father. I give you safe conduct. I make one appeal: that you bless me for the last time before we give you leave to depart from us. If we ever meet on the battlefield, you are free to kill me if you can. I release you from all our bonds.'

Few could resist such grace. Urien swallows down the memory of twenty years: the boy he taught to hunt, to shoot, to rob, to kill, all the wild education of a nobleman. He spins on his heel, so violently his swinging sword must have bruised his own thigh, and strides out of York. No farewell, to either of them, son or Morgan.

Only to me he flings a savage order.

'Get to Armorica as fast as you can. Find Arthur somehow and warn him of their treason.'

Me? I'm Chief Bard of Rheged, not a merman swimming the sea singing of doom. Too late. He's gone.

I turn, and there is Morgan. The tears have dried; her face is hard as granite. Very calm she seems, her hand quite steady. She's holding out a letter.

'Put this in his hand from me. But tell him the truth yourself, Taliesin, as only you know how. Tell Arthur he has lost everything.'

I think I know what she means.

So here I am, sitting on a cross-channel boat twanging my harp, like Trystan drifting to Ireland with a hole in his head. I never fancied myself as Essyllt's romantic lover; I have been wounded in a different place. I have loved song more than woman, though I serve both well. One I've lost already. Britain is dwindling on my horizon. Farewell, Morgan, lovelier than all the women of the world, more loving too, all that passion walled up in a too-strong heart like a closed furnace. Its outside has warmed me generously. I'm lucky to have escaped without a scorchmark. If her door should open, we may all be consumed.

Armorica is over our bows. Brittany, they are calling it now, since so many of our people fled there escaping the Saxons. A shore of song, like Powys and Dumnonia, a country of castles and dragons and giants, a land of legend. The legend of Arthur. Will you come again to us, great king, out of Europe, back to your true home, to the stirring sound of pipes and drums and the voices of noblewomen in the window-seats as they pluck poems from the lyre? Will the very peasants remember your deeds and the stones carry your name? Arthur, my song is still waiting, like a child unborn. Arthur, the news is bad. The battle that is coming is not the one I dreamed of singing.

Land at the harbour. Few folk about. The wind whips over the white sand. It might be the Cornwall I sailed from, save that this beach faces north, that the speech is stranger. My own, and not my own, like the batter-cakes we both make on the griddle. Light as lace they are here. Fairyland. Must I be the one to wake him from it?

I stumble on news. They've broken out of the siege. The enemy's routed. There's a camp around Howel's fortress with a good deal of roistering going on. Like schoolboys let out on holiday, they are. Grey warriors, remnants of Arthur's half-forgotten warband, and green boys, they're all brothers. They've slaughtered giants, they've revenged ravished maidens, they've put the world of chivalry to rights. Give him Morgan's letter.

I cannot watch him read it. Gone in the turning of a day. Queen, crown, son. Present, past and future. Love derided, honour smirched, hope snatched back. Great Arthur is a man destitute. Sing, Taliesin. That's all you're good for. Sing of a king who bestrides a hall like a warrior his horse. Of Gawain the golden knight bearing his sword before him. Of Modred with a battleaxe hacking at the timbers below. Of Gwenhyvar pulling the roof off with her own hands. Of the fall of many brave men. And Arthur, in all this ruin? He snatches his sword from fallen Gawain. He smites off Modred's head. His faithless queen he cuts to pieces and casts her down into a black pit. The tears are running down my nose. I face the window while I sing. This is not the song I meant. Where is comfort now? Where is glory, pride?

I see a wondrous lioness coming over the downs. I watch her break into a bounding run. Now she seizes the king by the waist and bears him straight into the sea. The waves drive them on. Fierce and gentle, that lioness. Strong and stealthy. Terrible and trustworthy. There is an island of peace beyond all storms.

'I will not believe her!' Arthur grates his teeth in a rage. 'She slanders my queen. She blackens my son. She dishonours the very crown of Britain. Morgan was always the destroyer.'

That stops me in my tracks. Tragedy's one thing. But how can you draw tears for a story that's not believed? Well, not credited in public, anyway. I see his drawn face in the morning. I catch his white fists on the drinking horn at breakfast. Too much beer too early in the day. Too foul a temper. Which of them is he grieving for? Gwenhyvar the fair, who must not have played him false? Or Morgan the dark, whose truth he can never accept? Or neither of them? A man's world, Arthur's. Is it Modred his son, dearer than either of them, found, and now horribly lost?

But now he must believe. More news comes from Bishop Bytwini. Gwenhyvar has married Modred, though Bytwini refused to perform the ceremony. Soon he'll be crowned. Arthur can deny the prince of poets, the truth-telling bard on whom his hope of glory hangs. He dare not disbelieve the Church.

War. Not games with giants. Britain is the maiden ravished now, by her own son, by his own son. I hear the screech of weapons on the honing-stone, the hammer of rivets in mail, the creak of leather sails on masts. Do you think my heart is merry because the great battle is finally coming? For all my lightness of the past, do not despise me that much. Believe that this is not the song I wished to sing.

Where can I turn for a foothold in all this mire? Where is faith, where is constancy now? Where is honour?

> Until my life ages,
> And death claims his wages,
> I shall not cease yearning
> Unless I praise Urien.

I'm off, before the fleet is ready. I am going home. Home! Is this how the landscape of the heart looks after an earthquake? We are invading our own country. Arthur of the Britons must attack Britain itself. Modred will take the crown with Gwenhyvar. Modred has married Gwenhyvar. Modred is lying in

Arthur's bed. The young king has come like springtime. The old king must die. He knows it.

But he will not accept it. Nothing from Morgan's hand. Not love, not death, not truth. Did they know, when they gave him back his son, what they were doing, Morgan, Margawse, Elaine? Have they borne, found and reared Modred only for this? Is this their vengeance? Arthur believes it is. Devastating the rage, the shock, the wound. Can they never be done, Arthur and Morgan, hurting each other?

The harp is silent on the voyage back. I cannot tune the strings against the seagulls' screams. It sits dumb on my knee. My heart is empty of poetry. This cannot be happening to us. Modred my comrade, my almost-brother. Arthur my king. Morgan, Morgan, what have you done to all of us? What have we done to you? An invisible tide creeps through the timbers, rises, chills me, chokes me. My song is drowned.

Chapter Thirty-two

Dry land again. I stand disconsolate on the quay. Pick up my bags. I'm flying north, like a lost child to its mother, a kitten snatched from its home. I belong to Morgan, to the slate and granite, to the hills of the west, to the rain of the tears of shattered constancy. She will need me, won't she?

I belong to Urien. I cannot serve them both.

But what's this? I've been expecting turmoil, revolution. Modred the tyrant holding on for both queen and crown by the might of the sword. Civil war, rebellion, cousin slaughtering cousin, the land trampled. But that's not the truth. Everywhere on the road I meet the smiles of summer. Gwenhyvar is queen. Modred is Gwenhyvar's husband. Soon Modred will be crowned king. Most men speak well of Modred, the women too. It's true, they love him!

A lot's been happening.

'He's made an alliance with the Angles.'

'He's calling a council with the Picts.'

'He's offering to treat with the Irish.'

'I left a sister in Saxon hands over by the Wash. I may see her children at last.'

'My son was taken hostage by the Picts. Another raid and they'd have cut his throat.'

'Three times our home's been burned by pirates.'

There's a great hunger for peace. Not for the tense truce of mailed men, not for heroes standing sentinel on the skyline, for watchers by the beacons peering out to sea, for armed suspicion on the Wall. One Britain, open roads, kin reunited. Who will make her laws? The common people shrug their shoulders. Just let us sow the seed and leave us alone to hoe and harvest. They've forgotten Hengist and his greedy axe-men. It's Arthur's troops they call the Red Ravagers.

There's gratitude for you! Wasn't Arthur the gift of Merlyn in our darkest hour? Arthur, their hero with the enchanted sword? It was Arthur who stopped the Saxons, wasn't it? And they'd rather have Modred! I've told you, very winning that family can be when they put their mind to it. Modred and Gwenhyvar rule not by force but with the people's consent.

But not from all the nobles, Arthur's generation. War's their god. No day worth living that's not greased with blood. Modred's a careful man; he can handle the sword too. He's taken a hostage from every hostile fortress, just to make sure.

It's a shock to the system. I am a heroic bard. How can I earn my immortality without battles? I'll hardly have enough songs left to make a living. Do you want me to go fasting like a monk to keep this peace? Peace! No fear of that, is there? I've brought the tread of battle stalking at my heels. You and your newmade friends must fight now, Modred, whether you want to or not. You must gird yourself for the war to end all wars, the new order to replace the old, the son against the father, the allied hues of nations opposing the red dragon.

Morgan, Morgan, is this what you want? Modred against Arthur? Can't you stop it?

I'm not safe here. The storm is close behind me. I'm in Gwenhyvar's country and I'm Urien's bard. I run for shelter.

I'm not the only fugitive. But I don't meet him where I might have expected. I've slept at Christian monasteries on the way, where I could hear of them. Decent places for guests, they have, and the food's good. They're pleased to see you, especially on a fast day. Gives them an excuse, you see, to eat like normal men and women. But they are not so many that you can find one every night.

As I move north the ways of Rome and Constantinople are slipping behind me like a cloak from my shoulders. The land of Urien, guardian of Rome's Wall, is still far off. I take to inns and ale-houses. The news is muddled here, with smoke and beer. I listen more than I tell. Will they believe me if I say that Arthur's coming? They think he's besieged or dead in Brittany. Tell Urien first.

A face listening in the corner, like me. Old, this one, ravaged with desperation and indignant wrath. He's attended by younger men plainly dressed, their faces pale mirrors of his own. Clerical gentlemen, these; I know that studious look. The old one's face leaps into focus, like a missing tile restored to a mosaic. I see the whole. Bytwini, chief archbishop of the land, skulking in a common inn. He sees me start and knows me too. Taliesin, Chief Bard to Christian Urien Rheged. Wry our grins across the firelight. Better than crying, anyway. He stretches and strolls to the door as if to take the air. I follow him.

There's a scent of lavender and rosemary outside as our skirts brush the herb patch. The air's grey, not fully dark. The hills brood, featureless.

'They will crown him!' he spits into the cabbages. 'The pagan son of incestuous parents, anointed with holy oil. But not by me.'

'Wasn't it to avoid this conflagration that young Arthur tried to douse the firebrand once?' I remind him. 'You churchmen gave him a heavy penance for that, I'm told.'

His grin flashes white, like an owl's swoop. 'Dreams! And only the witch-king Merlyn to interpret them. It was Merlyn he feared more than the saints, and after Merlyn that slippery Lady of the Lake. There was another way than killing. There is always another way.'

'What way is that, if our fate is written in the stars?'

'To change the enemy's heart. Christ always offers us a choice. To let the fire of love consume the rotten timbers of his sin and build a new and wholesome palace for them both.'

'Accept Modred as his son? He's done that, man. Look what happened!'

'Too late.' He shook his head. 'The child had formed the man. The boy that never knew his father turns on the father for denying his son.'

'*You* pity Modred?' That's stopped me in my tracks.

'Pity!' He fairly shouts at me. 'No! I condemn Modred. In the name of the Father and the Son and the Holy Ghost, I curse him. He has usurped the kingdom, made an adulterous marriage, reduced Christ's representative in Britain to a fugitive like our Lord from Herod. Can you believe the fiend

Nimue threatens me with death because I will not
crown him? I, that anointed Arthur's wife with these
very hands! I, pity Modred? But that's not to say I
don't understand him.'

'What would you say,' I murmur, 'if I were to tell
you I have talked with Arthur, that I left him on the
coast of Brittany not a week ago, that he is
embarking an army to regain the crown?'

Bytwini grips my arm. Even in the twilight I can
see his eyes glitter. 'Arthur is still alive and free! Is
it so? Our prayers are answered? Arthur will come
again to deliver Britain!'

New Britain, saved by ageing Arthur? The
Christians came with the legions. It is young Modred
that summons an older authority. Funny, that. He
was Urien's foster-son, schooled in priests' Latin,
growing up in the court of Christian Rheged. But he
is the one who can turn back the centuries for us.
Nimue has found her opportunity, a young man
standing in the shadow of Mabon's Stone. Mabon,
Son of Modron the Mother.

I totter then. The scent of herbs is heady in the
evening air. Morgan, those who blacken your name
have never known the power of your healing touch.
But we do well to be afraid of you. You are also
Morgan the Destroyer.

Bytwini is shaking my arm. He's a younger man
already. Hope is setting his agile mind racing,
planning, scheming. 'When you see Arthur again tell
him he will find Bytwini at Glastonbury. Tell him the
Church is for him. Modred, Gwenhyvar and all their
crew we have execrated. Bid him in the name of
Christ to cleanse the land and the Church will curse
these heathen as they flee.'

Another way than killing, did he say? Not this time. He pities Modred, but he cannot forgive him. The Saxons have savaged Christian Britain too sorely for that. As far as he's concerned, Modred's adultery doesn't stop at Gwenhyvar's bed.

'Tell Arthur? Sorry, man. I'm off home to Urien. When I see Arthur again, it will be on the field of his last great battle.'

I can't help myself, can I? The song is forming in my head already.

Chapter Thirty-three

I should have known the joy had left Carlisle. The ramparts are manned and watchful; the city's braced for war. The harp is no ready passport now. Even I, Taliesin Radiant-Brow, suffer the humiliation of being kept waiting at the gate. The captain's sent for; I'm recognised and passed through.

Inside, the fortress feels half-empty, though there are strangers about. Owain's in Brittany with the best of our warband. Urien has been gathering his second team. The men and women I pass in the street stare anxiously and do not give me good-day. King Urien decrees that Rheged opposes Gwenhyvar; they've no choice, have they? But Modred is a Rheged man too. He's talked with them, he understands them, he's helped them. Here, all men and women spoke well of Modred once. They may still in secret.

I'm at the palace already. Rhun is hurrying to meet me, Urien's behind him, the hounds are yapping round my legs. It's not in the absence of warriors that the awful emptiness lies. Where's Morgan? I'm searching for her in vain. She hasn't come home, has she? I see them speaking urgently to me, but I seem to be deaf. I'm gaping at them like a fish through water. Sense penetrates at last.

'She stayed for Modred's marriage?'

I can't believe that. Surely she's given herself more pain than she can bear already? Arthur and Morgan's time has passed, that never truly came. Modred and Gwenhyvar usurp their place.

He shakes his head. I think he'd like to shake me as well, for anger and hurt.

'Fool! She is still my queen. Elaine and Margawse were witnesses, but Morgan of Rheged never. But your own news, man, for heavens sake! Did you find Arthur? Is he dead? Or so hot besieged in Armorica that there's no help for us?'

'Arthur is on his way.' There's proud news to be bringing, if only the heart did not feel so hollow.

A silence, a sigh of breath released, a great cheer. The news is flying round the palace, through the city. The very hills will be ringing with it soon. Arthur is coming back!

Quick looks flash between Rhun and Urien, Morgan's forgotten. Rhun grasps his father's wrists. 'Modred must march to repel him. You must go to Arthur's aid. Carlisle is safe as long as they are fighting in the south. Leave Rheged to me. For all our sakes, you must not let Modred win.'

Hard that choice, to fight against his foster-son, to take arms for the Pendragon who so wronged Morgan, who laid lustful hands even on Urien's own daughter. Hard, but not long. Urien has always been as much in love with Arthur as with Morgan. The heart decides, and duty finds its reasons. His sword was pledged to Arthur in the budding of their manhood. Loyalty excuses all.

At once he gives the order. The whole household's busy in the yard or the storerooms. The smithy's working like a thunderstorm. A good job Woman isn't here. There's pain for you. A smith denied his hammer and tongs in such extremity. I should feel the same if I were robbed of song. The hall's a barn from which the swallows have fled in autumn. Iron and gold and bronze have been stripped from the walls. Patches of unsmoked wood show like fresh scars. This is the big one. No workaday cattle-rustling, this. They take the finest gear that will bear the shock of war. If Arthur falls, he will go richly attended to his hero's grave. If Modred dies, it must be by no common weapon. The crows of battle will wade through gold as well as blood. Such excitement!

My hour has come. I feel the sudden rush of joy confirm it. You must forgive me! I was born for this. Forget the anguish. Can I leave Urien bardless in such a battle? How can I feel the golden heat of Arthur catching the gorse on the southern downs of Britain and not bear witness to the conflagration? Who wins, who loses? I'm a bard before I'm a man. Tragedy, victory, Briton, Saxon, Christian, pagan, are all the meat of song. Great deeds I must sing, high praise I must make. Blood I must paint, graves I must name, for mead and gold and fame I must praise the valour of warriors. I shall hymn them all, the victors, the fallen. And the greatest bards that follow shall say, Taliesin made this song.

But it's real war. And war means bloodshed. Hard steel, blue blades, red gore. I've never actually taken part in a battle. I sang of Cynan of Powys's exploits from a safe distance, you understand. Now my hour comes, and with it danger. I'll need armour and a shield. Good stout ones, as well as handsome. How could I sing the battle-song of Britain with a spear

sticking through my windpipe? And a weapon?
Now's my chance to bear the beauty Cynan Garwyn
gave me. Just for the look of the thing, you
understand. I'm no hairy butcher. But, no, this is
serious fighting. We're going to kill each other. I need
a serious blade. I've a duty of self preservation, after
all. Whoever falls, it mustn't be Taliesin.

Only one man at the still centre of it, cool among
all this fever. I find Urien, of all places, outside the
walls, sitting on a boulder brooding over a flock of
sheep. I do not heed his stillness. I am breathless with
the glory of it all. Win or lose, we know how to live
and how to die, we the British. We will ride laughing
under the hill, fighting and feasting and singing till
the darkness falls and time turns over and the world
is young for ever. This is my song.

'Lord Urien! What shall I do for arms? And armour.
You wouldn't like to see a Saxon spearhead bedded
in this snow-white breast of mine, the blood of
Taliesin spilt where the breath of poetry once
thrilled. Just a little sword, but serviceable. And a
shield. Especially the shield. Nothing too showy,
mind you. I wouldn't want to draw attention to
myself. That comes later. But let it be stout. You
won't forget that, will you? You won't regret them.
When your turn comes to die, I'll sing you such a
death-song that your name will live for ever.'

He turns from the ewes and lambs and looks at me
sternly, as though I were a yapping puppy not yet
well trained.

'They will not be needed. There will be no battle
for you.'

'But I am Taliesin! I must be there, when all the
heroes of Britain are locked in combat, pagan and

234

Christian, west and east, Modred with Arthur. I have to be there to sing of it. I was born for this!'

'I forbid it.'

I read the truth in the grim furrows of his face. Warlord though he is, he does not want this mighty battle, and I confess now that I do. I must be there. I cannot be left behind like the dregs of wine, unwanted, to go flat and stale. I am choked with tears. I have to be simple.

'My lord!' I beg. 'Take me to the battle.'

Urien leans on the low stone wall of the sheep-pen. The din of the men behind us in the citadel is less than the sound of the wind in the gorse. For the third time he refuses me.

'This is a war that should not be remembered. This is a battle that should never have been fought. If Arthur defeats my foster-son, then I am shamed. If Modred kills the High King, it will be my dishonour.'

I sink to my knees at his feet to plead with him.

'But I am a powerful bard! I have the might of mockery. I can chant satires that will blister the enemy's face. I shall call curses that would make a dragon quake. I'll launch an assault of poetry like any druid! You need me!'

'You're well out of it, lad. This war is evil.'

Evil. A word the saints would use; my father perhaps, if I had ever known him. Does Morgan accept the meaning of it? Where is she now?

His hand rests on my shoulder, heavy and warm. He lifts one more gold collar from his neck and lays it round mine. He knows everything. I have not deserved his forgiveness.

I look about me. When the war is over, who will be king here, who queen? What will become of the

235

sheepfolds of Rheged, and the cattle raids across the Wall, the high-roofed halls and the leaping firelight? Will I, Taliesin, be left lordless, to see it prey to brambles and owls for the rest of my life?

> Until my life ages,
> And death claims his wages,
> I shall not cease yearning
> Unless I praise Urien.

'What shall I do?' I whisper.
'Find Morgan, and help her.'

Chapter Thirty-four

For a moment the guard drops from his eyes.

I'm left bewildered. Help Morgan? Against Arthur? Or does Urien understand more of his queen than I do?

I stare at him wordlessly as he threads his way through the lambs back to the castle. His back is straighter now. He's made his own choice.

I do not wait to see them march away, those ageing warriors who thought they had straddled a battle-horse for the last time, these lads with the bloom of childhood still on their cheeks. I've seen those stars in eyes before. We are the glory, the chivalry of Britain. We will defend Arthur. We will never be forgotten. I think of Modred's forces: the young warriors garrisoning the Island, hard Saxon frontiersmen who have grown up on foreign soil, Picts still smarting under the humiliations Arthur heaped on them. It will be bloody, this war. There will be mothers weeping. The bards will pile more stanzas on their grave-songs. Which of us will exult in victory?

Find Morgan. Where?

York's abandoned. Modred's coronation is done. With Nimue and all their allies he is marching south.

Almost without my knowing, my hands are turning

the horse's head that way. The harp on my back and
the burden of song in my heart can feel the pull.
Well, why not? As likely to find Morgan in the south
as the north, aren't I? And I shall be nearer the
battle . . .

The boughs of the may-trees lean towards me and
scatter their blossom in white tracks. This is her
doing. She has made, now she unmakes. She must
be there.

Not long before I come on news of armies. The High
Queen will wait in Winchester. I couldn't imagine
Gwenhyvar standing in a war-chariot, like Nimue.

Urge the horse faster. Morgan is lost. Now Nimue
holds the centre. I feel the Island unstable on its base,
breaking loose, beginning to rock on a dangerous
ocean.

Where's this? Garlot, where the great roads cross,
where the hills of the north go down beneath the
southern cornfields, where Saxon and Briton are
wary neighbours. Once the great throbbing heart of
our tribal kingdoms. Now? The twilight country, the
uneasy strand between the ebb tide and the flow,
the hollow that is the eye of the storm. Awareness
penetrates my brain more slowly than it should. Old
Nentres is king here, and Elaine queen. I leap as
though a bee had stung me. I know already I am
right by the pricking of my thumb. Where else
should Morgan be but with this eldest, this all-seeing
sister?

Knowing is one thing, acting is another. I find at
the last I do not want to turn the horse's head aside
and seek their capital, but I must. Rather the
battlefield, and the warfare of men.

Black Annis Hill. It's not an imposing place, no

stone-faced fortress-eyrie. Huge trees crowd it closer than is customary for a defended stronghold, so I know it is under another protection. Come to think of it, those old oaks themselves have a watchful look. I begin to see faces in them. My heart's beating faster than I like. Steady, Taliesin, Rome has been here before you; Britain is a Christian country, under Arthur. Was! An old hunger long denied is opening its jaws to feast on the ravens' leavings. But Gwenhyvar's a Christian queen; and Nimue can hold the balance, can't she?

Low branches shadow the hollow way until I near the summit. Dark ramparts jut against a sky bright without warmth. I tread in ancient footsteps. Crows peck the yellowed skulls staked on the walls. Some jawbones drop in silent screams. Once, Nentres fought against Arthur. Whose heads are these?

A young woman is one gatekeeper, and on the other side a man dwarfed by nature, though his head is bigger than mine and by the look of his powerful arms I wouldn't want to tangle with him.

'Go in, Taliesin Radiant-Brow; you are expected,' she says before I've opened my mouth.

The dwarf says nothing, but leers at my confusion. No, hold on to your wits, boy. The shape of the harp in your satchel is clear for all to see. Still, how did they know I was coming? Elaine the Fair can see more than I can. Ceridwen's clever boy is a blind baby here.

Nentres' house gives a more barbaric welcome than Urien's Carlisle. Rushes on the floor replace mosaics. Carved wooden posts support the roof. The smoke has dimmed those painted heads so their eyes stare darkly at me now. A cauldron dangles on a mighty chain. Pork seethes. No delicacies from Roman kitchens here.

In the dark hall Nentres broods on his couch. An old wound keeps him at home. He has sent his warband to fight for Modred, but he has a strong guard here. Elaine is seated, stitching as always, with her feet almost in the cinders.

I've found my queen. Morgan, standing over the fire, though the summer day's not cold. The face she turns to me is grey as the ashes. I did not remember that she so resembled her eldest sister. I feel like a stranger.

'You are not needed,' she says.

Oh, Morgan, Morgan, what words could hurt Taliesin more than that?

'Urien sent me,' I say, 'to help you.'

There's a small sigh, a little stirring of surprise. The harp nudges my back. I didn't call her Healer for nothing. Give me an hour. I will sing to Morgan. I will close her wounds. I will bring her back to life. It is a strange board-game they play, these two. They partly understand each other. There is a game they call the King's Table, the light side and the dark, the one striving to attain a distant goal, the other to encircle.

Presently Margawse appears, laughing delightedly to see me. I wish she wouldn't. She hastens towards me, tipping back her creamy throat, and I see that even her beguiling face is not unwrinkled.

'So Arthur returns in great anger? Modred has shamed him with this double incest. A true child of mine! We have bred him well. Arthur can overlook his own sin, but not his son's. The weapons are out now. This time he must shaft us with cold steel. How will you like that, sister?'

Morgan reddens like a stormy dawn.

Oh, Margawse, Margawse! Must you foul everything you touch? Was this what Morgan meant? Great Arthur, her brother, shamed by his own son? From the beginning you have soiled him for her. How could she take him cleanly after you, hating and loving him purely as she did? Arthur and Morgan. Because of you their day must end in death. There is no other way. His light will never split her darkness now.

She knows it. Too full to answer Margawse. Too proud. Too hurt.

Margawse is triumphant. 'The end is near. Soon Arthur will be a song that no one sings.'

The words pierce me. I am Taliesin. It is my destiny she strikes out with those words.

Morgan moves too, in a gesture of denial.

'It's no good. It is finished, little sister. You have looked your last on Arthur.'

Elaine does not turn her head. Her voice comes low and sleepy. 'She has not. Morgan will take our brother's hand once more. You will hold Arthur in your arms again, Margawse. Finally, he shall rest in my lap.'

Silence. Nentres stirs, the hounds whine.

'Where?'

'How?'

'There is an island, where red apples drop from the trees, and the ninth wave breaks upon the shore, and Avallach's daughters follow the path of the stars.'

Margawse and Morgan catch each other's eyes. I hear the distant neighing of horses from the stables.

Chapter Thirty-five

As I turn from Nentres limping across the yard to
bid us farewell, I find Morgan coming towards her
horse. She carries something white cradled against
her breast like a baby. I watch her push it into her
saddle-bag and catch the old stale stains on it. I
know then what this is she cannot bear to leave
behind. That shirt of Arthur's I stole for her in
Camelot. She has carried it all this time. And I'd
thought her love was dead! Surely that must mean
she still has hope?

The wind that brought Arthur's fleet is
strengthening. It buffets our faces. Our ears are
strained for news of the powerful tide that is
sweeping to meet us.

The sisters thread the valley of the Thames. I dare
not ask what they will do when they find Arthur.

A rise in our path beside the river. Difficult to see
what lies in the dip beyond it. Then our outrider tops
the crest and gives a cry. Too late for warning; we're
almost on each other. A smaller escort than ours, and
in a great hurry. A woman in a chariot. These are
tight-strung days. Weapons are levelled on both sides
before questions are answered. I've got my own
sword out, the jewelled gift of Cynan Garwyn. I've
never had to use it till today.

Close enough to launch a spear, close enough to see the woman's face. It's Gwenhyvar.

Fear, astonishment, relief, a careful calculation. I see all these in her face before she speaks.

'My sisters! Praise be!'

'We are the sisters of Arthur Pendragon,' calls Morgan, 'and he is no longer your husband.'

Not finely calculated enough, Gwenhyvar. But she's grown a bigger woman now. She's tasted sovereignty.

'All the women in Britain are sisters to their queen. I am Modred's wife now. But I hesitate to call such beauties by the name of Mothers.'

'It's you deserve that name, by the look of you,' says Margawse.

Oh, yes, strip away the stiff royalty of court dress and we can see she's thickening. It can't be Arthur's child. And she's not a month married to Modred.

'For this, and every child of Britain, I beg your help. Arthur has driven Modred from the coast. I fled to seek Cheldric the Saxon's help. We need more keels from Germany. Then terrible news overtook us. Winchester's fallen! My treacherous guard rebelled. This is all that is loyal. I am flying for my life.'

Morgan's gaze searches her keenly.

'Where is Tegau . . . and Morfudd? They would not desert you.'

Gwenhyvar shakes her head. Her look shows terror of this mother.

'I do not know. I have not seen them since.'

The finches twitter, and the river splashes over stones.

No sound from Morgan. If eyes could scream, hers would.

Morgan would never have abandoned her people.

'Help me,' pleads Gwenhyvar. 'For Modred.'

The sisters question silently and nod. Who knows what decision they affirm?

'You throw yourself on our protection?'

'I am his wife.'

Her independent royalty is soon forgotten. So shallow a root, to withstand such a tempest. Poor Gwenhyvar, kept in the shadow of the mighty oak of Arthur. How could this pale sapling make a sturdy tree?

Their tents are pitched in a clearing by the river. The soldiery withdraws. Gwenhyvar needs a stronger defence than shields can give. Morgan's eyes summon me. I shake my head. Help me Urien! But it is Urien who has ordered me to help Morgan.

'Let me only play the harp for you,' I beg. 'That's powerful magic enough.' She allows it.

Gwenhyvar's at the centre of the circle. She's shivering. The bishops have cast her out. This is not her rite. But she fears the loss of her life more than the loss of eternity. The women are all around her. Some men, like Teilo, that are called to the craft. They weave, now left, now right, the fires burn, almost without smoke or flame, the chants are circular, repetitive, monotonous, a looping chain. And Gwenhyvar kneels, fair, frightened, vulnerable, her belly swollen with Modred's child. Her hands have no size or strength to cover it. Her eyes stare. But the power of the ritual is strong on her. It confirms her queen yet.

Morgan questions Gwenhyvar's captain. 'Arthur is winning? Modred has fled?'

'Modred has many friends, madam. His fleet has

fallen back on Cornwall. More Saxons are coming. Arthur had no one but the warband he brought from Armorica, and they are dying with every battle. Great Gawain himself is dead.'

'Gawain the Golden!' The cry of grief bursts from Margawse's heart. Her eldest, dearest son.

'He was the first of the mighty to fall on the beach on the day they landed. They say that came as near as anything to breaking Arthur's spirit.'

Her sons are killing each other.

'Curse him who caused it!'

The imprecation hovers like a hawk, above whom?

Now the gale swirls us west, taking Gwenhyvar with us. The first town we come on is in high excitement. They've heard the news. Arthur Pendragon is back! Strong citadels fall to him. The natural order returns.

Ride, ride. Is Arthur ahead? Or will we hear the tread of his army on the highway behind us?

We race for Dumnonia that bred these women. Across the levels the island of Glastonbury mocks us with its ambiguous sanctuary. Camelot's no shelter now. We skirt Exeter. Custennin its king stands high in Arthur's favour. Even Cador, Gwenhyvar's foster-father, may find his loyalty straining. Fly further west yet.

Mark is a dark unknown. Once he was Morgan's jailer. But the bonds of blood are strong. The Pendragon killed his kinsman Gorlois, and Mark has suffered Arthur's mockery because of Trystan.

I think we're heading for his fortress on Tintagel. The sisters turn their eyes with a long gaze seaward. The air shimmers either side of this high ridge. It is more than summer heat, flickering in the eye.

There's the flash of mail and weapons below us, a field of tents. Modred's army.

Gwenhyvar's almost weeping with relief. 'Restore me to my husband.'

Morgan smiles. 'And which is he?'

At the same moment pain twists Gwenhyvar's face. A gush of water stains her skirt and makes a puddle leaking through the floor of the chariot. Again that look of understanding between the sisters.

'An armed camp is no place to give birth, your majesty.'

'Where else is safe? Help me!'

She is frightened of more than pain, as well she might be.

'Not long now.'

'I want to be with Modred. I am the High Queen.'

'He has no time for you now.'

The wheels are rolling on.

'Conduct me to your king. I command you!'

But the cries of a woman in labour are not regarded.

Gwenhyvar's not the only one who's glimpsed her salvation on the slopes of Camlann. I let the procession jolt past me along the stony track. I have a job to hold my own horse back. He's keen to be after his fellows. Too soon yet for him to get wind of the multitude of warhorses.

I'm deserting Morgan. Yes. I can't help myself. My place is there, beside the river Camel, no matter whose side I am on. Arthur is coming to his last great battle. Forgive me, Urien. I obeyed your orders this far. But I cannot ride past now, can I? The harp is pulling like a mastiff on a leash. If only the horse would stop bucking! I think he's caught the whinnying on the wind.

Morgan has turned her own mount. She's riding back. Her escort wheels and circles silently around me. No fighting or desertion among these men. The loyalty of Morgan's guards is never in question. They fear her, yes, but there is devotion besides. She has been good to them and theirs.

She has been good to me.

I hear myself plead, like Gwenhyvar.

'Let me go. Please! You do not need me. What use would I be to a woman in childbirth? My work is here. My destiny is here. This is the final fight, the great song of my life.'

Her hand cleaves the air in a sign crueller than any knife. It severs hope. Her voice intones.

'If Arthur wins, you must not sing of it. If Arthur dies, you shall not sing of it. That day will be as if it had never dawned.'

Her finger is stretched out towards me. She names her power. I feel the words in my throat whisper into silence like falling leaves. Is this how she punishes treachery? Margawse, Gwenhyvar, Ygerne, what have you done to me?

How can I tell her what she already knows: that I am the greatest bard that ever lived? I am not important in myself. It is my song, the song of Arthur I was born to sing. If I do not tell it, who will remember? The centuries will roll by like empty waves, and men will ask, 'Who was Arthur? Did he ever live?' If the song dies, then Arthur's name dies too.

Oh, Morgan, Morgan, I deserved better of you than this. I loved you truly. How many nights have I held you in my arms and comforted you? I would have surrounded you with flowers, wrapped you in fur, plucked serenades to charm your cares to rest. But you have forgiven nothing at all.

I cannot hold back my tears. I do not try. Let her see that when she kills my song she breaks my heart.

I am a child to her.

My horse carries me on past Camlann after hers.

Chapter Thirty-six

We leave them behind us, men in the last day of their life. Will those tents be full of wild laughter and singing tonight? Or will silence fall early over the fields where the fate of Britain waits?

Not Tintagel? Gwenhyvar starts as we roll past the road to the sea.

'Mark would protect me. Tintagel's impregnable. Where are you taking me?'

'No fortress is safe from the Pendragon.'

We wheel south now with our backs to the shining estuary of the Camel. Past Celliwig, that happy home, the favourite hunting-lodge of Arthur, nest for young lovers when the world was young and treachery only a word in a tale. Better steer clear of that. Gwenhyvar's wracked by the convulsions of her own body. Who knows what other pain brings a cry to her lips?

Moors hump their shoulders over us. Mist shadows pools. Wild horses start and run. Then the sun breaks and we are in a valley of apples on the banks of the upper Fowey. White huts of wattle, plastered, golden-thatched. A sound of singing and a chiming bell.

Margawse and Elaine look at each other. 'You would take her here?' as Morgan rides up to the gate in the low bank. A portly nun in an ample creamy gown comes hurrying to admit us.

Gwenhyvar has seen what this is.

'You cannot bring me here! The Church has excommunicated me. They are Arthur's friends!'

'These women know how to keep a sinner safe. They will protect your body. You must answer for your own soul.'

'I did not willingly oppose the Church.' Gwenhyvar's not without spirit, even now. 'Was I worse than Arthur? I tried to make the country whole. They cannot reject me.'

'Be sure they will not do that.'

Did Gwenhyvar shudder as she passed the holy threshold? Better she had trembled when Modred first crossed hers.

Another nun comes briskly to the door of the chapel and stands staring, as Morgan advances with her hands held out as if to an old acquaintance.

'Cigfa!'

'You, back?'

The sign that Christians make to ward off evil.

'A cool welcome for one who was your school's most able pupil! You are the abbess now?'

'Co-arb only still. Bryvyth's heir. Great duties and little power.'

'Bryvyth is still alive!'

For the first time in months, I see a flash of joy in Morgan's face, as if a treasure long lost beyond all hope had been restored to her.

'Wait there. I will send for her. Your friend is sick?'

A start. I truly think Morgan has forgotten Gwenhyvar.

'If the labour of women is counted a sickness.'

252

The nun Cigfa flushes strangely. 'The convent is no place for child-bearing.'

'So my servant Luned discovered when you expelled her.'

'Through your uncleanness the nuns lost their home.'

'I lost mine long before when you became my jailers.'

'For your own good, to save both your body and soul.'

Morgan bows her head slightly, abruptly ending the argument.

Others help Gwenhyvar to the infirmary. For us, the guesthouse. Margawse laughs wildly, though her face is ravaged by weeping for Gawain.

'These are the nuns that Mark threw out of Tintagel? Your teachers and keepers? And you bring Gwenhyvar here to have her child!'

'I know no surer sanctuary. They kept me safe from Uther.'

The tap of a stick outside on the herb-lined path. A slow but purposeful step. Morgan rises, her gaze on the door.

A tall old woman leaning on a staff. Her skin hangs like leather from her craggy bones, but her eyes are keen under the tufted grey brows and a grin splits her face as eager as a young maid's.

'Morgan, girl! By all that's wonderful! Let me look at you.'

I watch in astonishment as Morgan bows her head and makes a reverence like a dutiful student.

'Mother, I did not hope to find you alive.'

The gaunt old face looks at her keenly. 'I wish I could think that your coming means repentance. But

you have always spelled trouble to those who love
you. What is it this time? They tell me that Arthur
is on the warpath and Modred is near.'

'Gwenhyvar's time has come.'

The old abbess nearly drops her staff. 'That's
Gwenhyvar! That adulteress, here!'

A nun appears apologetically behind her shoulder.

'Mother Bryvyth, the children are born.'

'Children, did you say?'

'Twin boys.'

Twins. Modred's sons, Arthur's grandchildren.

'Two boys,' I hear Morgan murmur. 'They could
not keep the balance, even now.'

The women are hurrying to the infirmary. I'm not
invited, but I tiptoe after.

Gwenhyvar is lying in a plain, narrow bed. Two
purpled scraps of flesh wrapped in white bands are
held up to the abbess. They are frighteningly small.
They seem no stronger than the sticks that girls bind
with rags to make a doll.

'Bring me water,' orders Bryvyth. 'I'll need to
baptise them quickly.'

Elaine has already taken them in her ample arms.
Tears spurt from her puckered eyes. These babes
are not long for this world. They may not wait for
the avenging sword to find them. Is this all they
leave behind them, Modred so chaste, save in this
one great matter, Arthur so profligate? Is this how
it ends?

'Keep her,' says Morgan, staring down at
Gwenhyvar. 'Guard her closely. I do not doubt she
intends to make a full repentance. She will be a less
able scholar than I was, but she may make a better
nun.'

The High Queen's eyes, dreamy and spent, focus suddenly on us in alarm.

'A nun! Is Modred killed? What will happen to me? Say he is not!'

Bryvyth's face blazes. Infirm though she is, the staff lifts in her fist as if she'd like to cuff Gwenhyvar's ears.

'High Queen! And you do not ask what will happen to your country? Your sin has brought us to civil war.'

Morgan's smile stretches, like a cat's. 'Modred waits at Camlann. The battle is not yet. Whatever happens, it will not concern you. If Modred falls, this convent will keep you secure. If Arthur falls, you shall not enjoy his defeat.'

'What do you mean? I am the Queen! I am Modred's wife.'

'You are Arthur's consort,' Bryvyth thunders.

'You cannot keep me against my will.'

'And should not need to.'

'Arthur is coming. Would you rather we handed you over to him?' Morgan asks.

Modred, you have fished in deeper waters than you knew. To these women Gwenhyvar is Arthur's wife, but Arthur is Morgan's . . . what? I will not name the thought that swims beneath the surface of all our minds. Forget the facts. Forget who's in and out of whose bed. The truth is deeper, older than their history. This Gwenhyvar was never his true mate.

'You will not let him have me? Where are my guards?' The High Queen is appealing to the abbess now. The infirmarian soothes her. She should rest. Poor Gwenhyvar, too frail in every way to play the part they load upon her.

The abbess's grin is humourless, compassionate, shrewd, summing her up. 'This is a fragile place. Those that give all to the poor need few locks. But my nuns are discreet. We have fogous, pit-houses, where hermits live, with trapdoors opening to the sky, wind-eyes to God. We could find you a little cell for contemplation. You would not be discovered, I promise you.'

'But if Modred wins . . .?'

The arms fold like bars across her chest.

'I make the offer once, girl. Or you go back to your husband.'

'I was given no choice,' says Morgan softly.

The abbess rounds on her. 'We all have choice! You chose the darkness!'

'It did not seem so to me. I sought both light and dark.'

They challenge each other. Then the abbess's big arms reach wide. The two embrace each other with a strange intensity.

'Will you not repent, girl? It's not too late.'

There's an appeal, the vulnerability of human love in that furrowed face, beyond the duty of Christian correction. This formidable woman is in love with Morgan, like the rest of us.

'I tried to heal,' says Morgan, muffled. 'But there was no healing.'

'There is, in Christ.'

'Tell Arthur that.'

Gwenhyvar is weeping. 'Do not let him find me. He will not forgive me.'

'Do you forgive yourself?'

'I will do penance. Only keep me safe!'

'If you choose, the world shall not hear of you again, or you of it.'

A moment's panic in her eyes, then the lids close. They have taken her babies away. Gwenhyvar sleeps between chaste covers. Now, only now, the abbess's face softens and she bends over her to trace the sign of the cross.

'That one was never strong enough to be the Pendragon's wife.' She turns to the sisters. 'Will you stay the night?'

She bares her heart to the pain of rejection. Morgan shakes her head silently.

One last meal then, before we leave this place of peace. Margawse terrifies me. Even here, among the ordered sanctity of the nuns, even here under Morgan's nose, her eyes flash at me, still bright with the tears she sheds for Gawain. It is as though she knows the flower of all our manhood must be cut down, and the earth cries out in her: 'Renew me, renew me! Plough me, water me, seed me, make me fertile again.' Oh, Margawse, surely your time for that is past. What the sickle will reap tomorrow can never be restored.

Gawain is dead. Bright Gawain that carried the sun in the wild stiff rays of his warrior's hair. Firstborn son of the dark king Lot, a resurrection out of the land of shades. The promise wanes. Darkness at noonday. His strength is gone.

But his mother's blood rages to recreate what is taken, and even here, even now, I feel my new-found virtue begin to weaken to the urgency of her need. My eyes fly fearfully to my queen.

Morgan is quiet and serious among these women. She'd make a better nun than Gwenhyvar, though she denies it. Yes, even I who have been in her bed and deeper still, know I have never truly possessed her. None of us have. She gave what she did not regard, her body. The tool for which it was fashioned has never entered it. The rest of us are nothing. She might be the virgin priestess of the new moon. Now she talks soberly with Bryvyth.

I think I'm drunk, though I've only had two goblets of wine, watching these women play their several games, even on this night. I had forgotten that Morgan reads Latin and Greek, that she knows more of mathematics than the Bishop of Carlisle, that she can discuss the structure of an englyn as well as any harper.

Elaine eats in almost-silence, crumbling bread into her wine. She stares beyond the walls as though they were not there. For once I lean to her, as the only one of them that has understanding. I feel that she at least knows why we are here. Over that hill, Arthur is sharpening his weapons to kill Modred. Modred is preparing to destroy his father Arthur. Death is advancing. Does nobody but Elaine see him? Red Margawse beckons. Black Morgan talks politics. Grey Elaine opens her arms to receive their children.

I'm wrong. She's not the only one.

'Are you well, Mother? I can have food sent to your cell,' the co-arb Cigfa asks sharply.

The old abbess's face has deepened its lines of care. She's an intelligent lady. She doesn't need second-sight to warn her of catastrophe coming.

I make my excuses. Outside the sun is sliding towards evening. How close is Arthur now? I can see nothing but trees around me and the flash of the Fowey. I stand in the convent garden listening. I hear the rustle of a skirt against leaves.

What need has Margawse of tent or bed when the

grass is thick and soft under the apple trees? I'm caught on my uneven path up the hill. Is nothing sacred to you, Margawse? Or are all things sacred? All times, all places, even here, this eve? Nothing can come of it, but strife. Your sons are warring with each other. Must you make war between your sisters too?

Her will is stronger than mine.

The dew is falling on a last, still, chilly dusk. Morgan does not want me, but she knows. I try to jest. The wit withers under her gaze. I plead my youthful weakness. I know I've failed her. Men on the vigil of battle do not act so. Do not grow up, Taliesin. Never grow up. That is your only hope to stay alive. But the whole world is ageing, and Taliesin with it. Nothing is as it should be.

The kings are very near us, the old king and the young, the true king and the false. But which is which? The white nuns are back in their chapel, praying earnestly. They work at prayer. Like smiths, like armourers, physicians, warriors, they prepare themselves for battle, apply all their skill. Fortunate the army that has this warband on its side.

They are praying for Arthur. Arthur, begot by treachery in their own convent. Arthur, who has plundered what he wanted from many a churchland, who will never be done quarrelling with their bishops. Yet still they claim him for their own. He will be Arthur, the Christian king. Arthur, the champion of faith and honour. They need each other. He got his crown from them, and where he reigns, the Church has grown and spread.

We've untethered the horses. But at the last Morgan herself slips in at the back of the chapel and

259

lifts her hands. I glimpse the girl behind the woman. She was schooled as one of them. When she comes out I see the woman grown from the girl. They prayed for Arthur, while she wept for Modred.

Time to leave, though no one will tell me where we are going.

Morgan falls to her knees before Bryvyth and bows her head.

'The end is near. Will you bless me, Mother?'

There's a moment's silence. Margawse moves restively, but Elaine is still. The abbess's gnarled hands rest over Morgan's head. Her lips move. Her voice is too low for us to hear what kind of benediction this can be.

We leave Gwenhyvar and Modred's babies behind us.

We are on the road. Like an eddy in a river we are circling north. The wind whips a high colour in Morgan's face. Her eyes are overbright. Margawse looks at her curiously and smiles.

'So, there is no one between you and Arthur, at last.'

'No one but Modred,' says Elaine.

Chapter Thirty-seven

The armies can't be far off now. I'm not too late. I could break away. I can still be there.

No, I cannot run from Morgan. Not even Arthur himself could do that. She holds me, as she holds all of us, by the almost-offering of herself, the joys she seems to promise. More warmth than the full-blown generosity of Margawse. More comfort than our final resting-place in the lap of Elaine.

So we all follow the white tracks of Morgan's feet in moonlit meadows. We see her new moon rise and hope turns over like a piece of silver. It will be different this time, It will be new. It will be clean. No matter how many times the frost has charred the blossom. No matter how often the owl has robbed the nest of chicks. This spring the world will be created afresh. This month the new moon's flawless. The Maiden turns towards us. Morgan will embrace Arthur.

Taliesin, you're a fool.

On, then, on a cross-grained nag behind these queens. On to a last camp under the willow trees. The drums in my blood are loud enough to summon armies. Surely I can hear the din of men and horses? Why is she taking me so close if she's tied up my tongue? Why is she bringing me to the brink of such

frustration? Take away the stirring song and all I see
is sorrow.

A river, black between shelving banks. The
winding Camel, threaded with pools. I search the
night beyond for beacons, campfires. Nothing. Our
horses whicker. Our escort shift uneasily. We are all
awake. I am cold to the invitation of Margawse now,
though the firelight reddens her skin and kindles
green fire in her eyes. Morgan has silenced poetry
and chilled warmth. Elaine watches from the
doorway of her tent. How many dead men will sleep
in those arms tomorrow night? Margawse is starting
to keen, for generations of bitterness, for Gorlois her
father, Lot her husband, Gawain her son. I mourn
for what I may not tell.

Morgan walks away from us into the darkness. The
guards lift their heads and stir, but no one follows.
I start to rise, then sink back huddled in my cloak.
She doesn't want me, does she?

Each in our own way, we nurse our sorrows on the
eve of Camlann. Yet no one stops it.

A splash, more than a vole hunting under the river
bank. Our men are on their feet, swords drawn.
They're glad of action. Like me, they suffer
uselessness, more prisoners than Gwenhyvar in a
hermit's cell.

'Peace, if peace can be on such a night.' A woman's
voice.

A figure, glimmering in the starlight, steps from a
coracle. More females follow. I see the starlight wink
on the weapons they wear. Nimue, and her warrior
women. The bravest men step back a little. The
greeting was peace. I think they'd rather it was
Bedwyr leading a night-attack.

'I would talk with Morgan.'

'Morgan is the youngest of us.' Margawse rises to her feet. Always that lazy lateness with her that seems not to recognise alarm. 'I am here, and Elaine too. Will we not do to parley with?'

'You! You have done too much already. And we all know what Elaine is waiting for. But Morgan . . . with Morgan there is still possibility.'

I know what she means. Morgan can always surprise me. I think this tragedy's unstoppable, like a ship slowly capsizing. Perhaps it's not.

'Morgan is here.'

That low and lovely voice behind me. Morgan, on the edge of the firelight, that makes black silk out of her hair and leaves her eyes in shadow.

'Will you fight for us?'

'I am Morgan the Healer. It was you gave Arthur his weapons.'

'And you armed Modred.'

A catch of breath.

'You made him a man.'

'I am a woman.'

'You are Morgan the Wise. You must work for him now.'

'Where is the need, if he has the Lady of the Lake? Is your power not enough? You launched this war. You unshipped Gwenhyvar from Arthur.'

'Where is she? She was seen with you.' Nimue's look searches the unlit tents.

'Safe.'

'I do not speak of safety. She is our High Queen!'

'Was.'

'You have not deserted Modred! You have not betrayed us to Arthur? Tell me where Gwenhyvar is.'

Silence.

'Is her child born?'

Silence.

'You have destroyed them!'

'I leave that to frailty or to Arthur's followers.'

'Traitor to your kind! Have you forgotten Arthur's violence on Morfudd, Uther's stealing of Ygerne? Help Gwenhyvar now!'

'Help Nimue, rather! What was Gwenhyvar to you? A plant more pliable than Arthur, to be trained to your liking.'

'I served Arthur faithfully. Look how he rewarded me!'

'You taught and armed him. You gave him sword and scabbard. Yet you destroyed the balance. When you had the choice, it was the sword you saved for Arthur. This war is your doing.'

'It was you destroyed his scabbard!'

'I offered it to him. He would not make the marriage.'

'They were both his. What right had you to anything?'

Elaine and Margawse rise.

'The right to heal?'

'The right to bear?'

'The right to embrace?'

'We know your rites. Of poison, jealousy, possession.'

'I cast my power away, but Arthur keeps the naked sword.'

'So fight against him! Modred is your weapon.'

Silence again.

Elaine breaks it. 'We opposed Merlyn.'

'And you took Merlyn's place.'

264

I feel even Nimue draw back. She's a known enchantress. But there is something here. Too dangerous for her to use her magic. We mortals tremble, feel our peril standing so close, the limitations of humanity in the presence of these women. And Nimue feels it too, wise though she is.

'You would not reject the child you made? You cannot still love Arthur?'

A stillness follows, deepens. I, who a few moments ago felt the chill of night and strangeness, am aware how a warmth is thickening in the summer night, more than our paltry campfire could throw out. The heat I felt from Margawse magnified a hundredfold, emanating from the moonwalking, virginal, black-and-whiteness of Morgan the Fay. She is promising royalty, union, wonders beyond the stars. Oh, Arthur, why are you not here to feel it with us?

'Tomorrow Arthur Pendragon will surrender his sword to me.'

'There! I told Modred he had nothing to fear!' Nimue gasps a little as she finds her voice. 'I told him you would not change. I told him nothing could undo your hate for Arthur.'

I, Taliesin, am speechless with amazement. Can she really not feel the truth? Can the night so bewitch, so distort, so deceive her senses? Or do we find each in this story what we want to hear? Morgan the wicked witch, Arthur the noble king. Their tragedy is our misunderstanding.

Nimue moves off, still discontented. The high magic she came for has not been made. She has not reclaimed Gwenhyvar and the children. Her oarswomen paddle her away, like swans upon the river.

No one can sleep tonight. I watch the stars turning relentlessly. I hide my face. I, Taliesin the comforter, need solace now.

Do not grow up. That's what you said to save your skin, isn't it? Do not grow up, Taliesin. I'm only a boy still.

Only a boy, unblooded, on the night before Camlann. Only a boy, tied to the apron-strings of my queen, in the camp of women, while Urien is praying before battle. Only a boy, while all the men of Britain are quaffing mead, or testing armour, or stretched asleep in their tents at Camlann. Better if you had been a real man now, and died like them.

Queen Gwenhyvar is no more. But Arthur and Modred will still fight over her, blindly, unstoppably as the circling year.

Chapter Thirty-eight

I cannot sleep. I steal from the moonless clearing. Someone else is awake besides the sentry. Woman sees the path I am taking and growls a warning. I do not heed him. It's only Taliesin, a truant schoolboy. Nobody important.

I carry my shame and grief along the willowed water. The boughs hang sadly, trailing their fingers in the current. This is the time of night when the soul is lowest. The river beckons.

Is Modred sleeping?

The river is widening into a mere. The sky is lighter; not dawn, the night's glamour doubled in the sheen of water. No mist at midnight, a shadowed clarity.

There's a little beach. I'm walking delicately over star-washed sand. The water leaks cold through the deerskin boots that were new the day I rode out of Rheged. Very smart, I imagined myself to be, the brave little bard of battle. What do I care for damp now? The whole world is cold to me.

What is Arthur imagining?

Strange I'm not tired. The moon is rising now and the mere is lovely as Morgan's face framed in dark tresses. The water's still widening. The camp is far behind. But I can't get lost, can I? The river will guide me back.

I turn to be sure.

The campfire's gone. The lake stretches wide as a sea in both directions.

Don't panic, boy. A trick of the light. Too much imagination.

That's far enough. I'll just go up to that one black rock at the edge of the water and then start back.

Sand clogs my steps. The cold is creeping up my veins. I could turn here.

Wavelets are whispering. Clouds shroud the moon. The stone's ahead.

One black rock in a level land, humped and ancient.

Stand still, Taliesin.

Black rock.

Granite.

Do not breathe, Taliesin.

Rock, the form of a woman.

Morgan.

She is crouched, bent over the waves. Only her hands work, endlessly lifting and twisting, something white.

I cannot move.

Do not grow up! Do not grow up, Taliesin! How could you begin to understand? You must not understand what you are seeing!

A man's shirt.

Arthur's.

I know with sickening truth how she has come by it. I, Taliesin, entering Arthur's house, passing Modred. I, Taliesin, in Arthur's bedchamber, jesting with Gwenhyvar. I, Taliesin, with my own hands hiding under my tunic the muddied keepsake of Arthur's hunting.

I gave it to Morgan.

She is washing Arthur's shirt at the edge of the lake. And the water pours out of the breast, dark as blood.

The washer at the ford on the eve of battle.

The Morrigan.

No, Morgan, no! I would give anything not to have seen this. To believe still in love and life.

Not Morgan the Maiden? Not Morgan the Mother. The Morrigan is washing the shroud for the dead.

The moon slides out from a corner of cloud. It is more cruel still. Light touches grizzled hair. Bones poke through withered flesh. How long is it since my hands were stroking her body?

The Crow of Battle.

She is old, she is ugly, beyond bearing. I shudder and shut my eyes as I turn away from her. But I hear her voice croaking a tuneless dirge, like a rusty hinge, while she works. Oh, Morgan, Morgan! You who had Taliesin for your bard!

She must not see me, trapped in the emptiness of these sedges. She must not hear me go. She must not guess what I have learned.

But the buckskin boots are not soft enough on the squelching shore. And every rustling tuft of moss cries out, 'Look at Taliesin running away!'

Her elf-locked head begins to turn. In my ears the wind is shrieking. 'Return to me! Return!'

I'm racing madly now. I fling myself into the arms of the forest. Not kindly, those clawing limbs, but no place is dark enough for me to hide from her, and never mind about wolves. Far better to be eaten by flesh and blood. Better still to be a man at Camlann and die cleanly on the spears of Arthur, or of

Modred; it hardly matters which. I will run shieldless to the comfort of that war. No breastplate for the poor soundbox of Taliesin. I want to die and forget what I have seen.

Whom I have served.

Chapter Thirty-nine

I've lost Morgan; now I'm lost myself. The campfire's gone. And if I stumbled on either of her sisters, Elaine or Margawse, I should be more terrified.

I'm terrified anyway. I cannot find our men, our women, Woman. Did we exist, any of us? Are we a folksong spun when the true tales of heroes have been told over? Am I a figment of someone's else's imagination?

More like a nightmare. Brambles claw my back. I see less than I need to and more than I want to see: the groping fingers of branches aiming for my eyes, the swoop of bats across the moon. The rhythm of my sobbing breath beats under the cruel descant shriek of owls.

I stumble on, too senseless to stop. Another tearing twist at my tunic. I put up a hand to disentangle myself. Truth enters my disordered brain. I've lost her too.

Healer. The harp. As close to me as my own organs. My essential self. We have never been parted since the day my hands closed round her silky frame and my probing fingers plucked the first throbbing response from her. I do not know if I can live without her.

She lies beside the Camel, as lost to me as the land

of Lyonnesse that vanished under the waves. I cannot go back.

Slower now. What does it matter if I die?

Night's thinning into grey morning. I'm still alive. There's cruel irony. I, the bard Taliesin, escaped from the Morrigan, am free on the morning of the battle of Camlann. Free, but lost. I've lost my music, lost my heart, lost my awen.

I blunder on. For pity's sake, will no one tell me the way out of this wood?

The wind is rising. The branches clash like swords. The crows are thrown screaming into the air. How can I hear the tumult of battle above them? Where are Morgan's ravens? Where is Camlann?

Silence suddenly, only the crashing of my own progress deafening me now. I stop and listen. Is that how battle sounds? A far-off moaning, like the sea rolling for ever against some desolate shore. Hard to be certain which way.

I feel the loss of the harp on my back. I am too light, too unsubstantial without it. No armour either, only a toy of a sword not made for killing. What am I good for to anyone?

Difficult to force a way through the wood, even when I think I know which side the battle's on. Wet bogs, that wait to suck an offering down. Steep-banked ravines that will hardly let me out. Thickets of thorn where narrow deerpaths beckon only to end in tangled bewilderment.

She laughs at me. Out of the fecund earth her eyes are watching this. She weeps for Modred and Arthur, but me she mocks.

Brave men are falling even now. I can imagine it, can't I? The yelling warriors. The noble gold-torqued men. The plunging of gallant horses. The blood and foam that spatter like spray. The standards swaying against the sun. The struggling shadows. The splintering shields. Bared teeth flashing a grin of victory as the blade goes home.

I could make it up, like any competent bard. It wouldn't be the first time, would it? Cynan Garwyn's a hefty fighter. I kept a prudent distance from most of his scraps. What is a bard blessed with inspiration for, if not to paint the plain wood of reality with brilliant gilding?

But today history is ending, and I am choked with a sense of more than mortal struggle. Arthur the brigand; Morgan the Wise. Arthur the righteous king; Morgan the Faithless. All men spoke well of Modred in his lifetime; Modred the traitor. This day mows down the niceties of plus and minus. Legend is born on the field of Camlann. I must be there! I must touch the myth, the mystery, the magic and feel the bardic lightning in my soul. I could become a legend myself.

Will I tell you the truth?

Is this why Morgan cursed me and sends me stumbling in a swamp? Robs me of my harp?

She doesn't trust me.

She is right.

What's that? I glimpse a grey gown through the holly. Desperate for directions I run after it.

'Stop! Wait for me! Help!'

The hooded head turns. It's an old man, but he hitches up his skirt and runs off when he sees me, muttering to himself. He's nimbler than he looks. But I am fitter than he is, and growing angry now. I catch him by the arm and twist him round.

'Spare me, sir! Spare me! I will keep their secret.'

The grey eyes roll madly. He is witless and wandering.

'Where is the battle? Tell me which way to Camlann.'

'He lives! The king lives for ever. With his white mare beside him and a hundred warriors at his back.'

'Which king? The combat, you old fool! Where is the battlefield?'

The eyes go crafty.

'They are all sleeping. Till the horn of doom sounds and the drum rolls.'

I will not believe what he seems to mean. What use is this fool to me? He has lost his senses. I throw him from me and dash on.

Light promises ahead. The sun is out, but it sucks up a fog in the still afternoon.

Too still. Why is this calm along the Camel? Is it over so soon?

Sounds come like echoes, broken, long-delayed.

I'm hurrying downhill now. The hazel brakes are thinning. Cows have been here.

I see my shadow in the mist and take it for a stranger.

The jagged, scattered cries frighten me more than the full-throated roar of battle did.

A horse passes, riderless, wild-eyed and nervous. I stumble on, lower, into the thickest of the fog.

A trampled cornfield. Would that those were just sheaves lying ungathered on damp dark ground. Would that only the coulter of peasants' ploughs had furrowed the soil this deeply. Would that clean rain had watered it less thickly.

I am a royal bard, I was bred to sing of war and red slaughter and glorious death. Mead-singer, gold-getter, praiser of princes. But I stand surrounded by a harvest of corpses and I am weeping like a desolate child. All the tears of the poets of Christendom could not wash out these terrible stains of cruelty. Is this the field of honour I have hymned? The headless torso. Is this the glorious defence of all we love? The screaming of the wounded who cannot die. Is this the myth we raise our children on? I slither in the entrails of a disembowelled horse.

How should these wounded know the end for which they are still dying? I must guess the outcome.

Morgan has been here before me.

Daylight is fading, the mist weeps. And the crows gather, fattening, with eager eyes. I try to chase them off, but they are too many, too single-minded. I vomit instead, and they scream raucous laughter.

'Who's there? If you are for Arthur, name yourself. If for Modred, surrender.'

A handful of shadowy horsemen. The weapons they level at me are solid, though. Spears, swords, that have finished off braver men than me. I see the unnamed bloodstains on them. Unnamed, unsung. Is this the end of Taliesin?

'Taliesin?'

I am face to face with Urien Rheged. I fall on my knees and cling to his hand. Oh, the relief! My earthly king. My human, sane and Christian lord. Owain and half a dozen stern warriors behind him. and never mind the cloud of thunder in Rheged's face.

'I forbade you this battle. Why did you disobey me?'

'I was lost. I came too late . . . too soon. I . . .' I'm sick again.

'I charged you to find Morgan. Is this how you serve her?'

I shudder and cannot speak. His face confronts loss and shuts it away.

I feel his hand rest on my shoulder. 'There, boy. It's over. I fear we are all losers now.'

I cannot accept it.

'Arthur is . . . defeated?'

Yet they have no beaten look, these men. There is a sorrowful majesty about them. Still, they do not rejoice. I look at their set, exhausted faces. I think I know the truth before Urien speaks.

'Great Arthur is dead. Bedwyr bore him away from the battle, dreadfully wounded. He could not have lived. We seek his body.'

The warriors behind him keen like women.

I see it must be so. How could it have been otherwise? I have watched the Morrigan washing the blood from his shirt.

'Then . . . Modred is truly our king?'

'Dead also. Killed by his father's hand.' This, unflinching, from his foster-father.

So all is lost. No victor. No right restored. The High King Arthur and courtly Modred, the son of Uther Pendragon and the child of Arthur, that lately found and clasped each other in their arms. Where are the legends of Britain now?

The long dance is done, and the hobby-horse falls dead. This time he will not rise to the tap of the teasing bladder. The summer will not come. The dancers lie where they have dropped. The few of us that are left must limp away into the winter, leaderless.

I'm sorry, Urien. You're a good man, but it's not the same.

The great battle is over, and I am standing among its carnage. But I, Taliesin, will never sing of Camlann.

Morgan and Arthur. We shall not see them ever again. I do not wish to remember this day.

I will remember Morgan the Healer in Rheged. Let me try to recall her queen in Urien's hall. Lovely, she was. Her hair like the raven's wing and her skin soft as honeysuckle . . .

I'm sorry. I cannot sing of her. There are things a man may not look on and live.

I shall never touch Morgan the Wise again.

I will not go back to search the banks of the Camel. They will all be gone. Keep me with you, Urien. I am afraid.

Not hard to find a mount for me, after Camlann. Next day we turn our horses' heads to the north. Urien, Owain, Taliesin. To the open hills and the cold clean winds of Rheged. To the springing lambs and the fattening calves that lift their heads, expectant, for a lighter, quickening step that will never come. To the sober tale of history.

I have a new harp now, the gift of generous Urien. Its notes are true, but they cannot heal. Lift it down from the wall tonight, Taliesin. The world is waiting. I will sing the songs that I am paid to sing.

> Until my life ages,
> And death claims his wages,
> I shall not cease yearning
> Unless I praise Urien.

Why have you done this to us, Morgan? Why?

A selection of bestsellers from Headline

FICTION

A RARE BENEDICTINE	Ellis Peters	£2.99 ☐
APRIL	Christine Thomas	£4.50 ☐
FUNLAND	Richard Laymon	£4.50 ☐
GENERATION	Andrew MacAllan	£4.99 ☐
THE HARESFOOT LEGACY	Frances Brown	£4.50 ☐
BROKEN THREADS	Tessa Barclay	£4.50 ☐

NON-FICTION

GOOD HOUSEKEEPING EATING FOR A HEALTHY BABY	Birthright	£4.99 ☐

SCIENCE FICTION AND FANTASY

RAVENS' GATHERING Bard IV	Keith Taylor	£3.50 ☐
ICED ON ARAN	Brian Lumley	£3.50 ☐
CARRION COMFORT	Dan Simmons	£4.99 ☐

All Headline books are available at your local bookshop or newsagent, or can be ordered direct from the publisher. Just tick the titles you want and fill in the form below. Prices and availability subject to change without notice.

Headline Book Publishing PLC, Cash Sales Department, PO Box 11, Falmouth, Cornwall, TR10 9EN, England.

Please enclose a cheque or postal order to the value of the cover price and allow the following for postage and packing:
UK: 80p for the first book and 20p for each additional book ordered up to a maximum charge of £2.00
BFPO: 80p for the first book and 20p for each additional book
OVERSEAS & EIRE: £1.50 for the first book, £1.00 for the second book and 30p for each subsequent book.

Name ....

Address ....

....

....